The Legend of Amburgey Gibboney

BLOOMSPOONS ADVENTURES BOOK ONE

ROSA LEE JUDE

Rosa Lee Jude

ISBN-13: 978-1-942994-05-3

Rosa Lee Jude
Visit my website at www.RosaLeeJude.com

Books by Rosa Lee Jude

Contemporary Romance
I STILL DO
UNTIL INFINITY

Urban Fantasy
The Enchanted Journey Series:
TREMBLE
JASMINE
NEVERWRONG

Time Travel/Historical Fiction
The Legends of Graham Mansion Series:
(with Mary Lin Brewer)
REDEMPTION
AMBITION
DECEPTION
SALVATION
REVELATION

The Legend of Amburgey Gibboney

Prologue

IN HER HAND SHE HELD A LOCK OF HAIR, black as the night when the child was born. Between her fingers, she rubbed the fibers, silky and new, so like the hair she once ran her fingers through. It was another life, another existence. The locks were only days old when she snipped them from the tiny head. It was the only fragment Amburgey dared to keep. No photograph. No piece of clothing. It was proof enough of what once was. This connection to her. This link between them, forever. The child's hair was so like that which adorned his head. Ah, how she loved the man who had given her the child. It was the final piece of the puzzle. The final piece of the token which would enable the child to go where Amburgey had gone before her. The magic had been shared. The lock of hair was the force that could take the young life on a journey tainted with destiny that would answer all of the questions this child would one day have.

Chapter One

"ALWAYS LOOK FOR A SIGN. It will lead you where you need to go."

Symphony Wallace slid the cream-colored notecard back into the envelope. Holding it up to her nose, she took one long whiff before tucking it into the back of her suitcase. The paper still held a hint of White Shoulders, the perfume her grandmother had always worn. It was the last message Symphony received from her beloved Grammie Wallace before the woman unexpectedly passed a few months earlier. The woman's wisdom was strong in Symphony's heart. It gave her strength. She would need that strength on the journey she was about to begin.

"You know I am nothing but supportive of you, dear." The sudden appearance of Symphony's mother, Mariel, caused Symphony to jump as the woman walked up behind her daughter.

"I can't wrap my mind around why you have chosen such a small town to make a new life in. You've already built up a few years of experience. That combined with your master's degree should help you land a position with a larger museum."

"It's not about the size of the place." Symphony turned to face her crimson-haired mother. The woman's shoulder-length locks and freckled nose were in stark contrast with Symphony's ebony hair and dark complexion. Many found it quite unusual for mother and daughter to look so different, until they learned that Symphony was adopted. She was a child of Mariel's heart, not her womb. "Wytheville is a growing community. It's vibrant and friendly. I've never heard of such a small town having so many museums. I get to be the curator of four established ones and there are two more in the works. It's a great opportunity."

"I suppose." Mariel straightened some books that were lying on Symphony's corner desk. Her compulsively neat mother was always straightening something. "It's a pretty place, quaint, I suppose. Your father and I stayed there for a couple of days a few years ago when he was attending a conference. It was a nice place to visit." Mariel paused again as she stopped fiddling and returned to watching her daughter. "Your father says it has a low crime rate. I just wish it wasn't so far away."

"It's less than three hours. West Virginia and Virginia are neighbors you know. Besides, no one is far away when they have one of these." Symphony held up her cell phone. Noticing the time on the screen, she quickly put the phone down and turned back to her packing. "Good grief, it's almost two o'clock. I've got to get on the road. Dad wants me to get there before dark."

"Yes, he was mumbling something this morning about a cold front coming in." Mariel laughed as she closed an open dresser drawer. "Being the wife of a meteorologist all these years hasn't improved my understanding of the weather."

"He told me that there is snow in Wytheville's forecast tonight. It's best if I try to beat that."

SYMPHONY TAPPED HER hand on the steering wheel as Prince belted out *Little Red Corvette* on the radio. A flash of red flew by in the passing lane causing her to jump in her seat.

"No way." Symphony shook her head as she realized that a red Corvette had just sped by her. "Grammie would certainly call that a sign. Maybe I should follow that Corvette wherever it is going. Maybe its tracks lead to my destiny." Symphony laughed to herself as she watched the sports car zoom away.

While not reaching the Corvette's speed, Symphony did give her old Jeep Grand Cherokee a little more gas as she cruised along I-77 South. After paying the last toll a few miles back, she had begun to concentrate on the closeness of her destination and the change it would bring to her life.

A half hour later, a cold chill passed over Symphony as she watched the same red Corvette inch up the exit ramp in front of her. Without breaking the speed limit too much, she had managed to keep up with the sports car for the last thirty miles of travel. The realization that it was taking the same exit was more than her mind could fathom. She imagined that the car would stop at one of the gas stations or restaurants that she could see ahead. She soon realized that the vehicle was heading toward the downtown district. It was leading the way.

A feeling of excitement continued as her murky grey SUV

followed the bright red vehicle. Its speed had slowed as it followed Main Street toward the downtown district. Her mind was spinning with a thousand thoughts of who the driver of the Corvette might be. A ding from her dashboard brought her out of her thoughts.

"Low tire. I guess you are tired of hauling all my junk, huh?" Symphony patted the dashboard. "Don't fail me now, Gypsy."

The vehicle was a loyal friend. Bought by her father on the day of her high school graduation with an empty odometer, Gypsy had seen Symphony through four years of college, two more of grad school, and the last two years of her first real job.

"I guess this is a sign that I need to pull over." Symphony chuckled to herself before taking one last look at the red car in front of her. She put on the signal to exit into a gas station she saw ahead. She glanced at the license plate making a mental note of the Virginia tag's last four numbers – 1989. "What are the chances of that?" It was the year of her birth. The day had been full of signs. Grammie said signs were supposed to be heeded. The woman had never been too explicit regarding how to determine whether signs showed good or evil in your path. She had told her granddaughter that signs always came before a change—a change that would force life to move in another direction. The geographical move and new job she was undertaking could be a mistake. But, for Symphony, the possibility of learning answers to the mystery surrounding her birth was too strong to make her reconsider. She wanted to know who her birth parents were. She wanted real answers to the mysteries surrounding her heritage.

After putting air into the low tire and filling the vehicle with gas, Symphony found her way through the downtown to where she would spend the next two nights. The first Monday in January would be when she would start her new job as curator of a group of museums in the small town of Wytheville, Virginia. As part of her initial salary package, she would be living on the top floor of the oldest museum, the Haller-Gibboney Rock House. While she could not move in until her first day on the job, the director had arranged for Symphony to stay at a beautiful bed and breakfast in the historic district. As she maneuvered her vehicle to the side of the impressive brick Trinkle Mansion, Symphony picked up her cell phone and texted a brief message to her parents saying she had arrived safe and sound.

Symphony had filled a small rolling suitcase with enough items for her brief stay at the bed and breakfast. The outfit she would wear on Monday was hanging in the backseat between the Jeep door and several boxes of books. Retrieving the small suitcase, Symphony walked up the sidewalk that lined the front of the building and took in the view.

Four imposing white columns adorned the front of the large house giving Symphony a glimpse into the grandeur that awaited her inside. Her studies of historical architecture taught her that the Classical Revival style structure most likely dated to the pre-World War I era. For a small town of Wytheville's size then, it would have been a mansion, even in a time when most homes of influence were large and spacious. As she climbed the wide steps leading to the front door, it opened revealing a beautiful blonde woman waiting to greet her. The woman's smile was infectious and her accent oozed with southern hospitality.

"You must be Symphony. I'm Patti. Welcome to our home. I just love your name."

Photos on the business' website did little to prepare Symphony for the elegance of the old home. As she stood in the foyer with large parlor rooms off each side, Symphony's eyes were drawn to the large staircase that led to the second floor.

"We are so happy that you accepted a job here. You are going to fall in love with this little town, just like we did. Let's go upstairs and get you settled in your room, and then I will give you a tour." Patti began walking up the steps as Symphony followed. "We have four rooms on the second floor. I have put you in the Adel room. I think you will enjoy it. The room is named in honor of the town in Iowa where I used to be a postmaster."

"Oh, how interesting. I assumed that you were a native of this area." Symphony spoke as her eyes absorbed the rich colors of the room's décor. Scarlet, brown, and gold accentuated the dark furnishings of the room. The massive four-poster bed looked inviting after the long drive.

"Oh, no. Bernie and I have only lived here for a dozen years or so. It is home now though. I bet you will feel the same in no time."

After pointing out a few of the room's amenities, the innkeeper told her to return downstairs whenever she wished for a complete tour. Symphony collapsed on the bed as the woman left. Despite the excitement she was feeling about reaching her new home, her mind drifted to feelings of apprehension as Symphony wondered if she had made the right decision.

Symphony had been hesitant, at first, to apply for the curator's position for the multiple museums. Despite the small size of the area, the museums explored several different time periods with additional structures and new programming in the works. Prior to taking this job, the only position Symphony had held was at the entry level. For two years, she had worked diligently, at a large museum in Charleston near the West Virginia state capital, to learn all she could and to prove to her demanding supervisor that she had what it took to be given more responsibility. When she told her boss, Lyla Karrington, she thought the curator position in

Wytheville would be her dream job; Lyla picked up the phone and called the museums' director to offer her personal endorsement. Symphony felt her hard work and diligence had paid off.

At first, Symphony thought Lyla's quickness to call a stranger was unusual. Then, she learned that Lyla and the Director, Allison Emerson, were not strangers. Twenty years earlier, Lyla had done her college internship in Wytheville with Allison when there were two museums. Now, four were in operation along the historic Tazewell Street with two more under construction as well as an outdoor living history site in the works. Lyla had never mentioned to Symphony this portion of her college experience.

As her tired body sank into the comfortable bed, Symphony's thoughts returned to the day she told Lyla the reason behind her desire for the job.

"WHY IS THIS YOUR dream job?" Lyla Karrington looked up from the job description Symphony handed her. "Wytheville is over two hours away and is a much smaller community than you have lived in. There have been several similar positions open in Charleston. Did you apply for them?"

"No." Symphony swayed back and forth from one foot to the other—a nervous habit her mother had unsuccessfully tried to get her to correct. "I didn't think I was qualified for them."

"Then, what makes you think you are qualified for this one?"

Lyla should have been an investigative reporter or a private investigator. The woman could be ruthless in her interrogation. Symphony knew there was no use in trying to make up a story. She had learned that Lyla had a sixth sense when it came to the truth. Symphony had watched young interns try to get out of assignments with concocted stories and Lyla seemed to smell a lie before the person even said it.

"I want to work in Wytheville because it is the last place that I know my mother lived." Symphony paused as she saw a confused look pass over Lyla's face. "I'm sure it is not the last place she ever lived. She probably lives somewhere now. It's just the last place that I know about, for certain."

"Symphony, you aren't making any sense. Doesn't your mother live within a thirty-minute drive from Charleston? I met her and your father last fall when they came for the fundraiser."

"Yes, you did. Mariel and Peter Wallace are my parents in every sense of the word, except one. I was adopted by them when I was three months old."

"Oh, I didn't know that." Lyla paused. She seemed to be processing what Symphony had told her. "So, you have been searching for your biological mother?"

"I have, off and on, for a while. My parents never tried to hide the fact that I was adopted. Their love and devotion for me is strong, and I never felt I was missing anything." Symphony turned and walked toward the floor-to-ceiling window in Lyla's large office. "But, once I got into college and delved deeper into my major of history, the lack of knowledge about my own heritage seemed to shine in my eyes like a big bright light."

"I suppose that would be true. A history major without a history of her own would question her past more than I guess others might."

"Yes." Symphony turned back to face Lyla. "It's not been easy to find information about my birth mother. There's very little my parents know about her. I was one of those 'left on a doorstep' babies."

Symphony watched a look of bewilderment passed over Lyla's face before the woman caught herself as their eyes met.

"I'm sorry, Symphony, I don't understand."

"It's the stuff of old black and white movies. But, I meant what I said literally. I was left on the doorstep of a church. All that was in the basket with me was a change of clothes, a photograph, a pendant, and a note."

"May I ask what the note said?"

"It was just a few words. 'This is my daughter. I call her Symphony. I love her so much. But, I cannot stay here. Please give her all the love you have.' It was signed Amburgey Gibboney."

"Gibboney? That is a name that is deeply connected to the history of the Rock House Museum in Wytheville. Was your mother a member of that family?"

"I'm not sure. I've done quite a bit of research trying to find anyone with that name. It was unusual enough that I thought it would help me find her."

"It's an unusual name indeed. That's why you did your graduate thesis on finding lost ancestors. I thought that was an interesting topic when I read it on your resume."

"Since I had to do a thesis, I thought it might as well help me in my search. I told my professor my story, and he helped me shape the topic to best serve both circumstances. I found out later that his wife was adopted. He understood my dilemma."

Symphony sat down in the straight back leather chair in front of Lyla's mahogany desk. All the furniture in her office was large and old.

"My research led me to locate four women in the last two centuries named Amburgey Gibboney. All of them lived in or near Wytheville, so they must somehow have been related. As unusual as the name Amburgey is, I guess it must have been passed from generation to generation."

"Symphony isn't exactly a Mary, Sue, or Jane name itself. Your birth family must like names of distinction."

"It would appear so. If you start with my mother, who I believe was living in Wytheville in the late 1980s, and go backwards, there was another Amburgey that I found in 1950, one in 1924, and the earliest one in 1855."

"All had the last name of Gibboney and all living were living in Wytheville?"

"I was diligent in my research. I even looked for some alternative spellings. There are only four women in the last two hundred and fifty years in the United States who have been named Amburgey Gibboney."

"Good grief! Four in the entire U.S.? It would seem logical then that they are related in some way. This most recent one must be your mother and that is why you must get this job." Lyla looked back at the job description. "You go back to work. I will call Allison."

"Don't you want me to stay here in case you need to ask me anything?"

"No, young lady. I do not need you to listen to every word I say. I believe I know everything I need to in order to give you a strong recommendation."

Symphony sighed. She got up and walked toward the door.

"Symphony, you mentioned that there was a photo in the basket with you. Was it of your mother?

"Oh, no. It was an old sepia tone photo of a very handsome young man. My adoptive parents thought that the man must have been important to Amburgey. The photo does not seem to be from the right time period though. It is a mystery, like everything associated with me." Symphony shrugged her shoulders and smiled.

"It is amazing how one life can be filled with so many gripping layers. Your life is one big mystery waiting to be solved. You can go now. I will call Allison. You've got to promise me one thing though."

"What's that?" Symphony paused at the doorway.

"You'll let me know how this mystery ends."

"If I get the job. Absolutely."

"Oh, you will get the job. Trust me."

SYMPHONY'S THOUGHTS WANDERED back to her present. She was about to spend her first night in Wytheville. True to her word, Lyla had arranged for Symphony to interview for the job. It had gone splendidly. She liked Allison immediately and could see why Lyla had maintained a connection to her mentor. The two women had similar personalities and work ethics. Lyla had pointed out that the job would not be easy. Allison would demand excellence. She would do her best not to let Lyla down.

The comfort of the bed was enticing; she had not realized that the task of packing and the stress of driving would have tired her out so. Yet, Symphony knew she should make the most of her first Saturday evening in her new town and explore a little. Rising from the bed, she set to unpacking her small bag. Changing from her jeans and sweatshirt to a cardigan and nice slacks, Symphony touched up her makeup and put a few loose curls in her long black hair.

As she came down the stairs, she found Patti greeting a couple in the foyer. An energetic man came around the corner and introduced himself to Symphony as Patti's husband, Bernie.

"Patti is a whirlwind." Bernie smiled as he watched his wife. She was giving an animated description of some of the work that was done during the renovation of the house into a bed and breakfast. "I bet she was a hostess in the nursery when she was born." Bernie turned his attention toward Symphony. "You haven't had your tour yet, have you?"

"No. That's okay. I'll be here two nights. I can save my tour for tomorrow; it looks like it is getting busy. I'm actually getting a little hungry and thought I would go exploring for a restaurant."

"That sounds good. Let me give you something to help with your exploration." Bernie walked to the small welcome desk just below the stairs and retrieved a brochure. "There is a list of local restaurants in here with a map to help you find them. Of course, you can use your phone as well, but I prefer the old-fashioned way myself." Bernie flipped through the brochure and opened it to the restaurants section as he handed it to Symphony. "Although there is a little snow in tonight's forecast, I think it will hold off until after midnight. Those weather forecasters don't always know what they are talking about." Symphony chuckled as she thought of her father. He endured the 'weather guessers' jokes all too often. "Since it is unseasonably warm, if you are up for a walk, there are several restaurants a few blocks away. The Log House is a long-time favorite of the area."

"That sounds perfect. My legs could use a long walk after all the driving I did today."

Armed with her map, a jacket, and a healthy dose of curiosity, Symphony walked out of the front door of the mansion and headed toward the center of downtown. From her interview conversation with Allison Emerson, she had learned that the downtown had recently experienced an ambitious revitalization. The glow of new streetlights bathed the brick sidewalks to guide her from the upper Main Street area into the heart of the downtown district. She saw few empty storefronts as she passed by building after building that appeared to have a rich history attached. Even in the dark of an early winter evening, it was obvious that some of the storefronts sported fresh coats of paint and new façades. Symphony stopped under a streetlight to read the brochure and look at the map. A short paragraph at the front of the brochure indicated that the small town's history dated back to the late 1700s when it was first given the name of Evansham. After a disastrous fire in 1839, the name was changed to its current designation of Wytheville. Symphony laughed to herself as she read that there was only one town named Wytheville in the entire world.

"Another interesting fact to my heritage." Symphony spoke aloud to herself.

"What would that be?"

The voice came from behind, startling her. She dropped the brochure on the ground. Symphony turned to see who was speaking while bending down to pick it up. The stranger was also reaching down at the same time. They collided causing both of them to fall to the ground.

"I'm sorry that I startled you. I heard you speaking and thought you were asking a question."

As she stood up, Symphony noticed the stranger's face. He appeared to be about her age. When their eyes met, Symphony's attention focused on the color and intensity of his eyes. They were strikingly beautiful.

"Your eyes." The words came out of Symphony's mouth before she could stop them.

"Yeah." The man looked away as he picked up the brochure and handed it to her.

"Your eyes are so unusual." Trying not to make further eye contact, Symphony held the brochure in her hand and placed the handle of her purse over her shoulder.

"It's okay. I'm used to it." The man pointed to the brochure. "Are you visiting our fair town?"

"Actually, I am moving here."

"Great. By the authority vested in me by no one, I welcome you to Wytheville." With a flourish of his hand, the man bowed. "May I assist you in finding something?"

The awkward moment vanished. Symphony laughed at her new acquaintance.

"I just arrived in town about an hour ago. My name is Symphony Wallace. I'm staying at the Trinkle Mansion for a few days until I get settled. I've been driving for several hours and lunch seems like a long time ago, so I am starving. The owner of the B&B suggested that I might like to eat at the Log House."

"I'm Jason Newberry. Nice to meet you. Ah, the Trinkle Mansion, you will have a luxurious experience there. Patti and Bernie have certainly made a beautiful business out of that old house. The Log House is one of the best and most unusual dining experiences here. It just so happens that is where I am headed."

"Really?"

"Yes, really. I can prove it. When we arrive there, you will find my car is parked in their lot. I arrived at the Log House earlier than I expected, I thought it would be a great evening to walk down the street and stretch my legs. I never expected that I would become a tour guide for Wytheville's newest resident."

Jason extended his hand for her to lead the way. She paused and briefly allowed herself to take in the rest of his appearance. Despite the fact that he had on a heavy leather jacket that was a rich chocolate brown color, Symphony could see his broad shoulders complimented his average height. A thick head of brown hair curled slightly where it hit the collar of his shirt. Dark jeans and boots completed his look. He was casually dressed for a winter day.

"How far is the restaurant from here?"

"Hmm, about seven or eight blocks, I would guess. You will see the bulk of the downtown along the way."

They were silent for a few moments. Symphony took in her surroundings while they walked.

"Wow! I don't believe I have ever seen such a big pencil." Symphony pointed to a giant yellow pencil that was hanging from the second story of a building a block ahead. "What is the story behind that?"

"An interesting one, to say the least. The business associated with it is an office supply store. Back in the 1960s, the original owner thought it would be an attention grabber for businesses along Main Street to have three-dimensional symbols of their businesses attached to their buildings. This was before the interstates were constructed. This street was the main road through the area then. A few businesses joined him in the endeavor, but it never really caught on. Then when first, Interstate 81 and later, Interstate 77 were built, traffic was diverted. The family held on to his dream and have kept that pencil in sharp shape in the years since."

"Sharp shape, you are funny." Symphony shook her head. "How big is it?"

"It's about thirty feet long and is made of steel. Many people make a point to stop here and see it."

"There you go again."

"I know, I know, I shouldn't quit my day job."

"I don't know. What is your day job?"

"Well, that's a good question. It has several answers. I went to college and studied engineering. Most days, you can find me sitting in a cubicle designing mechanical parts for other people to make. But, I really think I am an entrepreneur at heart. I've been learning about the brewing of beers and ales. For the past six months, I have been working on the weekends at a brewery in a nearby town. I'm looking for a business partner to be the financial backer to open a brewery here."

"Interesting. I've heard that the downtown has recently experienced some revitalization." Symphony stopped to look through the glass of one storefront that was being remodeled. "Is the town re-inventing itself?"

"Rejuvenating is probably a better description. The main revitalization efforts have wrapped up. Lots of aesthetic improvements like these brick sidewalks we are walking on and façade upgrades to the older structures have been added. But, there is more work on the horizon. We just passed a building that was a movie theatre for many years that may undergo a restoration. A few other buildings, scattered throughout the historic district, are also being remodeled to become business locations. There's also a fair amount of work going on behind the scenes to lure entrepreneurs with incentives."

"There seems to be a focus on preservation as well."

"Definitely. I dare you to find a town this size or even bigger that has as many museums. It's astounding. There's—" Symphony watched as the man seemed to be counting in his head.

"Six museums in the town with two more in development, plus a host of historic mansions and other sites."

"How did you know that?"

"That's why I'm here."

The conversation paused as they stopped to cross the street. Symphony could see a large log structure on the opposite side that she assumed was the restaurant.

"The museums are why you are here?" Symphony could hear puzzlement in the man's voice.

"Yes, I'm the new curator for the Rock House and other museums that are operated by your town government." They had crossed the street.

"That's great. I heard about that new positon being created."

Standing on the sidewalk in front of the restaurant, Jason reached for Symphony's arm to help her out of the way as a couple came up behind from the steps leading to the restaurant's porch.

Symphony, by nature, was a fairly levelheaded person. She liked facts and organization. She did not put too much stock in 'fanciful notions,' as Mariel, her mother, would say. But, her Grammie Wallace's influence had taken her 'seeing is believing' tendencies and turned them on a dime. Grammie taught her to believe in signs, hunches, and the magic of serendipity. As Jason took hold of her arm, Symphony felt a jolt that made her a little unsteady on her feet.

"That was strange. Did you feel that?" Jason looked down at the ground. "That must have been a Southwest Virginia earthquake."

Symphony's heart skipped a beat. She wondered if her Grammie was sending her a message.

"I guess this is the restaurant." Symphony took a breath.

"It is indeed. 1776 Log House Restaurant. I was going to sit in the lounge and eat a burger. I presume you were planning to eat alone, I would love to invite you to have dinner with me."

"Oh, I wouldn't want to impose on you. I will be fine alone. No worries."

"It's not an imposition. I was going to eat in solitude with loud bar sounds all around. I would enjoy a conversation with the town's new curator. It would be a fitting end to my brief career as a tour guide." Jason smiled.

"Well." Symphony stalled for a moment. She looked into Jason's eyes. It was not just their unusual color; there was something mesmerizing about them. "Okay. That would be wonderful. You may regret it though. I have lots of questions about the area."

"I love to talk. If I don't know the answer, I will just make one up."

They laughed and began to walk up the steps that led to the restaurant's entrance. She noticed several large flower garden areas, dormant for the winter, with an eclectic assortment of art mixed in. Climbing a short, but steep, set of steps, Symphony caught the aroma of something delicious cooking as Jason held the door for her.

"Table for two." Jason nodded to the hostess.

"Right this way."

Following the hostess up the stairs to the second floor of the restaurant, Symphony looked at the varied décor that adorned the walls. The old tables and chairs were befitting a structure that dated back to the 1700s. The long menu the hostess placed before her had the heaviness of a piece of wood. She read a vast list of entrée choices. After serving their beverages, the waiter came back and asked them for their food selections.

"Are you ready to order?" Jason smiled at Symphony.

"It's hard to decide. Why don't you go first?"

"This young lady is new to our town. So let's start off with a

Log House specialty, the corn fritters with honey. Then, I will have the ribeye, medium rare, with stuffed squash and parsley potatoes."

"And, for you, ma'am?"

"There are so many appetizing choices. My mother says that you should always choose what first peaks your interest. So, I will have the stuffed chicken breast with wild rice and steamed broccoli."

"Excellent choices. I will be back in a few minutes with your appetizer."

"Symphony. That is certainly an unusual name. Are your parents musicians?"

"No, not hardly. My father is a meteorologist and my mother is a nurse." Symphony paused for a moment thinking whether she should reveal how she got her name. "I am told that they had some help choosing my name. It was a challenge as a child. Kids couldn't pronounce it and adults thought it was a joke. I went through a stage where I wanted to just change it to Cindy or something like that. I've grown into it since then."

"Well, it is beautiful. I am certain that I have never met anyone with that name before."

Jason took a drink of his beverage. Symphony caught another glimpse of his eyes.

"Since we are on the subject of the unusual, are you related to Elizabeth Taylor?"

"No, not that I am aware of. Why do you ask?"

A look of confusion crossed Jason's face. Symphony noticed his eyes turned a darker shade.

"Your eyes. The color is unusual. The only person I ever remember having naturally violet eyes was Elizabeth Taylor."

"Ah, yes. Just like your name has brought you unwanted

attention. So have my eyes. Girl eyes, they have been called. I was tortured on the playground."

"Children can be cruel. But, to have eyes that color without the aid of contact lenses is a beautiful thing."

"Thank you. They come from my maternal grandmother who hid hers behind thick glasses all her life. While beautiful, they did not offer her the best of vision."

Jason nodded to the waiter placing the appetizer between them on the table.

"The irony of that does not go unnoticed." Symphony paused for Jason to speak. When he did not, she continued. "Those look like hush puppies."

"They do. You will find, though, that they are much different especially when slathered with butter and honey."

"Really? Since you are a local, I suppose that I must take your direction."

Symphony picked up one of the ball-shaped fritters. Breaking it in two, she saw corn kernels were sprinkled in the fritter like blueberries in a muffin. She first spread butter, then honey, copying Jason doing the same. Taking a cautious bite, a drop of honey slid down the side of her mouth.

"Oh, my, that is delicious." Jason reached over with his napkin and wiped the honey away. "Thank you."

"They are addictive. I tell myself that I'm really eating a vegetable because of the corn."

With a big mischievous smile on his face, he consumed a whole fritter in one bite. His eye-rolling expression of pleasure made them laugh together. She had made a friend.

THEIR DINNER CONVERSATION covered a variety of topics, from his high school sports career to her year of college in Europe. When an embarrassingly big yawn interrupted her storytelling, Jason suggested that it was time he drove her back to the Trinkle Mansion.

"I'm so sorry. That was rude. I've been up since before sunrise doing last minute packing, and then making the drive from West Virginia."

"I understand. I made that drive myself today."

His comment caught Symphony off-guard and she stopped as they were walking out of the restaurant.

"On I-77?"

"Yes. Traffic wasn't bad at all."

"Where are you parked?" Despite the darkness, Symphony began to look around.

"I'm parked in the side parking lot. It's right through the garden."

Symphony walked ahead of Jason in the direction he pointed. The parking lot was full. She paused to let him walk around her and lead the way.

"Right back here."

A long Suburban blocked her view until she was at the back of Jason's vehicle—a red Corvette.

WORDS OF THE GRANNY WITCH

The woman drew in a long gasp of air as the darkness of the evening cast a shadow across the windowpanes of her small cabin. She knew the time had come. The presence of the girl was near. It was a certainty, every bit as much of one as the confidence the sun will rise after its nightly sleep.

"She will find her way here. The path has been laid. I will educate her as she takes in the depth of her destiny. The one who birthed her has prepared me. I shall not falter."

"The pendant is full of all the clues and magic needed to keep her journey safe. So heavy on her neck on the day of her abandonment, now she shall be able to bear the weight of her future."

The woman rose from her chair, made by her own hands from the branches of saplings when they were still young and agile. Like her, the chair was molded to be a nonconformist, weathered by the winds of time and the pains of heartache. Her voice was strong. Words only heard by those whose spirits lingered.

"I am the last of the granny witches. Given not this heritage by birth, thrust into it by the cruelness of time. Queens of Appalachia risen from the soil in which we grow the flora of our magic. No craft of sorcery, no white or black—granny magic bursts forth in the colors of nature, gentle to some, powerful to others. My name is spoken in whispers. Those who darken my doorway look over their shoulder for the guilt of association. Most never realizing I am the truest friend they have—keeper of their secrets. My secrets never even glimmer in their imagination. If they knew where I had been, they would not worry about who might see them darken my doorway."

A rumble of thunder made the woman look up into the sky of her cabin. Drying fragments of nature's bounty hung loosely in clumps in the air.

"Thunder in the winter, snow coming by week's end. Will it be in this time or one that has long passed? Shall this be a sign of the pureness of the child who has come back to these mountains? Or is it the vision of her first mother's cold heart of despair?"

Chapter Two

SYMPHONY AWOKE THE FOLLOWING MORNING laughing aloud. She did not remember the entire dream she had, but it ended with the red Corvette passing her on the interstate. Her Grammie Wallace was in the passenger seat waving at her. She thought at some point during the night she heard the rumble of thunder. She chalked that up to her dreamtime as well.

Despite the huge meal she had eaten the night before, she was more than ready for breakfast. After showering and dressing, Symphony made her way to the dining room she had glimpsed upon her arrival. Two couples were seated at the table, drinking coffee and eating small muffins when she joined them.

"Good morning, Symphony." Patti came out of the kitchen with a carafe of coffee. Symphony placed the linen napkin on her lap. "I hope you slept well."

"I did. Thank you. The bed was very comfortable. I didn't want to leave it."

"Everyone introduce yourselves. I will be back in a few moments with our first course. This morning, we will begin with Berries Romanof. Our main breakfast entrée will be my personal spin on Eggs Benedict. I call it Benedict Bundles. It will be served with Southern Potato Cakes. Our third course will be dessert, Mountain Man Cinnamon Rolls."

As Patti left the room, Symphony began drinking the orange juice that had been placed before her. One sip told her that the juice had been fresh squeezed that morning. Looking at the other guests, she saw another single guest besides the couples she saw when she entered the room. She smiled and nodded to them.

"Have you stayed at this inn previously, young lady?" An older man seated diagonally across from Symphony began speaking. His looks and voice reminded her of Sean Connery. Grammie called him a Silver Fox. The thought made Symphony smile. "Evelyn and I have stayed here several times in the last few years."

"No, sir. This is my first visit. It is a mansion. I cannot imagine the work that must have gone into the renovation and restoration."

"As I understand, Patti was involved every step of the way. Bernie told me that he was still working in Iowa and that Patti retired a year or so ahead of him and worked side-by-side with those she hired to do the renovation work. She stated it wasn't always easy to find the right craftsman for some of the aspects. So, Patti taught herself how to do some things."

"It was a labor of love." Patti placed a bowl of fruit in front of Symphony. "At times, I thought I was crazy. Now, I realize that I wouldn't have had it any other way. The work had to meet my standards, even when I was doing it." Patti laughed. She placed bowls in front of the other guests. "This young lady, I imagine, knows a thing or two about preservation. She has just moved here to become a museum curator."

"Bravo, young lady!" The man extended his hand across the table to Symphony. "I'm Hugh Portland. This is my wife, Evelyn. During our visits to the Trinkle Mansion over the past few years, we have enjoyed exploring this community and getting to know some of the people here. We've been retired for about a decade and have been wandering throughout the U.S. looking for a new home. We've just about decided that it should be Wytheville. I would love to get involved in the preservation work here. So many mysteries of history connected with this area."

Symphony was about to respond to Hugh's last comment when Patti entered the room with the second course. Everyone became quiet and enjoyed the meal. When Hugh began speaking again, he was deep in conversation with the others at the table. She thought about his earlier comment and wondered if he was referring to specific mysteries in the community's history. Symphony imagined that her breakfast companions might be surprised to learn she had a mystery of her own.

NO SNOW HAD fallen the night before and the weather continued to be unseasonably warm for January, so Symphony decided to take another walk on the quiet Sunday morning. Under the soft winter morning light, she wanted to take in the architecture of the downtown structures and glimpse a bit of the town's history along the way. For the walk, Bernie had armed Symphony with another brochure of a walking tour of the historic district. After flipping through the first few pages, she saw she could use her cell phone to listen to the audio version.

As she passed by buildings with histories that went back to the 1800s, Symphony could not help but wonder how her own heritage was intertwined with the community. She imagined that her mother had probably strolled down Main Street countless times. Perhaps her father had, too. She longed to know who they were and what brought them together. Symphony hoped that the story had an ending that would not haunt her for the rest of her life.

The sound of a church bell tolling drew her attention away from her own thoughts. Going back to the tour information, she realized that she was just a few feet from Church Street. The street sign ahead came into view as Symphony also saw an older man briskly making a right turn. As fast as he had been walking, she was surprised to almost run over him as she turned the corner. He was standing still in the middle of the sidewalk.

"Hello, sir." Symphony walked around the man.

"Greetings and salutations, young lady. What direction do you think the wind is coming from?" The man held one finger up in the air as if he was trying to feel the wind.

"I'm afraid I would not know that, sir."

"It is good to know which way the wind is blowing. It will tell you how your day will be."

The man was still moving around in a circle holding up his finger. She took the opportunity to study his appearance. A slender man of average height, his gray hair was buzz cut short. His profile revealed a pointed nose that reminded her of a bird's bill and unusually small ears. She wanted to know his name.

"I wish I could help you, sir. I have just moved here. My name is Symphony Wallace."

The man stopped and tilted his head, as if he was considering what she said.

"Symphony. You will make a great noise in all you do."

It was not the reaction that she expected, but it amused her nonetheless.

"May I ask your name, sir?" Symphony smiled. He looked at her warily.

"Everyone knows my name, young lady. I am the Father of Wytheville."

Symphony furrowed her brow. A car horn blowing on the street momentarily took her attention away from the man. She turned to see a driver waving at someone across the street. She turned back to the man; he was gone. She looked around. He was nowhere in sight.

"THAT WAS TOM BOYD. He is a curious fellow." Bernie offered Symphony a bottle of water. "He is a descendant of Thomas J. Boyd, the man who is called the Father of Wytheville. His ancestor was indeed an influential person in the beginnings of this town. Those wide streets you just walked on are some of his work. The first Mr. Boyd designed the layout of the town. You will see the more recent Mr. Boyd, Tom, walking all the time. He retired from the military. He was a high-ranking officer, as I understand. Tough as nails. He's mellowed since then and become rather quirky."

"He must be in great shape as well. I turned around for just a few seconds and he disappeared."

"Yes, that's another enigma about Tom. He seems to have the ability to vanish. Some of us have wondered if this is a skill he developed in the military. He refuses to discuss what his duties included."

"Intriguing." Symphony took an apple from the bowl that Bernie extended to her. "I hope to meet and get to know many interesting people here."

"There is no shortage of interesting people in Wytheville. Most of them will have a story or two for you. Since you will be working with history, you will find that many residents have ancestors that date back to the first settlers of this region. For many, heritage is still a sacred aspect of their lives."

"Heritage is something that I hope to learn about here." Symphony paused and looked at her phone. "It's not quite noon yet. My father thought there would be snow in Wytheville last night, but that never arrived. Actually, it seemed quite the opposite. According to the weather forecast, that snow might have been pushed into this afternoon. I don't think walking around town will be such a good option. Do you think I would have trouble getting a seat for the matinee at the dinner theatre?"

"Certainly not. January is a slower time of year for the travelling public. I believe that they start seating folks at around one o'clock on Sundays for the meal, and then the show begins at three. That would certainly fill your afternoon."

"Great. I have time to take a quick shower and change."

"I will call and make a reservation for you while you get ready."

SYMPHONY CLOSED THE front door of the Trinkle Mansion with just fifteen minutes to get to the other side of town where the Wohlfahrt Haus Dinner Theatre was located. Walking down the sidewalk to the gate, she noticed that a now familiar red Corvette was sitting out front and its driver was just exiting.

"Are you stalking me?" Symphony kept a serious look on her face.

"Hey, there. I was just going to come inside and see—" Jason stopped mid-sentence. "You are kidding me, right? You don't really think I'm a stalker."

"I don't know. I just met you yesterday. You passed me on the interstate. Then, you showed up last night while I was walking. Now, here you are sitting in front of where I am staying. You are either stalking me or someone is paying you to be nice to me."

"Passed you on the interstate? What are you talking about?"

Symphony forgot that she did not tell him that part of the story. Jason folded his arms across his chest and tilted his head.

"Listen, I would love to stand here and chat with you, on the street, again. But, I have a reservation at the dinner theatre and I'm about to be late."

"That sounds like fun. I would love to go." Jason walked to the passenger side of his car and opened the door.

"But, I didn't invite you."

"Of course you did." He flashed her a picture perfect smile. "I'm just trying to save you a little time since you are late. We can go through the formality of the rest of the conversation, if you want. It will only make us later."

"You have charm down to a science." Symphony put her hand over her mouth. She realized she said what she was thinking aloud.

"It's my hidden power." Jason winked and Symphony's blood pressure rose twenty points. "Could we continue this conversation on the drive over there?"

Symphony shook her head and got into the car. Before she

could get comfortable, he was in the seat next to her, putting the vehicle in reverse. Ducking down a side street, he had paused at a stop sign before he began questioning her.

"Where did you see me on the interstate?"

"It was after the last toll booth."

"What made you remember this particular car? Vettes are a fairly common sight on the road."

"True. But, not normally while the song *Little Red Corvette* is playing on the radio."

"The Prince song?"

"The one and only. It was quite unnerving to hear that song playing as a red Corvette drove by me."

"I'll say. That's a sign."

"That's exactly what my grandmother would say."

"See. We were destined to meet." Jason ran his fingers through his hair and grew quiet.

"It would appear so." Symphony laughed nervously. Jason pulled into the parking lot of the dinner theatre. "Wow. This is a big place."

"I think it seats a little over two hundred in the theater portion. There's also a pub with an outdoor dining area." He found a spot and parked the car.

"Do you come here often?"

"Not as often as I would like. Learning the brewing ropes has limited my free time." Jason turned toward her. "I'm not even sure what the current show is."

"Neither am I. Bernie at the B&B made my reservation."

"Was the reservation for one or have I really made a jerk of myself and crashed plans you had with someone else?" For the first time, Symphony saw a sheepish look cross his face.

"The reservation is for one. Surely, they don't have just tables for one. There's got to be at least one other chair at the table." Symphony reached for the door handle.

"Hold on a second. Let me say something." Jason touched her arm. Symphony looked down at his hand. He had a ring on his pinkie. The gold ring had an unusual design. Black onyx was the base with a large gold X in the center. She wondered what the letter stood for. "I come across all loud mouth and forward sometimes. Too often, really. If I am being too friendly, you just say the word."

"No, not at all. I'm glad we met. I don't know anyone here aside from those I met when I came to Wytheville for my interview. I want to make friends here. This is a great start. I appreciate your time." Symphony smiled and Jason returned it.

"Great. Let's go and enjoy some music."

They both got out of the car and walked toward the front door.

"If you don't know what the show is, how do know there will be music?"

"Didn't you read about the Wohlfahrt Haus in that brochure you are clutching so tightly?" Symphony looked down at the visitors guide. It had permanent wrinkles from the grip she had on it. "Their tagline is 'all musicals, all the time.' There's got to be music."

"WHAT A MEAL! All the meals I have eaten today were in courses. The Trinkle Mansion breakfast this morning was three courses and now this lunch has four. I'm going to gain five pounds before I ever start my new job."

"Yes, those two locations are hard on the waistline." Jason nodded as the server refilled his water glass. "Maybe you can start walking to work."

"Oh, that's funny." Symphony shook her head. She closed the play program she was reviewing. "I guess I didn't tell you where I am going to be living."

"No, I don't think it ever came up last night at dinner."

"I am going to be living in a small room on the top floor of the Rock House. I'm sure that will not be my permanent residence. But, it was offered as part of my salary package for at least the first few months of my probationary period, so I took them up on it. I have a feeling that Allison has a lot of work for me to do."

"I'm sure there is probably a backlog. I really don't know too much about the operation. There's been a lot of growth in the last few years in the number of locations and exhibits that the town operates. I imagine that has forced the curating work to be put on the backburner. Kind of like filing documents when you are overloaded with projects, I would guess."

"That's a good analogy. These types of positions seem to find me. My last job was basically two years of organizing and filing. I'm good at it."

"We never really talked about what interested you about coming to Virginia. Did it just happen to be where you found an opportunity?"

Symphony looked intently at Jason as she thought about how she would answer. She had not planned on telling too many people that moving to Wytheville was more than just a job to her. Yet, she already felt like Jason was becoming her friend. It might be good to confide her secret to someone.

"This job will be a great step up on my career path. The person

I worked for in my previous position did her internship here with Allison Emerson many years ago. So, I already have an idea about what it will be like to work with her." Symphony took a drink of water. "That's not the full story though. I'm hoping that living here will help me find my birth mother."

"Good afternoon and welcome to Wohlfahrt Haus Dinner Theatre."

A young man appeared on the stage to welcome the audience to the show. Jason looked surprised at her last comment. They turned their chairs toward the front to watch the show.

WORDS OF THE GRANNY WITCH

"Love blooms in the garden where it was planted. Like a wildflower, it may not end up where it started. This child who has returned came from a love that should have never been. It was impossible and, yet, she is the evidence that it was not. Her own love when she finds it might be the same."

The woman walked down narrow steps to the bowels of her cabin. A cold room lay at the end of the steps. No light could find its way there unless it was brought. The woman had for many years used nothing but a kerosene lamp. In recent times, modern ways had crept into the last room of her dwelling that remained in its own time.

Her bones ached in the coldness. She did not know if it was the passing of years or the wearing of time that had made her body feel so much. It was like a disease that consumed her body without ever entering her system. It made her wonder—would she ever quit paying for the sins of her younger self?

"My sweet favorite." She gathered up two bundles of lavender. It would be the foundation of her newest creation. She moved the bundles to her nose and took in a deep sniff. "The power is in the purple. It heals and soothes."

Slowly, making her way back up the steps, her mind wandered back to the child and the mother of that one. Like her bones and muscles, her heart began to ache.

"People think they understand love, like they think they understand time. They are fooled by the both of them. Love will lead you places you never should have been. It will give you your greatest gifts in the same breath as your strongest heartaches. This child comes from both. She will learn the truth of it. I will lead her as I have promised the one who brought her forth. She must travel a great distance to learn the real truth of her existence. Even though it is no further away than the reason that led her here."

Chapter Three

IT WAS AN EXCITING THOUGHT WHEN Symphony learned her living quarters would be within one of the museums. It would be a way to immerse herself in her new job. Upon her arrival Monday morning, the reality of it began to sink in.

"We don't include this portion of the house in the tour. The narrow stairs are a hindrance to accessibility. Since you are new to the area and we have a vast amount of work for you to do, I thought it might be convenient for you to stay here." Allison began to show Symphony around the Rock House. "Don't be afraid because I said vast amount of work. Think of it as job security."

Symphony released a nervous chuckle. She quickly stifled it when she realized Allison was not laughing.

"We've experienced so much growth in our archives and exhibits. I haven't gotten around to the true curating duties in a while. We've maintained accurate care of the items. But, the whole logging and cataloguing aspect has gotten out of hand because people have donated so many items during the last couple of years."

"Well, that's why I'm here."

As they made it to the top floor, Symphony studied the small room she would be making her temporary home. This was not part of the tour when Allison interviewed her. The lowness of the ceilings and primitive décor might be a detriment to someone accepting the position. Despite it being far different than anything she remembered in her life, she thought of it as an adventure—another part of the exploration of her heritage.

Symphony put her laptop case on the bed and continued to look around the small room. From what she saw, it was from an era over one hundred and fifty years previous. It was like stepping back in time. The room had an A-frame shape to it, making the ceilings on both sides slope down, giving the room the appearance of being smaller than it actually was. Two small windows brought bright sunlight into the room. There was a drafty feeling. Lines of age and repair ran through the plaster. Symphony noticed lamps were placed on the tables. It could be a dark place at night unless the moon peeked in. The floors appeared to be original, crafted from heartwood pine. The aged look of the wood made her wonder how many feet had passed over them. She figured her feet would get cold unless she wore thick socks or shoes. There was nothing modern about the room. Symphony fell in love.

Prying herself away from her exploration of the space, Symphony turned her attention to the young man carrying her boxes and suitcases into the room. He was quiet, in movement and voice, in his work. Symphony wished she had not brought as many belongings because he was making his third trip up the narrow stairs into the small space.

"Make yourself at home and get settled. I have a meeting until ten. Drew will stay here to help you with anything you need." Allison turned to the young man who had just placed a larger box on the floor. "I'm sorry. I forgot to introduce you two. Symphony, this is our newest intern, Drew Lassiter. Drew is a history major from North Carolina. Drew, Symphony Wallace is our new curator."

"Nice to meet you, ma'am." Drew extended his hand and smiled.

"I feel like I should be tipping you. I'm sorry that I didn't pack lighter."

"Oh, those things weren't heavy at all. Nothing like I am used to, ma'am."

"Drew grew up on a large dairy farm. I've had him moving lots of things since he arrived." Allison smiled as she walked toward the door. "Again, make yourself at home. Wander around the house. We will begin giving you the full tour later this afternoon. Despite that skiff of snow last night, it's a beautiful January day. We will try not to keep you inside all the time."

"Thanks for everything. I really appreciate this opportunity."

"Lyla says that we are lucky to have you. I've never doubted her opinion. I expect great things from you, Symphony. And, I expect you to solve a few mysteries while you are here."

As the heavy door click closed, Symphony examined the wood that created the closure. While Grammie Wallace had been a woman of signs and whimsy, her husband had been a craftsman and wood was his love and specialty. Symphony had spent many of her youngest days sitting on a stool in his workshop watching him create pieces of furniture that were as much works of art as items of functionality. Ever the student, she had absorbed his knowledge of the different types of wood he was using. Sadly, Gramps had passed before Symphony reached her teens, but not before he gave his granddaughter a wealth of knowledge that would serve her well as she pursued a career in preservation.

"The wood at my feet is certainly old pine." Symphony spoke aloud to herself opening the door to look at both sides of it. "This door is made of the heartwood of pine—the strongest part."

"You know wood." Drew spoke from the stairs below her, making Symphony jump. "I'm sorry; I didn't mean to startle you. Allison asked me to stay close by, in case you needed anything. I heard you speaking and thought you might be calling me."

"No worries. I am the jumpy sort. My knowledge of wood first began in my childhood with my grandfather. Did your upbringing on a farm give you yours?"

"No. Growing up on a dairy farm, there are times when you would do anything to get away from it. The summer that I turned seventeen, I got a job working for a company that was logging a deep, old forest in the western part of my state. There was quite a variety of tree species in that forest; some were hundreds of years old. I learned a lot about identifying trees and wood as it was cut. I'm not as good at identifying it once it has been made into something."

"I take it that you are majoring in some form of history?"

"Yes. I'm focusing more on the preservation aspects."

"Then, your education will certainly grow in identifying wood. I will remember that as we work together while you are here. Perhaps, Allison will allow you to work with me on the portion of the archives that has to do with furnishings or any documentation we do regarding structures, such as this one."

"That would be great." Symphony got a better glimpse of the quiet young man's personality and manner as a huge smile crossed his face. "What can you tell about this door from your initial examination of it?"

"I would say that this is longleaf pine." Symphony ran her hand over the door. "It's the heartwood of a pine—a very large pine tree. This wood was preferred by woodworkers because of its strength, hardness, and coloration. Around the time period that this house was constructed, there were massive pine forests from Virginia to eastern Texas. I've read historical accounts that indicated there were thirty to sixty million acres of this wood. It took over one hundred years for the trees to mature, but they could live up to five hundred years. Their massive trunks would produce a lot of lumber with the core, or heart, of the tree giving the strongest wood."

"It's amazing to think that this wood had a long history before it even became this door." Drew let his hand pass over the door as well.

"That's an interesting way of putting it. I guess it's like people. No matter your age, you have some level of history. Even a newborn has the history of how he or she came to be."

"I'm going to enjoy working with you, Miss Wallace." Drew turned to leave.

"Only if you call me Symphony." Symphony heard Drew laugh as he made his way back down the narrow stairs.

"I'll be right downstairs if you need anything."

Symphony smiled as she returned to examining her new surroundings. It was not the average attic. Built prior to the Civil War, she wondered if the small space had been used for any confidential meetings for the protection of the Confederacy.

Symphony surmised that was probably information she would be learning in the near future.

The small twin size bed that stood to one side had what appeared to be a new mattress on it. Her bed at home was queen size, so her mother had purchased two sets of twin sheets as well as appropriately sized blankets. As Symphony removed them from one of the carefully packed boxes, she breathed in the fresh fabric softener smell. Sheets never went from the package to the bed at Mariel Wallace's home. Symphony knew as surely as the sun would rise tomorrow that she would find sachets of lavender inside the blankets for her to tuck inside her dresser drawers.

As she packed during the previous week, Symphony did not know how much storage space she would have for her clothing. She was pleased to see that a tall dresser was located on the highest wall of the room. Allison had mentioned that they would make a small closet available to her on the next level down. It would be an interesting experience to get ready each morning on several levels of the house, as the bathroom was on the lowest floor. Being an early riser would be in her favor as there would be much for her to personally accomplish before the workday began.

Allison had referred to her new room as the children's room when they had first climbed the stairs. Symphony imagined that if it had ever been used as sleeping quarters, another small bed would have stood on the opposite side of the door as well. She was happy to see that the area now contained a comfortable looking chair with an end table beside it. Closer to the window, the smallest roll-top desk she believed she had ever seen was available for her use.

"I wonder how in the world they got that up those stairs and through this door. No doubt, it was more carrying that Drew had to do on my behalf."

"Symphony." A knock on the door startled her again.

"You seem to constantly be catching me talking to myself."

"My mother says that when she is talking to herself it is the most intelligent conversation she has all day." Drew bent down while coming through the doorway to leave her last box. "I missed this one by the door. You must have carried it in yourself. Allison forgot to tell you that the computer department left a laptop over there on the desk in the corner. It's under the roll-top. It is wirelessly connected to a printer downstairs."

"Is this my office, too?" Symphony was laughing until she caught a glimpse of the serious look on Drew's face. "I guess it is."

"Allison will explain in more detail. There's quite a bit of remodeling going on downstairs over the winter. I think that most of your initial work will be done on the next level below. That's where most of the Rock House storage is located. She thought a laptop would be of better use to you than a desktop as much of the cataloging work can be done on it."

"That makes perfect sense."

"She also forgot to tell you that the human resources department is expecting you at one o'clock this afternoon to complete your paperwork. You'll find a couple of files on your desk about the history of this house. That's part of the work that I am doing for my internship. There is a walking tour of the historic district that travelers can take."

"Oh, yes. I walked some of the tour yesterday morning. Good stuff. I like the online aspects."

"Allison thought that the online version about the Rock House could really be enhanced if we added more photography and stories. That's what I am working on."

"Sounds great. Before you leave, could you show me where

the bathroom facilities are? I might need to tour those later." Symphony chuckled and followed Drew out of the room.

"Have you ever lived in a house this old before?" Drew led the way downstairs.

"No, I have not."

"Then, I suggest that you might want to get some over-the-counter allergy meds. The dust in old homes is murder on the sinuses."

Reaching the bottom floor, Symphony noticed a tall antique clock in the corner next to the front door. There was something about the clock that compelled her to study it further. Standing back next to the stairs, she took in the full view of it.

"That's an unusual pendant you have on." Drew spoke as he waited for her to look at the clock. "My mother makes jewelry. She would love that."

Symphony nodded as her hand automatically went to the long pendant around her neck. In spite of his efforts to draw her into a conversation, she was still mesmerized by the unusual clock. Her previous experience with furnishings from historic eras told her that the clock could be an example of German craftsmanship. Gold numbers were surrounded by drawings of flowers. The drawings were intricate and simple at the same time. It made her wonder if there was a certain pattern that they followed or a message that they hid.

Despite the knowledge that she should not, Symphony could not stop herself from placing her hand gently on the glass. A jolt surged through her, as if the clock was full of electricity. Strange images passed before her eyes.

"Symphony, are you okay? Please say something."

Drew's voice was calling her back. Removing her fingertips

from the clock, she blinked a couple of times before he came into focus in front of her. His hand was on her forearm.

"What happened to you? I was about to call for help."

Symphony saw fear in the young man's eyes. It touched her that he was so concerned.

"I just got light-headed for a few seconds. It's probably like you just mentioned. The air is different in an old building."

"A few seconds? You've been standing there frozen for several minutes. Your body was rigid like you had gone into shock or something. I kept shaking you and calling your name. The only reason I hadn't called anyone was because I could still feel a steady pulse and your breathing seemed okay. I was on the rescue squad for a couple of years at home. I've never seen someone become catatonic and still be upright like that. Has this happened to you before?"

Symphony stared at Drew, trying to grasp what he had just told her. She touched the clock. She felt a jolt. Images appeared in her mind like a dream. It seemed like just a few seconds. How could it have been longer?

"No. I don't think so." Her mind raced. Drew was still searching her face.

"Hold on to the banister. I'll go get you a chair."

Drew placed both of Symphony's hands on the banister before he left her side. She wanted to sink down to the steps below her. She did not want him to see how rattled she was. He quickly returned with a folding chair. He placed it in front of the door. She felt it was too close to the clock. She pointed to an area closer to the stairs and away from the door.

"I'm going to call Marcella. Maybe you should go to the hospital."

"No. No. I don't think that is necessary. It was just a fluke thing. Let's chalk it up to first day jitters and too much rich food yesterday." Symphony forced a laugh and a smile. While his brow was still furrowed with obvious worry, Drew smiled at her comment. "Just let me sit here for a few minutes before you call anyone. I'm sure that I will be just fine."

Drew nodded and left the room. Before Symphony could relax and get her bearings, he had returned with a bottle of water.

"I'll be over in the medical exhibit area. All you have to do is say my name and I'll be back."

"Thank you, Drew. I appreciate it. Can this be our little secret? I really don't want Allison to worry that she has hired someone with some strange health condition."

"I understand. It can stay our secret as long as you are truly alright."

After Drew left the room, Symphony took a deep breath. She did not have a clue what had happened to her. It probably was just a fluke. Maybe her system was sensitive to the new environment that was filled with layers of settled dust and such. She would go to a pharmacy during her lunch hour and pick up some low dose allergy meds.

Unscrewing the cap from the bottle of water, she felt a tingling in her fingers. She made a fist, and then released her fingers. She took a drink of water and returned her gaze to the old clock. Standing tall in the corner, the grandfather clock had a semi-circle arched top of dark wood. Gold numbers were surrounded by an intricate flower pattern. From her previous preservation work, the pattern indeed reminded her of German clocks she had seen. The pendulum was large and had the gleam of brass. She wondered if it was original to the home or if it came as a donation in the years since the house became a museum. Nonetheless, it had an unusual look, and probably an identical history.

After a few minutes passed and most of the bottle of water was gone, Symphony took a deep breath and rose from the chair. Her legs wobbled a little at first. A strange aroma passed through her nostrils—antiseptic-like with a tinge of the sweat of a hot summer day.

"I hope I am not coming down with a bug of some sort." Symphony whispered to herself. "I cannot be sick my first week on the job. There must surely be some policy against that."

Symphony took a few cautious steps away from the foyer and into the adjacent dining room. Her thoughts were momentarily distracted while she took in the uniqueness of the almost two hundred-year-old room. On the front side of the house, there were several windows that brought in an unusual amount of light and made the room look large. A fireplace was in the center of the wall that faced the hallway.

"I thought I heard you talking." Symphony jumped when she heard Drew's voice behind her. "I'm glad to see you up walking around. Are you okay?"

"Yes. I think I am fine. I think it was an allergic reaction of some sort."

"I hope not. It would be awful to be allergic to your job." Drew smiled. "I've got to go out and pick up a large package that Allison ordered that was mistakenly delivered to the municipal building. Will you be okay?"

"Absolutely. I'm just going to spend a little time getting acquainted with the Rock House."

"Well, I'm going to go then. You know that you can call the main museum office, if you need anything." Symphony could tell by Drew's body language that he was hesitant to leave her alone.

"Don't worry. I'm fine. It was probably only first day jitters combined with all this new dust for my sinuses to become acquainted with. I'm sure I will get used to it in no time." Symphony laughed louder than she needed to in order to try to break the tension. "You have been kind. I appreciate your concern."

Drew nodded and left the room. A few minutes later, Symphony heard the side door closing. Looking around, she took in a deep breath. The doorway leading to the front foyer beckoned her. Slowly, she walked in that direction until she was standing in the middle of the foyer—the place where the incident occurred.

"I must have had some freak allergic reaction to old house air." Symphony eyed the clock next to the door. "There's something disturbing about a clock that no longer tells time. When it no longer serves its original function, what is left for it to do? Maybe it stores the time it ticked for." Symphony broke her gaze with the clock. She felt a strange tingle run down her spine. "Maybe I should quit talking to myself."

"Did you enjoy your stay at the Trinkle Mansion?" Allison led the way into her office. "It is amazing the work that has been done to restore the home to its former grandeur."

"It is a lovely place to stay. The owners are wonderful hosts. I'm sure it must be a popular location."

"I believe they stay quite busy." Allison sat down at her desk. "I'm thrilled that you have joined our staff, Symphony. We need a more scheduled process for our curation for future plans for growth. Lyla assures me that you have all of the skills to get us up to speed." Her phone rang and Allison momentarily looked at it before someone else picked up the call in another room. Symphony noticed that the woman pursed her lips when she saw the name on the phone's screen. She appeared concerned by the caller. "She also told me a little bit about why you were interested in coming to Wytheville."

"Oh, Allison, I am thrilled to be here and I want to assure you that my work here is my first priority."

"I don't have any hesitation as to why you are here. Lyla says that you are hardworking and dedicated just like she was. Lyla would not have any slackers on her team. I think it will be a grand adventure for you. I hope you will let us help you delve into your ancestry. Who knows? Your discoveries might lead us to learning some things about the history we are preserving here."

"I'm ready for any and all challenges that come my way." Symphony interrupted herself as she sneezed. "I do think I am going to have to get some allergy meds though."

"Working in old houses is hard on the sinuses."

"At my previous position, I had special gloves and a mask that I used when I was working in the archives."

"Absolutely. I believe we have those items you mentioned. Let me know if you need anything else." Allison looked at her wall clock. "It's about time for lunch. Why don't you take yours now, and then head to human resources to do your paperwork?"

"I think I will try to find a pharmacy and get something to help this sinus stuff until I get used to my new surroundings."

"Counts Drug Store is a couple of blocks down on Main Street. There are several cafés and sandwich shops between here and there." Allison rose from her desk and led Symphony to the outer office. She picked up a set of keys from the desk there. "Here are keys to all of our museum buildings. The one with the red dot is a key to lock your room."

"Thank you. I hadn't even thought of that."

"Neither had we. Drew mentioned it to me this morning. We had to dig to find it. After you finish with human resources, come back here. I will be in meetings for most of the afternoon, but Marcella will give you an overview of some of the things you will need to know about our general operation. I'm sure that you two will hit it off."

WITH ALLERGY MEDS in hand, Symphony sat at a high table at a small café within a complex called Old Stage Mall. She was ready to consume what a patron in the drug store told her was the best clam chowder in town.

"You made a good choice, young lady." A distinguished older woman leaned over from her table and spoke. "The clam chowder is the best. What are you having with it?"

"Thought I would go for something simple—a BLT."

"Excellent. You don't need anything fancy with that chowder. It will knock your socks off." The woman smiled and returned to her salad.

"I just moved here. My name is Symphony Wallace."

The woman put down her fork and finished chewing before she extended her hand.

"Delighted to meet you. Welcome to our town. I'm Nadia French. What brings you to Wytheville? I have got to say that you look quite familiar to me. I was about to ask if you have relatives in the area that I might know. Wallace is not a common name here."

Symphony felt a feeling of excitement pass over her to think that she might resemble someone from her mysterious family. She wondered how she might delve deeper into what the woman mentioned without seeming anxious.

"I have been hired to be the curator for the Wytheville museums."

"Oh, yes! I heard that Allison had hired a curator. I am on the historical society board. We are excited that someone will be devoted to the care of the archives. Do you have a connection to this area?"

There was the question again. Would Grammie Wallace say this was a sign?

"Ah, Mrs. French."

"Please, call me Nadia. I've always thought that when I hear 'Mrs. French,' I expect to turn and find my mother-in-law in the room. She was a rude woman. And, that is being kind." Nadia winked at Symphony.

A feeling of calm and trust came over Symphony. Something told her that she could trust Nadia. Perhaps, the woman could help her in the quest to find her mother. She would engage the woman further.

"Being on the historical society board, you must have a strong interest in local history. Is that because of your own heritage to the area?" So as not to seem too anxious, Symphony began to eat her soup. "Oh, my goodness. This is the most wonderful clam chowder. It's so rich and luscious. It must contain a thousand calories."

"Yes, indeed. It is delicious. You enjoy it and I will do something I greatly enjoy, I will talk." The woman laughed. The sound reminded Symphony of what it might sound like if a bird could laugh. It was lighthearted and fluttery.

"I love history, all sorts of it, even if it is not my own. I am not from Wytheville or the surrounding area. I came here after the passing of my husband to start a new life. There is something quite intriguing about the history of this part of Virginia. Wytheville has always been a crossroads of sorts. Long before the interstates brought the streams of traffic we see today, the roads around it still brought many people to this community."

"I've read some of the history about transportation through the area. It seems as though being on a well-traveled road has figured prominently in the success of this town."

"Indeed. I think there is something about the hustle-bustle combined with the calm quaintness that is especially attractive about this community. It's like something large surrounding something small. I've always felt at home here even though I am a stranger in many ways. The town has embraced me."

The server filled Nadia's coffee and placed Symphony's sandwich in front of her. Looking at her watch, she realized she only had thirty more minutes before her appointment at the human resources office.

"I'm sure it is your welcoming spirit that laid the groundwork for the community embracing you. I've only been in your company a few minutes and I feel like I have known you all my life."

Symphony looked down at her sandwich. Her eyes glimpsed Nadia's purse hanging on the back of a chair that sat between them. It was a burgundy Etienne Aigner bag, just like her grandmother had carried. It was a sign. Symphony took a deep breath as she thought about what she was about to say.

"What I am about to share with you may seem strange for me to be revealing since we just met. Something tells me that I can confide this in you."

"Oh, goodness, my dear. I would be honored to listen to you." Nadia moved her chair closer to Symphony. "Old women are good at keeping confidences."

"It's not exactly a secret. It's something that few people know about me. I came here to become the curator and work on the preservation of the museum collections. But, I do have a connection to Wytheville. I believe my mother lived here once. I may have even been born here."

"I'm not sure that I understand what you mean. You don't know where you were born?" Nadia furrowed her brow and tilted her head to one side.

"No, ma'am. Not exactly. I was adopted. I grew up in a small community north of Charleston, West Virginia." Symphony took another deep breath before she continued. There were few people to whom she had revealed the circumstances of her adoption. It was easier to leave it simply—she was adopted. "I was left on the front steps of a church in Bluefield. There were a few items left with me, a birth certificate was not one of them."

"Oh, how sad. How do you know who your mother was then?" Nadia looked away from Symphony for a moment. She thought the woman suddenly seemed sad.

"There was a note left with me. It was signed."

"Goodness. This sounds like the makings of a good mystery novel. It's giving me chills." Symphony watched as the woman took a drink of her coffee. She looked a little uncomfortable. "I know that I probably shouldn't be this bold. Something tells me though that you may need a listening ear. I know many people in the area. I would be honored to help you on your quest to find your mother. May I ask what her name was?" The look of sadness returned to the woman's face. The look made Symphony wonder if the woman had lost someone dear to her. "I know that I am just a prying old woman. I am a trustworthy one though."

"My Grammie Wallace, that's my father's mother, believed in signs. I've not even been in Wytheville two days and I've met so many kind people. Grammie would say that was a sign." Symphony looked at the woman. She thought she saw an understanding smile. "She would say that meeting a nice lady in a coffee shop on my first day of work who offered to help me was a sign that I should trust her." Symphony took in a deep breath. "I've got to start this search somewhere. When I was left at the church as an infant, there was a note with me. It was signed with the name of Amburgey Gibboney."

Nadia's eyes grew large and her expression completely changed. Symphony could have sworn that the name made a look of horror cross the woman's face. Nadia quickly looked down at her hands. Symphony could see that they were trembling. The woman moved her chair away from Symphony and took another drink of her coffee. The sudden change frightened Symphony. She wondered what her mother's history must include for this woman to have such a sudden and strange reaction to hearing her name. Perhaps, it was a torrid past that led her mother to abandon her child.

"Young lady, I have kept you from finishing your lunch."

"Did I say something wrong?" Symphony searched the woman's face for some sort of explanation to her sudden change in behavior.

"No. Do not worry about what you said. I'm sure you have to get back to work soon. I have interrupted your lunch long enough." Nadia lifted her head and looked Symphony straight in the eyes. "I now know why you looked so familiar to me."

Nadia's eyes were full of emotion as she hurriedly collected her belongings. Symphony could not decipher what the emotions were. She chose to remain silent. She wondered what her mother could have possibly done that would invoke such a response from someone. Symphony tried to figure out what to say while she watched the woman prepare to leave. Nadia took out a small pad from her purse and wrote something on a piece of paper, her fingers trembling, before tearing the paper off and handing it to Symphony.

"Your grandmother is right. You should pay attention to signs. I should do the same. I wasn't prepared for there to be a sign that was from so far back in the past." Nadia looked around the café like she was just realizing where she was. "I never go out for lunch on Mondays. I don't know what possessed me to do so today." Nadia looked back at Symphony. "Well, I suppose that is not an entirely true statement. I now know why I am here. It was so that I could meet you, my dear." Nadia's face softened. She had regained her composure, but still seemed a little rattled. "Amburgey Gibboney was my daughter."

The woman's words hit Symphony like a slap in the face. Her mind tried to grasp what Nadia said. It was like Symphony suddenly heard a foreign language, one that her brain could not compute. It was like the woman was speaking in slow motion from somewhere far away. For a moment, Symphony wondered if she was having a stroke, she felt like her spirit was leaving her body. Just as quickly, the feeling disappeared and Nadia sounded normal to her again.

"I'm sorry. I cannot speak any further about this right now. We will need complete privacy and the comfort of my home in order for me to go back into the past." Nadia's expression looked strained. Yet, she stopped again and stared at Symphony. "You have her eyes and some of her expressions. It's like seeing a ghost."

"A ghost?" Symphony found her voice. It was trembling almost as much as her hand was she clutched the piece of paper Nadia gave her. Her mouth was dry as she formed a question she did not want to ask. "Is Amburgey dead?"

"That's a question that I cannot answer. I don't know for certain. I have not seen her since about two months after you were born. I don't know where she has been since."

Symphony's mind raced with questions that she could not put into words. She felt afraid. Afraid of what she might learn.

"That's my address and phone number. You call me in a few days. I need time to grasp this. I need time." Nadia turned to leave. Stopping before she reached the door, she turned and walked back to Symphony. Gently, the woman touched Symphony's face with the fingertips of her right hand. Her eyes filled with tears. "I've always wondered about you. I wished that she had left you with me."

Before Symphony could react, Nadia was out the door. Symphony numbly watched through the window. Nadia rushed to her car and immediately drove away.

"Is everything okay, ma'am?" The owner was hovering near the table with a concerned look on his face.

"Yes." Symphony's voice was barely above a whisper. "I think I will need to take my sandwich to go."

WORDS OF THE GRANNY WITCH

"Being a granny witch has its benefits—one is solitude. Humans have a fear of anything connected with the word 'witch.' That is, until they think they need your services. Few people, outside of those who grow up knowing, understand what a granny witch really is. Most are born into the occupation. The best ones come from long lines, deep in their blood. The roots of the heritage in these Appalachian Mountains are as deep as the old trees that grow here. Grandmothers pass the mystery to mothers who pass it on to the daughters. All my skills were learned; I have no genetic tendencies to make the magic pure. I must rely on what I have learned sitting by the side of one of the last true Queens of Appalachia. The ways of the granny witches are fading, replaced by the lure of technology, killed off by the pain of poverty, forgotten by the tragedy of not believing."

Flexing her fingertips, the woman heard a crackle come from them. It had been a normal sound and feeling for longer than she wanted to remember. She wished to be able to converse with another of her kind—another who held the magic of time.

One day the child would understand. The woman sensed her presence. The child was full of secrets; most she did not even know herself. Yet. Her instincts would lead her to seek those who could help her. The woman hoped that those who had raised her had nurtured the strength that was deep within.

"The body can stand all sorts of shocks and afflictions. It can heal itself. The mind is another story entirely. The mind holds on to all that is happy and sad unconditionally. The shock of what she is about to learn will never leave the child. The one who birthed her put all her confidence in the finding out and none in the scars the reality would leave behind. I shall help her when she finds me. It will be small comfort for all the secrets she will one day know."

Chapter Four

IN A DAZE, SYMPHONY GATHERED HER belongings. Her mind was a murky mess, swirling with information and emotions that she dared not try to immediately process.

Looking at her phone, she saw there was just enough time for her to get from the café to the Rock House, deposit her food in the staff refrigerator, and run to the municipal building for her appointment with the human resources department. The urgency of it being her first day on the job was the only thing holding her together emotionally. Logging through stacks of paperwork and personnel policies was ideal; it would force her to think about what was in front of her in black and white. Not about the knowledge that had smacked her between the eyes and would certainly change her life.

She tried to not appear too frazzled when she arrived at the municipal building. Friendly faces greeted her in human resources and all of the other offices during the tour she was given to orient her to the nucleus of the municipal government operation. Symphony welcomed the order and structure that she glimpsed in each department. She recognized how crucial to her sanity this day-to-day life would become as the emotion of her heritage might unfold.

"Have you signed your name enough today?"

Allison had instructed Symphony to report to the main museum office after she was finished with the paperwork. Marcella was the marketing coordinator for the multiple museums. From the looks of the woman's desk alone, Symphony imagined that Marcella was the backbone of the internal operations.

"My hand is a little cramped from filling out all of the forms. I'm surprised that more of the paperwork isn't purely electronic by now."

"Less paper would completely defeat the emphasis on technology, don't you think?"

Symphony could already tell that she had found a kindred spirit in Marcella. They had only spoken a couple of times. Yet, it was crystal clear that the woman had a sarcastic side.

"So, besides starting a new job and writing your name a lot, what have you been up to since you arrived?"

"Well, I stayed at the Trinkle Mansion for the first two nights. That was a wonderful experience. My room was luxurious and the food was out of this world. I've already thought about my parents staying there on one of their visits to see me. It would make a great anniversary present for them."

"Indeed, Patti and Bernie have a successful business. Guests just rave about staying there. The structure is a thriving example of the profitability of historic preservation." Marcella handed Symphony a large notebook, explaining that it was filled with scripts and photographs for the different types of tours that were conducted at each museum. "You may have already gathered that our department is a rather small one. Even though your primary duties will involve curating, tours are a high priority on everyone's list of duties. Allison wanted me to orient you to the different tours we offer for each museum. She doesn't expect you to learn these immediately. It would, however, be helpful if you could begin to become familiar with them. Circumstances will probably arise sooner than later when you will be called upon to help give tours."

"I gave a lot of tours at my previous position. I understand about museums never having enough staff. I think learning the tours will help me with my preservation duties." As she began to go through the pages, Symphony realized the vast amount of learning she would need to do to begin to understand the items she would be curating. It was one thing to give the items proper care. It was even more important to understand the significance of each piece and how it fit into the historic story it helped preserve. "I've only learned a little so far, but I can already see that there are so many levels of history that are covered in each of the museum buildings."

"It may seem a little complicated to you, at first. Hopefully, you will soon see how all of the different aspects fit together." Marcella motioned for Symphony to sit in a chair next to her. "Let me show you a little bit about how our files are set up on the computer. There are different drives where we store files. The laptop that you were given to use is wirelessly connected into this network. The archiving software that we use is loaded on your laptop and on my computer. This is new software for all of us. When Allison decided to create your position, she also purchased this new software. It has more functions and archiving abilities than what we previously used. That other one was ancient. Every time I tried to open the program, it locked the whole computer up."

Symphony watched Marcella roll her eyes and shake her head. Glancing at her desk, she noticed that while neat and organized, it was filled with many projects. Symphony's first impression was correct—just about everything that happened within the operation of the museums passed through Marcella's desk in one way or another. The woman's present task involved logging a stack of purchase orders into a computer program for bill payment. Perhaps, it was time to begin a friendship.

"I met this guy."

Marcella never stopped typing, yet gave Symphony raised eyebrows look.

"A guy?"

"Yes. His name is Jason and he is going to start a brewery. I keep running into—"

"Jason Newberry? Drives a red Corvette?" Marcella stopped typing and looked at Symphony.

"Yep. That's the one. He drove right out of a Prince video and passed me on I-77 when I was driving here on Saturday."

"You're joking." Marcella went back to typing.

"No, I'm not. I was minding my own business, listening to the radio during my drive. I was tuned into an oldies station. Prince was in the middle of singing *Little Red Corvette* and this flash of red speeds by me in the passing lane. I thought I had dozed off and was dreaming I was in an MTV video. But, right there on the interstate was this Corvette passing me by. I basically followed it to Wytheville. It turned off of the main exit. I really didn't think any more about it after that."

"That is quite an interesting story." Marcella smirked.

"I'm not finished telling it. Later that evening I was walking around downtown and Jason knocked me down. Then, he asked me to have dinner with him." A sly grin crossed Marcella's face. Symphony thought she heard her mumble something. "The next day, he showed up at the B&B and went with me to the dinner theatre. I'm actually surprised we haven't seen him walk in here today. He's everywhere." Symphony could hear the exasperation in her own voice. She was not sure if hearing her chance meetings with Jason repeated was unnerving or exciting. "I thought maybe he had been asked to welcome me or something."

"I'm sure there is a long list of young women who would love for him to follow them around. He's known around town for his beautiful eyes and elusive dating habits. He's the uncatchable catch."

Symphony stopped looking at the tour notebook and stared at Marcella.

"Close your mouth, Symphony. The shocked look is not a good one for you." Marcella chuckled and returned to her work. "Jason Newberry is a busy man. He's an engineer at one of the plants in the industrial park. He coaches little league sports teams. And, as he told you, he is trying to start a brewery downtown. If he has taken the time to get to know you, it's because he has an interest in you. The man doesn't have a lot of free time."

"But, why?"

"Why what?"

"Why would he be interested in me?"

"Why is any person attracted to another? Something about the person draws you. You met accidentally. I guess there was a spark there or he saw the opportunity to make a new friend. Only time will tell."

"Marcella, I've got to head to the Gas Station Museum to check on something." Allison came out of her office and interrupted the conversation. The woman was wearing a bright red sweater paired with a navy and white striped shirt and navy slacks. The outfit paired well with Allison's ivory complexion and silver hair. She had a hip chic style for her sixty-something age.

"Symphony, you will get used to our short names for the museums. The one that Allison has just referred to as the 'Gas Station' is actually the Great Lakes to Florida Highway Museum. The building was once a gas station."

"Yes, Marcella is correct. Sorry, if I confused you. Why don't you come with me? I'll give you a tour."

"Sure. That sounds great." Symphony darted her eyes to Marcella. The woman had a smile on her face. "Can I leave this notebook on your desk? I would like to study it more this evening."

"Certainly. It will be here when you and Allison return."

"I'll just get my coat." Allison returned to her office while Symphony made a small stack of her belongings on top of the tour notebook.

"I enjoyed our chat, Marcella. Thanks for listening."

"Our chat is far from over. I expect to be kept informed regarding further developments."

The phone rang as Marcella spoke. Symphony waved to her new friend and followed Allison out of the office.

Sleep did not come easy to Symphony on her first night at the Rock House. Not only her bed and surroundings were far less luxurious then what she enjoyed at the Trinkle Mansion, her mind was haunted by the conversation with Nadia French—the woman she now assumed was her grandmother. It made her feel, on the second morning of her new job, like she was walking in a haze.

"Good morning, Symphony. Did you rest well?"

During the previous evening, Symphony purchased a few breakfast and light meal items and was just finishing washing her plate and utensils from her simple bagel breakfast when Allison entered the small staff kitchen.

"I rested." Symphony returned the items to their cabinet locations.

"That doesn't sound very convincing. I'm sure that little twin bed looked pitiful after the big comfy one at Trinkle Mansion."

"The bed is fine. My room is great. No issues with that. It's kind of like being in a college dorm again, without the other people." Symphony forced a smile. "I'm not sure that you are interested in your newest employee confiding in you. But, I've got to talk to someone about this."

"Goodness. I'm talking about mattresses and you have something really bothering you. Let's go into the parlor and sit down. The first tour doesn't begin until ten."

"I thought a lot about the Hallers last night." Symphony began speaking as she and Allison sat down on two folding chairs Allison had brought into the parlor. "Marcella gave me the tour notebook to study. I spent a couple of hours reading it. It was a good mind diversion. I couldn't help but wonder about the Hallers' lives in this house. I imagine it would be beyond their wildest dreams to think that their home would one day be a museum and that their lives would be studied and preserved."

"That is an interesting thought. I don't think I have ever considered what the Hallers would have thought about what we are doing here. With Dr. Haller being the first resident physician for the area, they were certainly a cornerstone family of their time. I doubt that they imagined there would be a legacy to follow them. It makes you wonder who historians will be honoring in another two hundred years."

Symphony looked around the room. The simple furnishings on display told a story of what life was like in the era that the original Haller family lived in the home. Chairs and small couches that looked quite formal by today's standards. A pianoforte in the corner for the family to be entertained on or for a child to learn to play. A large fireplace for warmth to sit by as the good doctor read his newspaper or expanded his knowledge with a medical journal. Mrs. Haller sitting in the corner embroidering or tatting while listening to a child recite schoolwork aloud. Somehow, the thoughts of her imagination made Symphony happy and sad simultaneously. Lives gone with few to remember them.

"Symphony, I can tell by your expression that you may have already had an adventure in your first few days here. Tell me what has been happening. You look troubled."

Symphony pondered Allison's words. The woman appeared to be genuinely interested. Symphony knew it was slightly unorthodox to be confiding in and seeking personal advice from your new boss on your second day of work. It felt like the right thing to do though. Few knew of her special circumstances and she preferred to keep it that way, at least for a while.

"While I was having lunch yesterday, I met Nadia French."

"Nadia. Delightful lady. She is quite active in the historical society. Sits on the board, chairs several sub-committees. There is no one better at fundraising then Nadia."

"I think she might be my grandmother."

Allison's eyes grew wide with a look of surprise. After she thought for a moment, the look changed and she began to shake her head.

"I think you must be mistaken, Symphony. I do not believe that Nadia has any grandchildren. I've barely heard her speak of her daughter. It's like she is a forbidden topic."

"How long have you known Mrs. French?"

"Ever since I moved back to Wytheville in the early 1990s." Allison unscrewed the cap of the water bottle she had carried in with her as if she was preparing to take a drink. She quickly screwed it back on. "What makes you think that she could be your grandmother?"

"Because Mrs. French told me she was."

The shocked look returned to Allison's face. She did not say a word. From the rapid succession of changes to her facial expressions, Symphony could almost see Allison's thoughts racing around inside her brain.

"She told me that Amburgey Gibboney was her daughter."

"Amburgey Gibboney? That is who you think is your mother?"

"Yes. I forgot I hadn't told you her name."

"Oh, my goodness. Now, I understand more fully why you felt like you had to get this job. The legend surrounding the life of Amburgey Gibboney is vast and complicated."

"Which one are you talking about?"

"Which one? I don't understand what you mean."

"I've done extensive research on Amburgey Gibboney. Obviously, it is an unusual name, so I did not find too many instances of it. My research revealed that in all of the United States there have only been four women in the last two centuries named Amburgey Gibboney. All of them lived in or near Wytheville. I was born in 1989. The first Amburgey Gibboney I found was living in Wytheville in the late 1980s. I assume this one was my mother. Then, if you go backwards, there was another Amburgey that I found in 1950, one in 1924, and the last one in 1855. So, a total of four in different time periods."

"All with the last name Gibboney and all living around Wytheville?"

"Yes."

"And you are certain that Amburgey Gibboney was your mother."

"As an infant, I was left in a basket on a Sunday morning on the steps of a church in Bluefield. There were only a few items left with me. One was a note. In the note, the person identified herself as my mother. It was signed Amburgey Gibboney."

"Well then, that would be a good confirmation. The research you have done is accurate and quite thorough, I might add. I'm glad to see that you have honed those skills. I will put them to work even further." Allison smiled. "I hesitate to bring up this topic so soon. Yet, it's not going to go away, so we might as well address it. When I spoke of the legend of Amburgey Gibboney, I meant that in a literal sense. Her story is a complicated one. As strange and unorthodox as what I am about to say will seem, there are a list of researchers through the last couple of decades who have come to the same conclusion." A feeling of dread passed over Symphony, like an omen foretelling bad news. "There's quite a bit of evidence to indicate that there was only one Amburgey Gibboney."

"Only one? You mean others assumed that identity?"

"Another logical thought process regarding this mystery. The problem is that it does not fit the facts we know."

"I don't understand. I found concrete evidence of women

by that name in four different time periods. Newspaper articles, public records—one Amburgey Gibboney couldn't have lived that long." Symphony chuckled nervously. "Especially if she gave birth to me."

"I know this sounds crazy. Everyone who has researched her has closed the book on the research with disbelief and the curiosity of possibility." Allison shook her head.

"Please tell me, Allison. You are making her sound like an alien or a witch or something."

"There are some who might certainly brand her in that way. It's hard for me to even begin to wrap my mind around the possibility. Some things are impossible to explain or ignore. Even Albert Einstein thought it might be possible."

"What? What might be possible? What do you think that Amburgey Gibboney did?"

"Much of the research points to one thing—Amburgey Gibboney was a time traveler."

"What?" Symphony had risen from her chair as Allison began answering. Slowly, she eased herself back down. "You don't mean a time traveler, like you see in the movies."

Allison's wide-eyed look and affirmative shaking of her head took Symphony by surprise. She rose again from her chair and walked toward the doorway that led to the foyer near the front door. She glimpsed the grandfather clock. A cold feeling passed over her. She walked back into the parlor where Allison was still sitting. She felt embarrassed to be having the conversation with her new boss. Yet, perhaps it was a sign. A sign to confirm what she had not allowed herself to think about, but somehow knew. The same thought had crossed her mind while she was doing the research. She just refused to accept it. Every tidbit of information that she was able to gather about each Amburgey Gibboney could almost be laid on top of the other as a complete match. It was like one person had lived the same way four times. Amburgey was a ghost in her own life.

"I'm sorry, Symphony, I've shocked and upset you. That was not my intent. I should have waited to reveal this information. Perhaps, I should not have revealed it at all." Her voice was so caring and apologetic.

"No, you have nothing to apologize for. The last couple of days have been so wonderful and so scary at the same time. I think I am trying to process too much at once. I've thought I was crazy for quite a while when my research led me to the same conclusion. I was just never brave enough to say it aloud."

"You can say it here and there are others who have come to the same baffled conclusion. Amburgey Gibboney may have transcended time and lived to talk about it."

"Are you sure about that? Mrs. French did not seem to know whether her daughter was alive or not."

"This connection to Nadia really baffles me. I've never even heard of a whisper of connection between Nadia and Amburgey. Maybe there are others who know about the connection and just assumed that I knew. I wasn't living in Wytheville when Nadia moved here. But, she and I have worked closely over the years since. Sometimes, it amazes me how well we think we know a person superficially and how little we really know about who the person is." Allison tilted her head and thought for a moment. "Did Nadia indicate that she wanted to speak with you further?"

"Yes, she gave me her phone number and address. She said for me to give her a few days before I contacted her. She said she wanted time to think about what I had told her."

"I would say so. Nadia is a very complex person. Her personality presents her as outgoing in most situations. That's why she is a great fundraiser. She has no trouble talking to people and asking difficult questions. Yet, I have found her to be quite private in many ways. What you have revealed may indicate why. A missing daughter who might be a time traveler would be quite a secret to keep. A secret that has been well kept, at least from me."

"Yes, Mrs. French went out of her way to be friendly to a stranger that sat down at the table next to her. She may have wished that she hadn't been."

"I would not go that far, Symphony. Finding you might turn out to be the best thing that could happen to her. If it doesn't dig up a painful past." Allison took a drink of water. "Before you see Nadia again, perhaps it would be a good idea for you to meet her closest friend. I think I could arrange for that to happen. Her name is Millicent Monroe and she is also on our historical society board. Millie, as most of us call her, is an expert in the history of the McGavock family. She is also a direct descendant. Millie was a teacher and school administrator for most of her career. She was able to retire early and has since devoted her time to researching and preserving the history of the McGavocks and other first families of the area. Millie and Nadia have a close friendship, and I believe it has been that way since Nadia first moved here."

"Is everyone you know connected to history somehow?"

"It would seem that way, wouldn't it? I've spent twenty-five years working on historic preservation. I guess I don't get out much beyond that." Allison laughed and rose from where they were seated. "We have been planning to create a special exhibit that showcases the significant impact of some of the region's first families. Millie would be our resource about the McGavocks. Since you also have a reason to meet her, I'm going to go ahead and set that meeting up. We will just make your first week a hodge-podge of assignments about many different topics."

"Maybe you can think of it like a big overview of my entire job."

"I like the way you think, young lady. It's similar to how I do. Beware."

WORDS OF THE GRANNY WITCH

"Love. Love comes right through the door without knocking. It hits you in the head like a tall oak during a wicked storm. If you go looking for it, the end is never pleasant. It's got to sneak up and climb inside you for it to really take hold and last.

"People show up at my door asking for a love potion. It's all foolishness. You can't make a potion for love. I mix together spit and vinegar with a dash of honey and crumbled lavender. It smells pretty and tastes sweet going down, but the spit and vinegar is still there. It's of no worth. All in folks' heads.

"Love glides into you like a panther sneaking up in the dead of night. You don't know it's there until it's too late. People think that love begins and ends like a storybook. Love has no beginning or end. Your love for someone is always in you. Your heart knows who you love long before you ever see the beloved. It keeps that person in there long after you've given him or her away. Your heart knows all your secrets. It doesn't break because of what someone does to you. It breaks because it knows that love has been used. You can never give it to another soul. That love is done."

Chapter Five

"YOU HAVE CERTAINLY HIT THE ground running. Allison must have great confidence in you to already have you out on assignment. She told me on the phone that this is your first week on the job."

The wind was strong on the hill where Millie Monroe lived. Overlooking the two interstates that crossed nearby, her home had a beautiful view of the Blue Ridge Mountains, even in the winter setting. Millie met Symphony at the side door and welcomed her inside.

"I'm happy to be able to get into projects immediately. It's very kind of you to take the time to meet with me today."

"When you get to know me, you will realize that I never turn down an opportunity to talk about history."

Symphony moved quickly trying to keep up with the small

woman. Her house was quite large and appeared to be at least a hundred years old. Symphony wondered if it had always been in the McGavock family.

"I'm sure that you are wondering if this is a historic McGavock home." Symphony wondered if the woman was also a mind reader. "It is not. The main family home has long since been destroyed. The most historic McGavock home still standing sits out there on the interstate."

"Oh, I believe I saw that as I was driving here."

"Yes, it is open for tours during many seasons and is also a restaurant."

As she followed the woman through the house, Symphony stopped to look at the elegantly furnished large rooms. The house looked more like a museum than a home and had the feel of an old southern mansion. She soon found out that Millie could move rather quickly to be such a small person; she caught up with the woman in the front foyer. Millie was looking at her reflection in a breath-taking full-length mirror at the bottom of the staircase.

"Allison told me that you retired from education. Did you teach history?"

"That would be a logical conclusion. Sadly, it is not an accurate one. I taught high school business and accounting classes for twenty years. Then, I moved into the world of school administration as an assistant principal."

"That must have been stressful. I imagine that focusing on family history would be a refreshing change."

Symphony studied Millie's appearance while the woman adjusted her outfit in the mirror. Millie was quite petite in stature. She was no more than a few inches over five feet and probably barely weighed one hundred pounds. Her smallness gave her an appearance of floating when she moved. It was hard to imagine the woman being a tough school principal.

"It is indeed. Please forgive me, dear. I don't always stare at myself in the mirror. I am not *that* vain. It's just that I believe I have lost one of my earrings in the layers of this blouse. My daughter-in-law gave me this blouse for my last birthday. It is certainly beautiful, but it is way too complicated." Her attire consisted of lightweight slacks in a cerulean blue with a billowy blouse that was loose and airy. It was a cream color with small flowers that almost perfectly matched the color of the slacks. Millie pulled her hand out from the bottom of the blouse. "Finally, I've got it. What an exploratory mission that was. I would hate to lose an earring."

While Millie retrieved the piece of jewelry and repositioned it to her ear, Symphony looked down at the woman's shoes. She had to bring her hand to her mouth to stifle a laugh.

"Don't you like Crocs, my dear?"

Symphony looked up wide-eyed at Millie. The woman looked amused.

"Oh, I do. My mother wears them all the time."

"Does she? Does she wear fashionable ones like mine? Or, is it those ugly green ones people wear while they are gardening?"

"No, my mother is a nurse. She has lots of pairs that match her scrubs. Yours just don't seem to fit you." Symphony knew it was a bold statement to make about someone she just met. With her education background, Symphony had a feeling that Millie could smell the truth. She needed to earn this woman's trust, if she was going to learn anything from her about Nadia.

"That was bravely honest; I like that. I can smell fear. You have none. That's a trait that will serve you well, especially if what I have heard about you is correct."

Symphony started to question the woman, but thought better of it. Millie returned to looking at her reflection. The woman's gaze went to her shoes.

"I suppose you are right. The shoes match my outfit in color, but not in style. My feet have seen better days. I put miles on these feet in the classroom. You have to be on a good foundation if you are going to work. Hard work deserves good shoes." Allison had not mentioned that the woman talked in circles. Again, as if the woman could read Symphony's mind, she continued. "You didn't come here to talk about shoes though. We'll get to the real reason over lunch. Right now, I'm going to give you a lesson in the McGavock family."

TWO HOURS AND two hundred years of history later, Symphony sat down across from Millie at her dining room table.

"It is so kind of you to invite me to have lunch, Mrs. Monroe." Symphony accepted a finger sandwich from the plate that Millie offered her. "I have been impressed with the kindness that everyone has shown me since I arrived in Wytheville."

"Southern hospitality is a way of life here, for the most part. This community has welcomed visitors for over two hundred years. It's an important part of our economy and our mindset. You should call me Millie, by the way."

Millie ladled out a bowl of steaming hot tomato soup from what looked like an antique china soup tureen. She handed a bowl to Symphony.

"It's my own recipe, creamy tomato basil. It pairs nicely with my homemade pimento cheese sandwiches."

"It smells delicious. My grandmother used to make her own pimento cheese. It's a southern delicacy, isn't it?"

"Exactly, my dear, and wonderful with soup on a winter day."

Symphony sampled a spoonful of the rich looking soup. It was the most delicious tomato soup she could remember eating.

"Before I get my first paycheck, I am going to have to purchase larger clothes." Symphony took another finger sandwich from the plate that Millie held out to her. "I feel like I have done nothing but eat since I arrived on Saturday."

"It is a downside of living in the South. That's why an active lifestyle is so important." Millie paused and tasted her soup. "I understand that you have met my friend, Nadia."

Symphony choked on the sip of lemonade she had just taken.

"Yes, I met Mrs. French in the café near the Rock House." Symphony cleared her throat before taking another spoonful of soup. "She seemed like a lovely lady."

"The same could be said of you, young lady. Good genes, no doubt."

Symphony could only describe the expression on Millie's face with one word—coy. A game of cat and mouse had begun.

"I prescribe to the theory that we are a combination of nature and nurture. The environment in which we are reared is equally important, in my opinion." Symphony moved an imaginary chess piece in the game.

"Indeed, you would certainly be an excellent example of that, would you not? You have told me that your mother is a nurse. Such a noble self-sacrificing profession with an immeasurable impact on others. What does your father do?"

"He's a meteorologist." Symphony swore she could hear a comedic drumbeat behind her.

"Oh, I see. That's interesting."

"Sometimes, he predicts dangerous storms."

"Yes." Millie seemed to be very interested in her soup.

"Tornadoes and blizzards, and such."

"Of course."

"And, often, his predictions are wrong."

Millie looked up at Symphony with a serious expression. A smile quickly replaced it.

"Certainly."

"He's been a really good dad though."

"That is an obvious conclusion, my dear. Your parents have raised a lovely, intelligent, and brave young woman."

"Brave? What makes you think I am brave?"

"It is brave for someone to confront her past. You, my dear, are not just confronting yours, but that of those who caused your birth. You are daring to find out who you are and have come to our fair town all alone to do so." Symphony started to speak, but Millie held up her hand. "Nadia and I have been friends for over twenty years. I came into her life right after her beloved and only daughter disappeared into thin air, to use a clichéd and, in this case, appropriate, term. You will not make this journey alone though. There will be many who will walk beside you and aid you in your discovery. Ultimately, though, it will come down to you and your tenacity. You are braver than you realize."

Several long moments of silence passed between them as Symphony digested what the woman had said. Many times, she had thought herself foolish to go looking for someone who had left her behind. She imagined that she was setting herself up for heartbreak and failure to try to find someone who quite possibly did not want to be found. Never once, had Symphony thought of herself as brave to undertake such a process.

"I might be chasing a ghost, Millie. There doesn't seem to be much evidence of my mother's existence since my birth." Saying the words out loud caused a lump to form in Symphony's throat. She had not allowed herself to really consider the possibility that her birth mother could be dead. "My search may be futile."

"No matter the present state of Amburgey, I do not think your quest shall be futile. You may not know that there is quite a bit of mystery surrounding your mother." Symphony started to respond but thought it might be better to not reveal what Allison had already told her. "There are those who have unsuccessfully searched for her. While many of them put in the time and diligence, they lacked the key to making their search successful. You possess that key."

"What would that be, ma'am?"

"Your existence is the reason she was willing to sacrifice her life. You are the one reason she would like to be found."

"What makes you think Amburgey is still alive?"

"Only because I know of no reason why she should be dead." Millie rose from the table. "It will soon be time for you to return to work. Come sit with me in my sunroom for a few moments before you leave."

Symphony did as Millie suggested and followed her from the dining room down a long hallway to the back of the large house. Hidden, like a closet, was a door that opened up into a sunroom. Large glass windows were three stories in height and lined two sides to enclose what would have been a dreary outdoor space into an indoor room of magnificent light. Even in the cold of January, there were beautiful blooming plants in every corner as if willed into thriving existence by the simple presence of an opportunity to be there.

"This is incredible." Symphony spoke as her eyes continued to drink in the beauty of her surroundings. "It's like you have your own botanical garden."

"Your observations are precisely correct. The late Mr. Monroe was a botanist. He loved plants and he loved me." Millie raised her arms up as if she was reaching for the ceiling. "From our early years as a young married couple, I dreamed of having a beautiful sunroom that would give you the feeling of being able to reach the sky. He dreamed of being able to have plants growing year round within our home. This is how he made our dreams come to life."

"It's amazing. It feels like it is a summer day in here. How wonderful that you were able to enjoy this together."

"It was a dream come true. Sadly, my Beau only lived for a year after it was completed." Millie's tone turned somber. "But, I have spent most of my relaxing hours since in this room, enjoying it for the both of us. Please sit down for a moment."

Symphony spied a white wicker chair in the corner with big comfy cushions of periwinkle blue. Easing herself down, she thought how easily it would be to drop off for a short nap in the chair. Millie chose a loveseat to sit in. A table next to it indicated that it might be a frequent location for the woman as there was a small basket of yarn, a pair of reading glasses, and a hardback novel with a bookmark on the table.

"Allison was wise to arrange this meeting. I can help prepare you for your next meeting with Nadia."

"I'm afraid that I might have seriously shocked her during our introduction. Something told me that I could share my secret with her."

"Your heart recognized her. Your spirits were reintroduced and you were made to feel comfortable. Your revelation was quite a shock for Nadia. It had been too many years, basically your whole life, since she has seen Amburgey. She had no knowledge of what had become of you. All she knew was that Amburgey had given you up."

"Mrs. French told me that she wished that my mother had left me with her. Why did my mother choose to give me up? Why not give me to my grandmother to raise if she did not want me?"

"Symphony, I do not feel comfortable with sharing intimate details with you that you should hear from Nadia. That is not my purpose for having you here today. I will say though that Amburgey's reasons for giving you up had little to do with not wanting you. Her situation was far more complicated than that."

"Was it complicated by my father?" Symphony was now sitting on the edge of her seat. Her curiosity was taking control of her manners.

"Your father was just one of the complications. I think that is a topic best left for your discussion with Nadia. Let me tell you a little about my friend so that you will understand her. Sit back in that comfy chair and relax. That is Nadia's favorite chair in my entire house."

Millie paused and allowed her words to register. Symphony gave her a nervous smile. Took a deep breath and, again, reclined in the chair. The thought that her grandmother favored the chair made it extra comfortable.

"As I believe I mentioned, I met Nadia over twenty years ago; it's probably closer to twenty-five. My husband and I moved here around that time. He had retired early because of some health issues, and I was taking one last position in administration. Nadia was a substitute teacher at my school. We became fast friends. I soon learned she was a complex individual with an interesting past and what was then, a captivating and heart wrenching present. I will try to make this as brief as possible."

"I think we are okay on time. I had to work yesterday evening to attend a meeting with Allison. She said that I could use some of that time today if our conversation about Mrs. French took longer than my lunch time."

"Allison knows a great deal about the mystery surrounding Amburgey. She will be a valuable resource for you." Millie's statement surprised Symphony. Perhaps Allison was trying to tell her things in small doses. "Nadia was born into a very poor family in a rural town in West Virginia. The family was a large one. I believe she may have had as many as a dozen siblings. Nadia was the youngest. I believe her next oldest brother or sister might have been as much as ten years older than her. It was like she was an only child with her brothers and sisters mostly grown and away from home before she was old enough to know them. Due to such an age difference, Nadia's mother was older than most mothers when Nadia was born; and, as I understand it, her father died shortly after her birth in a coal mining accident. Times were hard for her mother and the whole family."

"West Virginia, how interesting. I wonder if it was anywhere near where I grew up."

"That, I would not know. Nadia was beautiful from a young age. She thought her looks might be her ticket out of the poverty she was growing up in, so she began to enter beauty contests. Ultimately, she won the Miss West Virginia pageant and was sent off to Atlantic City to compete for the title of Miss America at the age of seventeen."

"I didn't know that contestants could be that young."

"I'm sure Nadia was probably one of the younger ones that year. She made it to the final ten contestants but did not place any higher. It was, however, a life-changing experience for her."

"I would say it would be for a young girl who had been raised in rural Appalachia. That might have been her first experience with a large city."

"I'm sure that it probably was, and the pageant experience would have been exciting. But, the biggest change in her life was sitting in the audience. A man named Tyler Gibboney came to Atlantic City to watch the pageant with a friend whose sister, Miss New Jersey, was also competing. Tyler took one look at Nadia and was smitten. He arranged for his friend's sister to introduce them. Nadia did not return to West Virginia after the pageant was over. She rented an apartment with Miss New Jersey and found a job. A few months later, Nadia and Tyler were married. They had one child, Amburgey."

"Oh, wow. That's a neat story. I presume that since Nadia's last name is now French that something happened to him."

"Yes, sadly, Tyler was in a plane crash while Amburgey was in her early teens. They moved to Wytheville shortly thereafter to live in a home that Tyler had inherited years previously. Nadia thought it would be a good place for her and Amburgey to get a fresh start."

"Does that mean that Tyler was related to the Gibboneys of the Rock House?" A cold chill passed over Symphony as she uttered the statement.

"Yes and no. Tyler was not a descendant of the Gibboneys who once lived in the Rock House. He was a distant relative and that is how he inherited the home in which Nadia lives today. I cannot remember the exact connection. I think he inherited it from a great or great-great uncle who was a bachelor. Like Tyler, he had inherited the property, yet, never lived in it."

"Interesting. I guess I was destined to work at the Rock House."

"You certainly have had the right connections. Whether you knew it or not."

"So, Nadia's last name is French now. Was that her maiden name?"

"No, during the early years after Nadia and Amburgey first lived here, Nadia met Nathaniel French. Nathan, as we called him, was the principal at a nearby county high school. Nadia met him while she was substitute teaching. Nathan was a widower with two grown children. After Amburgey graduated high school, Nadia and Nathan married."

"Why is it that I feel like there is another sad story coming?" Symphony frowned.

"Because you have already figured out that Nadia's life has been full of challenges and heartache. She really is the epitome of someone who has not let life get her down, despite what it has thrown at her." Millie paused for a moment. It gave Symphony time to reflect on what Millie had said. "Shortly before you were born, Nathan had a fatal heart attack. Nadia has partly blamed herself for Amburgey leaving as she did. Nadia thinks that if she had been more focused on her daughter, she might have been able to convince her to not have given you up and leave Nadia's life."

"Do you think there is any validity to that?"

"It's hard to tell. From my vantage point, I think that Nadia did the best she could. Amburgey had her own reasons for how she handled things. I don't think it had anything to do with her relationship with her mother."

"Then, why didn't Amburgey stay in contact with Nadia? I assumed that there might have been some disagreement that caused her to leave." Symphony took a deep breath and fingered the pendant that hung around her neck. "I assumed that it had something to do with me."

"My dear, absolutely not." Millie reached over and grasped Symphony's hand. "I cannot for a certainty say exactly what transpired between Nadia and her daughter. I only know what Nadia revealed to me afterward. I can say with confidence that Nadia would have loved nothing better for both Amburgey and her child to continue living here. It is all that Nadia talked about in the weeks and months after Amburgey left. Nadia even hired a private investigator to try to find Amburgey and you."

"I wonder why the investigator couldn't find us."

"Well, for one thing, you two were not together. There was no way to know where Amburgey had left you. Amburgey liked adventure. She could have been anywhere in the world. For the investigator, it was like looking for a needle in a haystack."

"It's still hard to imagine just leaving your mother like that and never having contact with her again. Amburgey had to know what that would do to Nadia."

"I suppose she did. I hope that what I am about to say does not upset you." Millie released her grasp of Symphony's hand and leaned back into her chair. "I agree that I think it would be hard for Amburgey not to have any contact with Nadia for this amount of time. They had their challenges like any mother and daughter during Amburgey's teenage years. But, there was still a strong bond there."

"You said earlier that you had no reason to believe that Amburgey was dead."

"No, I have no information to substantiate that conclusion."

"But, you think it would be difficult for Amburgey to stay away for this long. What do you think happened to her then?"

"I think something prevented her from returning."

"Something or someone?" Symphony rose from the comfortable chair and began pacing.

"Symphony, I do not want to be the one to reveal ideas that are purely speculative about her."

"I will say it." Symphony stopped in front of Millie and looked the woman straight in the eyes. "You are referring to the idea that some think my mother was a time traveler. You think she went on a trip and became stuck in another time."

"It's unimaginable. Yet, in this situation, it is amazingly the only possibility that really makes sense to those who knew her."

"My investigation into my birth mother's life began long before I even considered moving to Wytheville. None of my research led me to anyone with the name Amburgey Gibboney after the year of my birth. If she is still in this time, she has altered her identity."

"You will no doubt, if you have not already, hear her life referred to as the legend of Amburgey Gibboney. For the most part, it refers to the speculation of the mind-boggling adventures that some people believe she had before your birth. I suppose it is interesting and what fuels many theories. It is far more interesting to me to wonder what has happened to her in the years since."

WORDS OF THE GRANNY WITCH

"People think they can run from their troubles. It's like saying you can escape your own skin." The woman's hand twitched as she took a long drink of a steaming hot beverage of her own creation. "The biggest mistake I ever knew anyone to make, myself included, was to try to chase something that isn't really there. You know what I'm talking about. Folks look for answers in the strangest questions. If I run away from this life, nothing from the past can hurt me. It's worse than ignorance. You take your past with you everywhere you go. It's like playing on a train track. You can get out of its way for a moment. Maybe it won't get you that time. But, sooner or later, that train is going to catch up with you. You can't get off the tracks of your past. At least, not without leaving this life. Who knows, it might even go with you to the next."

Chapter Six

THE FOLLOWING DAYS WERE A WHIRLWIND of activity for Symphony. Every day was full of new things to learn and new people to meet. She woke up early and walked to a nearby coffee shop or café each morning to get a little exercise and experience something different about her new small town life. After long days filled with learning, she grabbed a takeout meal and spent time in one of the many rooms of the Rock House studying the history of the area and, more specifically, the history of her new home.

Several times during that week after her visit with Millie, Symphony considered calling Nadia. She would take out the slip of paper that the woman gave her and gaze at the address and phone number, trying to conjure the nerve to reach out to this link to her past. Each time, she would fold the note and think that the time was not yet right. There were none of Grammie Wallace's signs to lead her to the action until Friday when a big sign revealed itself.

"Symphony, this is Marcella. Nadia French is here to see you."

Symphony almost dropped the phone when she heard the name. Her mind raced with a mixture of fear and excitement.

"Symphony, are you there?"

"Yes, Marcella, I'm sorry. I will be right down to see Mrs. French."

"Good. She said that she would meet you in the parking lot. She has something for you."

Symphony acknowledged the last statement before returning the handset to the phone cradle. Her hand lingered on it for a few minutes while she wondered what the woman could have possibly brought her. Symphony quickly ran back upstairs and grabbed a coat. The weather had turned colder overnight with a skiff of snow falling. Walking out of the door of the Rock House and through the wrought-iron gate to the sidewalk, she felt a burst of wind. Walking a few steps up the sidewalk, the wind ceased and she did not feel it anymore until she reached the parking lot at the main museum office.

"Are you sending me a sign, Grammie?" Symphony whispered as she turned the corner toward the tall brick building and saw Nadia French getting out of her car. "You're still my favorite, no worries." Symphony took a deep breath and crossed the parking lot.

"Symphony, it's good to see you again." A small red felt hat was pulled down over Nadia's ears. The band of the hat held what appeared to be a peacock feather. Coupled with the grey tweed coat that snuggly fit her small frame, the woman had a look resembling a British spy in a James Bond movie. "I have something for you."

"I'm glad to see you." Symphony started to say more but

stopped when she saw Nadia turn her back to get something out of the backseat of her car. When she turned back toward Symphony, there was a box—a fancy storage box like you might find filled with beautiful stationary—in her hand.

"This is my Amburgey box. During the first couple of years after she left, I was in denial. I thought that surely she would show back up on my doorstep. When it became evident that wasn't going to happen, I started putting items in this box that I associated with her. Some of them actually belonged to her; some only reminded me of her. Before you start asking me all of your questions, I want you to look at it. You can return it to me when you come to visit tomorrow."

"Tomorrow?"

Nadia put the box into her arms. Symphony was at a loss for words. Everything that was being said and done was hard to face. Everything was happening so quickly. Her mind felt like it might explode from all the revelations that kept appearing, one after another, as the week had progressed.

"I should not assume that you do not have plans for tomorrow. You might have to work."

"No, I don't have any plans. I'm adjusting to my new home and learning all I can about the area."

"Allow me to do this properly then." Nadia looked Symphony straight in the eyes and smiled. "I would like to invite you to spend Saturday afternoon with me. I would like to begin to get to know you."

Symphony was not sure if it was the gentle tone of the woman's voice or her own realization of whom this woman was in relation to her. A surge of emotion hit her causing tears to form in her eyes. Nadia saw it and reached out to touch Symphony's face with her gloved hand.

"I would love that." Symphony tried to maintain her composure.

"Wonderful. You have my address. I'm sure that your new friends here can give you directions. Please come around noon."

Before Symphony could say anything further, Nadia turned and got back into her car. Symphony noticed that the woman's fingers went to her cheek to wipe something away. Symphony stepped away, clutching the box, while Nadia put her car in reverse and swiftly drove away.

SYMPHONY SAT IN the floor of her room at the top of the Rock House. Despite the winter weather and the draftiness of an old house, Symphony had found a way to make the small space cozy. It involved several oversized pillows and flannel blankets her mother had wisely sent with her.

She had spent several evenings that week sitting in the same position pouring over notebooks and files about the history of her new home. That evening, she put the work aside to do homework of another kind—a lesson in Amburgey Gibboney. Apparently, her classes in the subject would begin the following day. She must do her homework.

"It is a beautiful box."

Symphony spoke aloud and ran her hand over the top of the box. She could barely wait for the evening to come after receiving the box and placing it in her room. The remains of a large container of stew and fresh baked bread she had purchased from the Log House lay on a nearby table. It had been the only distraction between her workday and the mysterious box.

"It looks like it once contained stationary."

The box was predominantly a soft green tone with a multicolored floral design. Rather than the feeling of cardboard, the exterior was like soft fabric, but still had a sturdiness that had stood the test of time. Symphony remembered seeing a similar one when her mother's grandmother had passed. Great Aunt Jenny had been a packrat by nature but a neat one. Upon her death, in her home, a closet was found with stacks of boxes similar to the one now in front of Symphony. Each was filled with something different—photographs, bills, buttons, and school mementos. Symphony remembered her mother returning to their home with a peach-colored box that was filled with photographs of Mariel's father.

"Mrs. French said that this box contained items that reminded her of Amburgey." Symphony spoke to herself. "I guess I need to remember that as I look at the contents. The items were not Amburgey's prized possessions."

Taking the lid off the box, Symphony immediately saw a mixture of mementos. She remembered her father once telling her that you could tell a lot about a person by what they kept. On the top of the pile of things was a baby's bib. It was pale pink terrycloth with 'Ambur' embroidered on it, along with a couple of yellow and white daisies. While still in good condition, the bib showed signs of wear—a remembrance of a mother's love.

Setting the bib aside, Symphony saw a pile of newspaper clippings. As she thumbed through them, Symphony noticed that Amburgey's childhood interests seemed to focus on music— she had played the flute in the high school band, and equestrian activities—including a show horse named Prince Edward. Besides the clippings, there were several ribbons related to both endeavors.

"I wonder if Mrs. French was involved in these activities with her daughter. It could be that these were interests they shared."

Small pieces of arts and crafts items like a Thanksgiving turkey that began from the outline of Amburgey's hand and a clay paperweight were abundant in the box.

"Gifts that a child gives a parent." Symphony speculated as she opened a green birthday card with a turtle on the front. 'Happy Birthday Dad' was written on it with the 'i' in birthday replaced with a 'u.' "I don't see any ribbons from spelling bees in here." Symphony chuckled to herself. As the laughter faded from her lips, a melancholy feeling passed over her.

"It's like spying on a life you weren't invited into."

Hearing the words aloud, Symphony realized that what had started out being a search of her ancestry, while she was in graduate school, had turned into something far more personal. She was embarking on finding out not only who her mother was on the surface but also the depths to Amburgey's most personal moments.

"I'm not sure that I am ready for what I am about to get into."

No sooner had the words left her lips then her fingers touched a tiny lock of hair. It was not the ebony color that adorned her head. These locks were golden with a tint of strawberry. Tied in a pink ribbon, there was no need for a tag to identify. The mother who had given her the box had one child. Within her fingertips was a bit of Amburgey. Symphony's biological mother was once someone else's beloved baby girl.

WORDS OF THE GRANNY WITCH

"True Granny Witches, Sacred Queens of Appalachia, do not mix black magic with their craft. We would not even call our magic white, as that is not as pure as the earth magic we honor. Our magic has all the colors of nature. It is not good or evil. It is natural. As natural as the sun rising each morning. As natural as the sprigs of life that burst forth each spring, reaching to the sky in praise. What is more magical than new life coming into the world? Human or animal. Flora or fauna. You want to see magic, witness the birth of something—that magic is pure, pure as a drop of rain falling from a green leaf with the sun shining through it.

"I've seen birth. I've felt birth. The Granny Witch who taught me this pure craft, she had a saying about birth. She said that birth was the closest a woman could come to death and survive. Too many died in her day, she said, and the days before her. Too many women gave up all the strength of their life so that another life could burst into the world. I used to ask her if a mother dies while her child enters the world, does the child get her soul, too? She said she knew many a child who seemed to be carrying the burden of the mother all the days of its life. She said my words might be true.

"The child who comes now. Her mother did not die giving her life. But, her life ended just the same. Has the child carried her mother with her? Can the child ever be free?"

Chapter Seven

"WE ARE GOING FOR A RIDE."

Symphony's apprehension regarding her visit with Nadia soon changed to wonder as the woman met her at the front door. Nadia's house was on the outskirts of town. While the home was fairly close to the road, Allison had told her that the woman owned extensive acreage all around it.

"Going for a ride?"

Nadia walked down the steps past Symphony and down the sidewalk to a path that went around the house. The snow from earlier in the week had disappeared and unseasonably warm temperatures had returned. By midday on Saturday, it was already in the low fifties with bright sunshine almost feeling like an early spring day.

"Are you coming?" Nadia yelled from the side of the house.

"Yes, ma'am."

Symphony quickly followed the woman and was surprised to see a brightly colored golf cart parked on a concrete slab near the garage. Nadia was waiting in the driver's seat. Symphony had barely sat down before the woman began speeding off while Symphony held on for dear life to the bar that connected the cart to the shade canopy. Nadia seemed to only have one speed that she drove—fast. Symphony swore that the wheels left the ground on her side on the last left hand turn they had made.

"I like to explore my property this way."

"Explore, okay." Symphony wondered what she had gotten herself into. "I've never seen a hot pink golf cart before."

"It was special ordered. This is my signature color. It's called Panther Pink."

Where most golf carts were white, this one was painted bubblegum pink. Stripes of black and pink outlined the front seat covers. Two additional seats were back-to-back in the rear. Symphony imagined dangling feet from the back as Nadia made hairpin turns down the gravel path that led to a wooded area. The color of the cart and the manner of the woman's driving seemed in stark contrast to the demur, refined woman she had seen in their two previous meetings.

"Do you have a license to drive this?" Symphony laughed half-heartedly. She wondered where the woman was taking her.

"That's only required if I am driving it on a public highway. This is all private property." Nadia stopped the golf cart inches in front of a large oak tree.

Symphony took in the surroundings and slowly got out of the cart. Nadia was already a few feet away looking back at her.

"Don't be afraid. I am not a crazy woman. I just have some wild

tendencies, at times. You will soon learn that it is a family trait."
Nadia walked a few feet and then turned back again. Symphony
had not moved. "You are too young to be that slow. Life flies by
quick enough, you better keep up."

Symphony realized that the woman's pace was like her driving.
Nadia's agility walking the pebbled path again made Symphony
wonder about the woman's age. While a few trees were seen every
ten feet or so, the path was mainly framed by small bushes and
shrubs. It appeared that the trail had been there for some time
as the path was well worn. It was not long before she saw a small
structure before them. She stopped and watched Nadia pause in
front of it for a few moments with her back to Symphony. All of a
sudden, the woman turned. Her face was filled with sadness.

"If you want to learn about Amburgey, you need to begin here.
It was her favorite place."

In comparison to the grand house that Symphony caught a
glimpse of upon her arrival, the little structure looked out of place.
It was a log cabin, a very old one. A small door stood in the middle
with two large windows, one on each side. The windows almost
made it look like there were three doors.

"Those windows are rather big to be in an old cabin like this,
aren't they?"

"You are observant and correct. Those are not the original
windows. They came from what once was a grand hotel on Main
Street. The hotel was torn down a century ago. I don't have the
slightest clue how Amburgey knew where these windows came
from. She took me to an old warehouse where an estate sale was
being conducted. She begged me to buy them. She wouldn't tell me
why. She just asked for the windows to be put in this old cabin."
Nadia turned away from Symphony and walked to the door. "My

daughter wanted to live here. She seemed set on it. So, I had a few things upgraded, like electricity and running water. Despite my better judgment and desire to keep the cabin historically accurate, I conceded to her requests and put in these lovely tall windows in this tiny little cabin."

Nadia opened the door. Symphony walked closer to the windows. While she counted fifteen panes in each window, the seams were so thin that it created the illusion of one large piece of glass. She jumped when she realized that Nadia was now on the other side of the glass looking at her.

"Come inside." Nadia's muffled words were coupled with her motioning to Symphony.

As she walked across the doorstep, a familiar feeling came over her. Symphony knew that it could not be déjà vu, yet, a surge of remembrance passed through her that she could not ignore. She stopped and drank in her surroundings. As tiny as the space was, it was huge with character. Symphony marveled at how a room could look so new and so old, simultaneously.

"Look around, Symphony." Nadia let out a long sigh and sat down in an old chair in the corner. "If you are indeed the daughter of Amburgey Gibboney, then this is the room in which you were born."

Symphony stopped moving. A cold chill ran down her back. She clutched the pendant that lay hidden under her clothes around her neck. A dizzy feeling came over her. Images flashed quickly before her eyes and her ears filled with snippets of strange sounds.

"Born here." Only two words escaped her lips.

"I suppose I should have been more delicate in my revealing this information. However, there is very little of this story that will be gentle and mild. If you are going to hear it, you need to be ready for the truth. It's not all as pretty as you."

In spite of Nadia's words, Symphony's eyes were drawn to an old wrought iron chair. The design of twisted metal created a heart shape for its back with four feet that were braided iron. It had been painted red. The years had faded much of the paint. As unusual as seeing the wrought iron chair appeared in the room, it was what was located in the seat that intrigued her. Where once a cushion no doubt had been was now a large pot with small purple and white petunias and little blue flowers cascading to the floor. It soaked up the afternoon sun from its window home and flourished in its place of honor in the room.

"No matter the season, there must always be flowers in this room." Nadia bent down and passed her hand over the arrangement to pet it. "Always."

Underneath the chair was a braided rug. The colors of burgundy, pink, orange, and cream were combined in an unusual swirling flower design. It was far different from any braided rug that Symphony had seen before. She walked closer to get a better look at it.

"Amburgey made that rug. She was quite creative."

Symphony bent down to touch the rug. It was soft.

"Something that Amburgey made."

"Yes, like you."

The words were simple and logical. Yet, they pierced Symphony's being like an arrow striking her. Amburgey had created her. It was true.

After she rebound from that thought, Symphony continued to look around the room. It was a living room and parlor combined. While it did not look lived in, it was far from abandoned. In the back right hand corner of the room was a small kitchen that opened up onto a side porch and sunroom. She moved her gaze to the right side of the room. In front of the other large window was an artist's easel with a painting ready for the next strokes of a brush. A light layer of dust was visible as the sun shone from the window.

"I wish I had such a talent."

"What makes you think that you do not?"

"Let's just say that I failed finger painting in kindergarten. I did not like getting my hands dirty."

"Perhaps it is a suppressed memory." Nadia's comment made Symphony look at the woman with a confused expression. "Look down at the right hand corner."

Barely visible was the outline of a tiny hand in paint. Symphony looked down at her own hand, and then back at the small painted one before returning her gaze to the woman.

"You don't mean—"

"I most certainly do. I was here for that moment." Nadia's eyes filled with tears. "Even at your very young age, you didn't like the paint on your hands. You held out your tiny hand to me to get it off. I took soap and water and quickly took the paint away." Nadia turned away, wiping tears from her eyes.

"I remember holding out my hands to my teacher in disgust. She didn't seem to understand why I disliked it so much."

"Our memories are a strange device. I suppose somewhere inside our heads we have stored everything we have experienced." Nadia walked toward the kitchen. She picked up a small teapot on the stove and filled it with water. "It is mysterious to me why we can only recall a relatively few moments of our lives. There are so many things I wish to remember, but I no longer know what they are."

Symphony thought about the woman's words. She wondered

if the key to finding the secrets of her past was somehow locked within her own memory.

"That tapestry on the wall came from Spain. I spent a year there when I was young. The beautiful colors bring back the feeling of being in those captivating ancient villages. I cannot recall the woman who sold it to me or what her story was. I know that I knew it then. It is engrained in my personality to seek the story behind the object—to learn the living behind the life. Yet, her existence is now locked away in this gray matter between my ears. I doubt if it shall ever reveal itself again."

The depth of Nadia's words caused Symphony to sit down. She found a rocking chair near the center of the room. She heard Nadia pouring tea into a cup.

"Oh my." Nadia's face paled. Symphony quickly rose and grabbed the cup from the woman's trembling hand.

"Are you okay? Perhaps, you should sit down." Symphony led Nadia to a chair at the small table that bordered the kitchen.

"I'll be fine. The sight of you in that rocking chair shocked me. Of all the many chairs in this room, for you to choose that one—"

Symphony looked around and did a mental count. There were at least fifteen chairs in the room. Quite an unusual number for such a small area. There were indeed many different places where she could have chosen to sit. Even the table where Nadia now sat was a more logical location. She had been drawn to the rocking chair.

"I've always liked rocking chairs."

"That one was the first one you were ever in."

Nadia's words made Symphony's heart skip a beat. She felt herself gasp.

"What?"

"Amburgey held you in her arms in that rocking chair in this room on the days after your birth. It was where she would rock you to sleep."

"I suppose that I should be careful with my questions. But, after all of this lost time, it seems rather foolish to worry about how I phrase them."

"Speak freely, Symphony. You are correct that there is no time to waste. Amburgey has robbed us of that pleasure. Ask whatever is in your heart. Say whatever needs to be said."

"Your words conjure the feeling that I was loved and wanted. It conflicts with what I know to be a different reality. Why did my mother give me away? Why did she leave me to be taken care of by strangers? From the quick glimpse I had of your home, money does not appear to be a worry that you have."

"My daughter had nothing but love for you. I know that to be a certainty. You are correct that I have enough wealth to take care of all of us." Nadia took a drink of her tea. Symphony could not help but think that the woman was struggling to explain. "You came into her life in a very unconventional way."

"Unconventional? Was it something she was ashamed of? Was my father a married man or something?"

"No. Nothing like that, at least, not that I am aware of." Nadia furrowed her brow. She seemed to be searching her thoughts. "Your conception did not occur in the most natural of circumstances."

"First you say unconventional and now you say that the circumstances were not natural. I do not have any deformities or abnormalities that I am aware of. You are making me wonder what might be wrong with me."

"I'm sorry, my dear. I should have thought this out better. I should have formed the way I would say this before you were sitting across from me."

"You don't seem to be a person who minces words. What was so horrible about how I came to be that it made my mother want to get rid of me?"

"Again, Symphony, I do not believe that she wanted to give you up at all. I was angry with her for many years because of her decision. During these latter years, I have come to understand perhaps, why Amburgey felt she had to allow someone else to raise you. I believe it was fear. Since she has never returned since giving you away, I can only conclude that her fears were right." Nadia took a deep breath. "I can only accept that her fear of what would happen to her was fulfilled and that she is no longer alive."

"Unconventional circumstances, unnatural conception, her fears for her life—what does all that mean?" Symphony stood up and began to pace in the room.

"Oh, it was not my intent to tell you so much so soon. I do not want to overwhelm you. You need to be enjoying these first few weeks of starting a new life."

"Mrs. French, I have spent most of my life wondering. I never felt unloved, because my adoptive parents made sure that I knew that they wanted me more than anything else in their lives. But, they didn't try to hide anything from me either. When I was old enough to understand, they explained that I was not their biological child and that they had no records of who my natural parents were."

"It must have been difficult to create a legal identity for you, without a birth certificate or such a document. I wondered about that later. Did Amburgey even note your birthdate?"

"I think there must be some law governing what must be done when a woman leaves a baby. She left information on the note that was found with me. I asked a similar question about how my parents handled the legal aspects of establishing my identity. They said that the church where I was left made sure that was dealt with in the proper way. When the judge approved my adoption everything was in place for me to be Symphony Mariah Wallace."

"It is a beautiful name."

"I've had a beautiful life. Yet, there has always been something missing. A veil of mystery hangs over me, haunting my thoughts. I realize that the truth may be hard for me to accept. I need to know it though to feel whole."

"Indeed. I will tell you this story. Like any good book, let's tell it in chapters. Today is the first one. I wanted you to see where you were born and feel a little of your mother's presence here. You might wonder why it is still so well kept twenty-five years later. It is because I spend a good deal of time here. It is the one way that I have been able to still feel close to her. Perhaps, now, I have another way to do so." Nadia's expression turned from a sad one to a happy one.

"Another way?"

"Through you."

"I only share the biology of her though. That can't feel much like a link."

"Oh, I am a silly old woman. I have forgotten that you know nothing about her." Nadia reached out for Symphony to sit back down beside her. "Symphony, I think somewhere inside I knew who you were before you even sat down in the restaurant. Consciously, my mind would not allow me to see the physical similarities. Subconsciously, I recognized all of the qualities you share with her. It is remarkable. You have so much of Amburgey in the subtlest of ways. Why even the expression of disbelief you have on your face right now is so much like her. I saw that look a thousand times while she was a teenager. I saw that look the first time that Amburgey—"

"The first time what?"

"I must remember this is chapter one. There are many things left to reveal." Nadia looked at her watch. "Goodness, it is already the middle of the afternoon and I have not fed you lunch yet. Let's go back to my house. I have a nice meal prepared for you. I will show you some photos of me when I was Miss West Virginia. Millie told me that she gave you a little summary of my young life. Your grandmother was a looker."

Grandmother. Symphony thought for a moment about what the word meant to her.

"I realize that you have had your own grandmothers who, I'm sure, were wonderful women who loved you unconditionally. I hope that you can someday think of me in that fine company. I don't expect you to call me such a name of endearment. I haven't been around to earn that. But, maybe we could settle on something less formal than Mrs. French. Your proper upbringing dictated for you to use such a term. It hurts my heart to hear it. Way too formal for even the beginning of our relationship. Why don't you call me Nadia? It, at least, denotes that we have known each other for a while. In a sense, it is true. I am one of the first persons you met in this world. Even if you do not remember it."

A light laugh escaped from the woman. The tone was whimsical in its innocence. This woman wanted to be in her life. She wanted to love her. How could anyone turn down such a request?

"I think that would work, Nadia." Symphony reached out and took the woman's soft hand. "Thank you, for chapter one. I must warn you that I am the type of person who stays up all night to finish a book. I will be diligent in wanting more chapters."

"That diligence, my dear, may have come directly from me. I promise not to make you wait too long. You've seen how I drive."

"THAT WAS DELICIOUS." Symphony wondered if her mother would be unhappy with her table manners as she felt as if she had gobbled the lunch without chewing. "I didn't realize I was so hungry. I slept in a little this morning and missed having a full breakfast. So, I ate a breakfast bar and a banana that I had left over from my shopping earlier in the week."

"I am glad that you enjoyed it. I made quiche thinking that we would eat earlier than we did. This was actually Allison's recipe. She and her husband used to have their own café in the same location that we met the other day."

"I didn't realize that."

"You are living on the top floor of the Rock House. I didn't realize that there was even a room big enough for you to do that."

"Well, I'm not really sure that it is big enough." Symphony accepted more water from the pitcher Nadia offered. "It is okay for now. They were very kind to offer it as part of my package. I will get an apartment soon."

Symphony's phone beeped. She had been so engrossed in their conversation that she almost forgot that her phone was in her pocket. Looking at it, she saw that it was a text from Jason. She had not heard from him all week and imagined that his introductory friendliness might be over.

"Do you need to answer that?" Nadia rose from the table and picked up a couple of the food dishes. "I'm going to wrap up a few items of food for you to take back with you for later. You have access to a refrigerator, right?"

"Yes, I have run of the house after touring hours. There is a small kitchen and a full bathroom on the bottom floor. I don't have to reply to this now. Let me help you."

Symphony picked up the dirty dishes on the table and followed Nadia.

"That was a text from a new friend. I can respond to him later."

"Him?" Nadia gave Symphony a raised eyebrow look as she took the dishes from her.

"Yes. The first day I arrived I met a man named Jason Newberry."

"Jason Newberry? I know Jason. He's an engineer or something and is learning how to make craft beer. I plan to be one of his investors whenever he gets ready to go out on his own. You've met a fine young man there."

"Okay. You seem to know a lot of people."

"Well, I've lived here a long time and have not been a recluse."

"But, few people seem to know that you have a daughter."

"Many people know I had a daughter. Some knew Amburgey. Those I have met in the years since she left may not know. Out of respect to me, many of those who knew Amburgey don't mention her. I suppose to some it would seem like she died. I don't know that for a certainty, but it sure does feel that way." Nadia's expression turned somber. Symphony thought it made her look much older than she was. "Let's not talk about that. I want to hear how you met Jason. He is one of the area's most eligible bachelors."

Symphony watched Nadia's expression change to an excited one. She recounted her initial and subsequent encounters with Jason.

"You do realize that he doesn't have much time for a social life? He was not just being friendly."

"That's what Marcella said. I don't know if I believe that. He just happened upon me and wanted to be courteous."

"Inviting you to have dinner after accidentally knocking you down was being courteous. His parents taught him those manners. Showing up at the Trinkle Mansion the next day was interest, pure and simple. So, what did the text message say?" Symphony gave her a surprised look. "I'm a nosy old woman. If you didn't want to talk about him, you wouldn't have told me."

"You got me, Nadia. I'm just not used to having attention like this."

"What? A smart, beautiful, outgoing young woman like you, I don't believe that."

"I've had my share of boyfriends. It's just that most of them have resulted from meeting through school or work or something we were both doing. Then, later after knowing each other for a while, we would start going out. I've never just met a guy and started dating him."

"Maybe that's because you hadn't met the right guy." Nadia dried her hands with a dishtowel and stood next to Symphony. "Aren't you going to let me see the message?"

Maybe it was the eagerness in her voice or the gleam of excitement in her eyes, but something about that exchange with Nadia gave Symphony a feeling of kinship with the woman. Almost like it was just another conversation in a list of many from a long life together. The thought tugged at her heart. For the first time she allowed herself to think about what she might have missed.

"Okay, but I'm not letting you hold the phone."

"Why?"

"I'm afraid that you might respond to him yourself."

The small laugh that she heard earlier was nothing like what now came out of Nadia. Symphony began to laugh as well and realized that she might have just found a grandmother that she could truly call a woman after her own heart.

WORDS OF THE GRANNY WITCH

"They say this magic came to these mountains from the old world. Stowed in the belly of the ships that crossed the waters to the new world from Ireland and Scotland and the lands of another time. Most of the magic was passed from one generation to the next closely guarded in family tradition. Like the land where they dwelt, outsiders weren't welcome to learn. You had to have the same blood coursing through your veins to learn the craft. Some were called 'Water Witches' or 'Witch Doctors' depending on where their gifts were more powerful. Some were more in tune with dowsing water, ley lines, or energy vortexes. Others had their specialty in healing, midwifery, and the making of charms and potions. My strength lies in the latter. My Granny Witch saw something in me that had no business being there. There were no witches in my family tree that I had heard of. More than likely, my ancestors would have run the other way. She said that I had the magic in my fingertips. She made sure it worked its way back into my soul.

"Her name was Orenda. I stumbled onto her cabin high up in the mountains on a day that I was running from myself. The thing about running from your own self is that just when you think you've run far enough, you turn around and realize that you haven't moved at all. I ran right up to her door when she opened it that day. She told me that my special gift was time and that she would teach me the rest of what I needed to know.

"Why time? I asked. Her time was running out, she said. I came looking for a way out of time. There was no one for her to pass the craft to—it must be a sign."

Chapter Eight

"I'M SORRY THAT MY MESSAGE WAS SO last minute. You are going to think that I never plan anything ahead of time."

Symphony got into Jason's Corvette a few minutes after seven that same evening. His text message asked her if she would like to have a late dinner and go see a movie. Her carefully worded reply met with two thumbs up from Nadia.

"No, I understand. You said you thought you would be working tonight. What changed?"

"Well, I was supposed to be helping one of the brewers who I have been apprenticing with as they bottle up a new flavor. But, the brewer ended up having to go to Bristol this afternoon to see his mother who is in the hospital there."

"I hope she is okay."

"Well, she wasn't. She had some sort of complication from

a surgery she recently had. They were able to go back in and fix whatever was wrong and she is already on the road to recovery. Anyway, that changed my day dramatically. I thought that I might be lucky and find that you were still too new to town to have a full social calendar."

"Today has been a full one."

"I would have thought you might be resting after a busy first week on the job. What did you do today?"

To most people such a question would just be small talk over dinner. Since arriving in Wytheville, Symphony was not sure that she had experienced any small talk. Every conversation seemed to either have a purpose or could reveal hidden aspects of her life.

Looking across the table at her handsome dinner companion, she contemplated what she should do. She had almost revealed her secret to him while they were at the dinner theatre a week earlier, but the timing of the beginning of the show had been an interference or perhaps a cue for her not to do so. Symphony looked around her. There were no diners at the adjacent tables. No one was walking toward the table. Everyone told her that Jason was a great guy. He was trusted and respected even by those who barely knew him. He had obviously made an effort to see her. She thought from the first meeting, if nothing else, he was going to become her friend. She needed someone who was slightly removed from the situation to be her sounding board. She also needed to hurry up and answer him before he started making up things she might have done in his head.

"I visited Nadia French."

"Really? That's not even remotely close to what I thought you might say."

Symphony was about to share the rest of her story. Jason's response stopped her in her tracks.

"What did you think I was going to say?"

"I thought you might have said that you had worked or gone exploring around town again. I thought that you might have even gone to get your nails done. Then, I looked at your nails and realized that wasn't the case."

Symphony looked down at her bare nails. She could not remember the last time she had a manicure. That had been something she and her mother used to do together, before Symphony had moved away from home.

"I might have done one of those things if I hadn't been invited over to Nadia's house."

"You sound like you have known her for a long time."

A sly smile crossed Symphony's face remembering what Nadia had revealed to her earlier regarding her birth. Looking up at Jason, she saw that he was concentrating on his salad and not her face, for a moment. She really needed a Grammie Wallace sign. Just then, she heard a familiar voice coming up behind her.

"I think I see Jason Newberry over there. Millie, let's go say hello."

Symphony shook her head. She was sure that she did not tell Nadia where she and Jason would be dining. Symphony had not known herself until he picked her up. She imagined that Nadia and Millie had driven through all of the local restaurant parking lots until they found Jason's red Corvette.

"Hello, Mrs. French. Mrs. Monroe. Funny to see you two. Symphony was just telling me that she visited you today." As the women approached the table, Jason rose to greet them. Nadia motioned for him to sit back down.

"Now, Jason, we have both counseled you on calling us the missus names. We've known you long enough for you to call us by our first names. We will not tell your lovely mother that you are being disrespectful."

"Okay. I will try to do better. Nadia, Symphony just told me that you have met her. Millie, do you know Symphony?"

"Yes, Jason, I do. Allison Emerson sent her to meet me a few days ago as part of her research for a new exhibit." Millie winked at Symphony as Jason sat back down. "We had a nice chat."

"Wow. Already working on a new exhibit?" Jason smiled. "I'm impressed. She must have a lot of faith in you."

"Oh, it's more likely that she has a lot of work for me to do."

"That's not a bad thing. I had just asked Symphony how she knew you, Nadia. She seemed like she might have known you for a while."

Symphony gave Nadia a wide-eyed look. Nadia responded with raised eyebrows and a tilt of her head. Symphony noticed that the woman was biting her lower lip. She wondered if that was one of the woman's signs of nervousness. Behind her, Millie nodded her head in encouragement.

"Why don't we ask these two ladies to join us and I will explain?" Jason winked at Symphony.

Symphony thought she saw a look of understanding pass over him. Like he already knew what she was going to say. He motioned to the server.

"Oh, no, we don't want to crash you dinner." Symphony gave Nadia a look of disbelief. "We already have a table waiting on us over in the next section."

"Are there people at that table?" Jason stood up again while the server prepared two additional settings.

"No, we weren't meeting anyone. We just have a table reserved over there."

"Then, I bet the restaurant will not mind for you to sit here with us. This sounds like the makings of a good story. It will probably be better than the movie Symphony and I are planning on seeing later."

Once the two women were situated, had received their beverages, and placed their entrée orders, Jason pointed to Symphony.

"So, you were saying."

Symphony took a deep breath. She looked from Jason's kind face to Nadia's nervous one to Millie's understanding look. Grammie Wallace might say this was the trinity of signs.

"I had not actually met Nadia until this week. Although, I found out that we had actually become acquainted many years before. I was actually an infant, so I'm not sure if that counts."

"Okay, there were three 'actuallys' in that response. But, I'm not actually understanding any of them."

"I was there when Symphony was born. I wouldn't expect her to remember that."

"Oh, were you a nurse or something?" Jason's question was a logical one. Symphony was beginning to understand that he was the asker of logical questions. It must be the engineer in him. It could become a problem.

"No."

"Then, I've just got to ask why you were at her birth."

Symphony closed her eyes and shook her head. She tried to build up the strength to reveal her real relationship with Nadia. As she opened her eyes, she met Jason's gaze. Before she could say a word, he spoke.

"I can see this is hard for you. You do not have to talk about this."

And, there was her sign from Grammie Wallace. She could trust him.

"Nadia is my grandmother."

Symphony watched Jason's face for any signs of shock or confusion. The blank look that she was seeing confused her.

"Is that supposed to surprise me?" Jason looked from Symphony to Nadia to Millie. "You told me that night at the dinner theatre that you were looking for your birth mother. Nadia is not a nurse but was at your birth. It's not a wild stretch that she would be a member of your family."

"It doesn't bother you that I am looking for my birth mother?"

"Why should it bother me? I assume from everything I have observed about you so far that you were raised by great parents who saw to it that you were taken care of and educated and grew up with a semblance of sensibility and sanity. Hey, that's a lot in your favor these days." Jason paused for a moment and tilted his head as he looked at her. "You are a woman who works in history. It's not unusual that you would want to know your own. If Nadia is your grandmother, you've hit the jackpot. She is one cool lady."

Symphony watched as Nadia beamed, wiping a tear from her eye.

"Does that mean that you have found your mother? Would that mean that she is Nadia's daughter?"

"Yes, my birth mother is Nadia's daughter. Nadia doesn't know where my mother is though, or even if she is alive."

"Wow. That's tough. I'm sorry to hear that." Jason took a drink of his iced tea. "So, is this why you took the job in Wytheville? You came here to get to know Nadia?"

"No, I didn't know Nadia existed until last Monday, my first day at work."

"Really? This story is getting more and more interesting. Keep going."

"I sat down in the café across the street from the Rock House to have lunch. Nadia was at the table next to me and she struck up a conversation."

"You can imagine my surprise, Jason, when this lovely girl decided to reveal a secret reason why she had come here to a nosy old woman who was sitting next to her."

"In Symphony's defense, you do have a way of getting people to talk to you and tell you things. Actually, you have a way of getting people to do what you would like to have done. I've seen you work your magic." Jason winked and smiled at Symphony

"Listen to him, Symphony. He's been the recipient of Nadia's persuasion." Millie laughed and shook her head. "I believe that she persuaded Jason to draw up architectural plans, free of charge, for a project that the historical society was working on."

"Guilty as charged. He did a wonderful job, too." Nadia reached over and squeezed Jason's hand.

"It's still an incredible coincidence for you to have been sitting in the café that this brand new person to our town decided to eat in." Jason gave Nadia a look of disbelief. "Are you sure someone didn't tip you off to her arrival?"

"No, Jason. It's not possible." Symphony spoke in a soft calm tone. "Nadia had no idea what my name was or who adopted me. After spending a little time with her yesterday, I feel certain that she would have tried to find me, if she had any idea where to look."

Before Symphony realized what was happening, Nadia had reached over and pulled her into an embrace. She could feel the woman's tears hit her check as she whispered in her ear.

"I would have done anything to find you." After a few moments, Nadia gently let go and bowed her head, trying to regain her composure.

"I was a needle in a haystack. My birth mother made sure of that. Nadia and I would have never met if I had not been determined to find out the story of my past. My adopted father's mother was a wonderful woman who I called Grammie. She was a great believer in signs. Grammie has shown me several important signs since I have been here and one of them led me to Nadia. I'm happy to have found her. But, my quest has only just begun."

WORDS OF THE GRANNY WITCH

"Time is a strange thing. We often ignore the present when we go back and visit the past or dream about the future. It's a crime against all that is natural to not appreciate each moment as it occurs. Every Granny Witch knows the importance of time. People like to meddle in it. Time has the upper hand. No amount of magic can undo what it has done. No amount of manipulation can make it conform to what you want, if it is against time's nature. People talk about forever; it can be a very short time.

"It's the reason this girl exists—this messing with time. Nature's highest powers took pity on the babe and did not punish her for the sins of the mother, the dangerous sins of the mother. I'll have to be the one who tells her about this. It is my dark duty to be the one to explain to her how it happened. I know in my heart, it will make her want to see it for herself. That's why the mother made that token that hangs around her neck. Her foolish, youthful notion her daughter would want to transcend time. It's a blessing that the wisdom of another, a real Queen of Appalachia, laced the token with the flowers that would protect the girl in case she inherited her mother's blind determination to test the rules of time. Only love can conquer time—only time can justify love."

Chapter Nine

Over the next few weeks, Symphony became consumed in learning her new job. While she wanted to spend as much time with Nadia as possible, she realized it was probably a blessing that her newfound grandmother had already scheduled a month long trip to the Caribbean with some of her friends.

"Every time you come out of storage, you have a layer of dust on you." Marcella laughed as Symphony entered the business office of the museums. "You almost look like a ghost in that outfit."

Symphony looked down at herself. She had spent the entire mid-February morning in a cramped storage area going through collection items that had not seen the light of day for many years. She was wearing a long-sleeved white blouse paired with a long tan skirt that skimmed the floor. White 'archiving gloves,' Symphony called them, completed her outfit. Marcella handed her a small mirror that she pulled out from her desk drawer. A quick glance told Symphony why she looked like a ghost. A thin layer of dust was resting in her hair with smudges of the same on her face.

"I like to get into my work." Symphony smiled and shook her head, handing the mirror back to Marcella. The movement left a layer of dust covering the papers on the desk.

"Yes, you do." Marcella rolled her eyes before she picked up the top papers and poured the dust into the trash can under her desk. "I bet your allergies aren't happy."

"No, I've done my share of sneezing this morning. I think that's how I got these smudges around my nose." Symphony carefully took off the gloves and gently placed them in a plastic bag that Marcella was holding open for her.

"We'll get these cleaned. Get a new pair next time you enter the dust dungeon."

"I am thankful to find that most items are well-protected in storage. All of this dust is mostly from the outside of the containers or drawers."

"It's like in your home; dust accumulates quickly no matter how often you clean." Marcella handed Symphony several pieces of mail and a small box. "I love cleaning."

"Careful, Marcella, your sarcasm is showing." Symphony smiled at her new friend. Marcella had helped her learn many things about the operation of the museums. She enjoyed the banter they exchanged throughout the day. "Allison is off for a few days, right?"

"Yes. She and her sisters have gone on an excursion. There will be stories when she returns. Have you enjoyed staying at Nadia's house while she's gone?"

On the premise that it would be a big empty house, Nadia

had invited Symphony to housesit for her while she was on her trip. Symphony agreed to the ruse with the understanding that it was really her grandmother's way of inviting her to live there. While Symphony still had a few of her belongings in the attic room of the Rock House, she knew that once spring came, she would completely move out.

"Nadia's house is incredible. There's so much space."

"I'm sure it is much more comfortable than the attic." Symphony had confided in Marcella, who Nadia was in relation to her as well as her quest to find her birth mother. "Nadia's home has an amazing close to everything, yet remote, feel."

"It does. You feel like you are far away from everything, but it's only a few miles from here though."

"It looks like she has sent you a postcard from her travels, and I believe the package is from your parents. You haven't mentioned what they think about your new living arrangements."

"I think it worried them at first that I was moving into a stranger's house. Then my father said the most wonderful thing." Symphony paused for a moment and took a drink from the water bottle Marcella had handed her. "He and my mother were skyping me so that I could tell them both about Nadia. My mother made a comment about it being a stranger's house. My father said that I was left with strangers as well, and they were certainly thankful for it."

"That is a lovely statement. It is a happy and sad truth, I guess."

"They were as surprised as I was that I found a connection to my birth mother so quickly."

"You say surprised. Yet, didn't you imagine that you would encounter some connection to her?"

"I had hoped I would. But, I did a lot of research before I

came, and I couldn't find a connection to Amburgey Gibboney online anywhere. I started to think that maybe my mother had been the last of her family line, or something."

"I'm going to go pick up our sandwiches for lunch. Why don't you go and de-dust yourself while I am gone? I want to talk more about Amburgey."

Symphony followed Marcella out the door. Walking around to the corner of Spiller and Tazewell Streets, Symphony saw a streak of red pass by. She smiled. She saw the brake lights and the turn signal. Jason turned into the parking lot across the street. He was out of his car and walking across the street toward her by the time she reached the area between the Rock House and Boyd Museums.

"You're a vision in dust." Jason laughed as he walked toward her. "When you texted me earlier that you were sitting in dust, you weren't joking, were you?"

"I don't want you to think that everything in storage is as dusty as I am. But, I have been working in several different corners this morning, and I seem to have taken something away from the experience. I was on my way back to the Rock House to clean up a little while Marcella goes and gets our lunch."

"Great. I'm on my way to a meeting, so I guess I won't hold you up. I'm going to work at the brewery this evening, but I will call you later."

"That sounds good. Talk to you later."

Reaching the door of the Rock House, Symphony turned and saw Jason get into his car. Their relationship had slowly progressed over the past few weeks. Both of them stayed quite busy, so time together was limited. Their conversations were deep and meaningful though, and Symphony had begun to feel like she was beginning to understand who this man, and she liked him.

Setting her mail down on one of the tables in the side foyer, Symphony walked down the hallway toward the front door and the staircase that led to her room upstairs. No one was touring presently, so the museum was empty. Before she entered the building, she gave herself a good shake on the porch to get rid of as much dust as possible. That shake must have awakened a bug she had carried with her. Symphony felt like something was crawling down her shirt. She quickly pulled her shirttail out of the skirt. While moving her pendant to the outside of her shirt, she momentarily leaned on the clock that stood near the door. Instantly, Symphony began to feel lightheaded. Everything began to spin around her. At the same moment, it felt like a gust of wind was passing through the space even though all the windows remained closed. Symphony released her hand from the clock and everything stopped.

"I thought that was just a fluke." Symphony spoke aloud as she eased down to the floor in front of the door. "This is way stranger than just allergies."

Symphony took a deep breath, closed her eyes, and tried to calm herself. The feeling that had come over her was frightening and confusing. It troubled her that it had occurred in the same location. Thinking Marcella would soon return to the office and be looking for her, Symphony began to rise; her fingertips touched the base of the clock and the swirling feeling instantly returned. She jerked her hand away from the clock like someone touching a hot stove. Rising to her feet, she stared at the large timepiece.

"There is something strange about you, clock. I think I am going to have to break down and tell someone about what is happening to me each time I touch you."

"This is the second time this has happened to you?" Marcella and Symphony had about finished their sandwiches before Symphony began telling her friend what occurred at the Rock House. "Why didn't you say something when it happened the first time?" A concerned look crossed Marcella's face.

"It was my first day. I didn't want Allison to think she had hired someone with a crazy sickness or something. I swore Drew to secrecy."

"Drew knew?"

"He was there when it first happened. I guess from your reaction that he was true to his word to keep my secret." Symphony looked at the clock that hung above Marcella's head. "Is that clock right? Can it really be almost two?"

"Yes. I wondered why you didn't beat me back to the office. I had to go to the post office to mail some items that the gift shop sold. I thought you would be pacing in hunger when I returned."

"I must have blacked out again. I didn't think any time had passed. Maybe I should go to the doctor."

"Symphony, earlier when we were talking about Amburgey Gibboney you said that you thought she might have been the last of her family line. What makes you think that?"

"Well, I found four people with that name from 1855 to 1989. I didn't find anyone with that name before 1855 or after 1989. It made me think that my mother, the Amburgey who was alive in 1989, might have been the last one. It seemed strange to find such an unusual name used for over a hundred and thirty years and then, all of a sudden, it stopped."

"I realize that you've been concentrating on your job and haven't had too much time to do any further research, but have you talked with Allison regarding what you know about Amburgey?"

"We had a brief conversation when I first arrived. She's been so busy with the new building project, I haven't wanted to bother her."

"Did she mention that there were several researchers who looked into the lives of the women associated with that name?" Symphony had a feeling that Marcella was carefully selecting her words.

"Allison mentioned something about that. Do you know what they learned?"

"I'm not sure how to tell you this."

"Just spit it out. It cannot be any crazier than what I have thought myself."

"I wouldn't be so sure about that." Marcella took a deep breath. "Some of the researchers seem to think that Amburgey liked to travel."

"Travel?" Symphony knew where the conversation was going.

"There seem to be several theories about her travelling. The strongest though seems to indicate that her travelling wasn't about geography."

"Her travels were about time?"

"Yes." A surprised look crossed Marcella's face. "You've heard this before."

"Allison briefly mentioned it. Frankly, my research took me to the same conclusion. I couldn't bring myself to say it. What makes you mention this now?"

"I've been looking for the right time to share it with you. I wanted you to get to know us first before you learned about these theories. I didn't want you to think we were a town of crazy people." Marcella smiled.

"I would hardly call speculating about time travel crazy. Albert Einstein theorized about how space and time could warp, bend, expand, and contract through unknown links. Science fiction is used to explore those ideas and the idea of cyberspace. With the internet and the cloud, sometimes it feels we live in cyberspace now."

"A term that was penned by a former Wytheville resident." Marcella gathered their lunch trash and threw it away.

"What?"

"The term, 'cyberspace.' William Gibson coined it first in a short story, then in his novel entitled *Neuromancer*. It came out in 1984. Mr. Gibson spent most of his childhood here in Wytheville."

"Really? That's very interesting. I wonder if Mr. Gibson believed in time travel."

"It's hard to say. It's been several decades since the man was in Wytheville. Perhaps his novels would offer a clue to his philosophy on such."

"Hmmm, I might have to check them out, in my free time. I am a fan of science fiction."

"Between this job, your research, and Jason Newberry, I'm betting that you will not be having much free time." Marcella raised her eyebrows at the mention of Jason's name.

"I saw him when I was walking back to the Rock House. He was on his way to a meeting."

"Have you told him about your quest to find your mother?"

"Yes, when we were at dinner one night, and Nadia and Millie showed up at the restaurant. They joined us and I got up enough nerve to tell him some of my story."

"And?" Marcella stopped working on her computer and leaned in to listen.

"Jason reacted perfectly. He was interested and understanding."

"Told you. He's a keeper."

"Well, I don't know if I can say that in regard to myself. But, I most definitely think that I have made a friend in him. We have a lot of fun. He's busy and I'm busy. There's no time right now for any deep romance."

"But. I know there is a 'but' coming there."

"I like him a lot, and I think he likes me, too."

"I'm sure of it. The man just doesn't have much time for a social life. There have been a dozen local single girls who have vied for his attention. He always seems to graciously bow out of any commitments beyond casual ones." Marcella looked back at her desk. "Jason has carved out time for you from his busy schedule. He's not a welcome wagon representative. You have shown up on his radar."

"His 'Little Red Corvette' radar."

THE WORKDAY WAS long and tiring. Symphony spent the morning and afternoon going through dozens of boxes of items. Examining each item and logging the details into the software program was tedious, yet an interesting process. She opted to get a takeout meal for dinner from a nearby restaurant and take it back to Nadia's big house.

Nadia's golden retriever, Psycho, met her at the door. He was anxious to go out and run a little before the darkness enveloped his path. Symphony had made quick friends with the animal on her first visit.

"I don't really have any fears living here." Nadia had said when Symphony asked about his name. "But, if I am walking closer to the road and anyone strange walks toward me, I can yell for Psycho, and the person is quick to put as much distance as possible between us. It's like packing heat with a wagging tail."

Symphony laughed to herself thinking of her grandmother's response. Psycho was one of the friendliest dogs she had ever encountered. The canine companion also had some interesting eating habits that Symphony was given strict instructions to follow. Every morning, Psycho enjoyed a bowl of cereal—Cheerios or Special K—with a sliced banana and milk. Symphony thought it was a joke. She soon found out differently when she put dry food in the dog's bowl and he went psycho after her bowl of Special K. Evenings were all about regular canned food.

After settling in from their short walk, Symphony gave Psycho his food, and then took her own meal and sat down in the living room with her mail. The day was so busy she had not even stopped to read the postcard Nadia sent her. After she took her first bite of food, Symphony's fingers immediately went to the small box from her parents. She was certain that it must contain one of her mother's wonderful sweet creations.

Symphony did not take time to read the note before breaking open the package within the box. She held the cookies up to her nose and took a big sniff—gingersnaps, her mother's homemade ginger delights. It was like heaven in a box. She might eat all of them at once. She could certainly blame it on the stress of adjusting to her new life. After giving one of her precious cookies to Psycho, she went through the rest of her mail. The pile mostly contained advertisements, which she quickly flipped through before finding the postcard.

"Dear Symphony," the postcard began. "Having fun in the sun, but missing my mountains. Hope Psycho hasn't shown you why I named him that." Symphony stopped reading and looked at her canine companion. As if he knew what she was reading, he rested his head on the floor and covered his eyes with his paws. "I forgot to tell you that I left a special present for you upstairs in my bedroom. It's a suitcase on top of my cedar chest. It contains some of the items that your mother collected on trips she took before you were born. Thought you might find something interesting. Running out of space. Love, Nadia."

"Well, Psycho. Now, that we've both had dinner, why don't we go outside for a few minutes so that you can be one with nature, and then I will go investigate what Nadia left me?"

Symphony rose from the couch with the dog close on her heels. After disposing of the trash from her takeout, she grabbed her jacket and opened the kitchen door that led to the backyard. Psycho sprinted outside and immediately began sniffing. A tall pole nearby held a dusk-to-dawn light that blanketed the backyard in a muted brightness. She could feel a change in the air. Winter began to shake its boots off to welcome spring.

Back inside a few minutes later, Psycho's tail wagged in sweeping motions while Symphony dug in his treat box for a big new bone. She laughed for a moment thinking about her mother's spunky toy poodle, Choo Choo. The size of Psycho's bone would dwarf her little friend at home. Once Psycho was settled on his big brown pillow next to the fireplace, Symphony climbed the stairs to the second story of the house. Her schedule had been so busy that she had not really explored her grandmother's home. Nadia had suggested that Symphony use the bedroom on the far end of the hallway. Each day since, she had passed by the other three rooms with not much more than a brief glance as she began or ended a busy day.

Entering Nadia's large bedroom, Symphony spied what appeared to be a small vintage suitcase sitting on a cedar chest at the bottom of the bed. Her eyes were also drawn to a quilt under it. She moved the small, yet heavy, suitcase to the side and unfolded the quilt onto her grandmother's king-size bed. From the knowledge she gained doing archiving work during her college internship, she thought the design of the quilt was called 'Trip Around the World.' It used small squares of fabric in circular rows of different colors to create the design. She had seen many vintage examples during her time on that project, but had not seen any other versions since. As Symphony looked at the quilt more closely, Psycho walked into the room and plopped down on his large pillow beside his owner's bed.

"Psycho, have you seen this quilt before? The colors are amazing." The dog panted a moment before laying down his head. Symphony returned her gaze to the quilt. The colors were rich and vibrant and included burgundy with several shades of blue and green as well as contrasting paler shades of white, pink, and cream. The placement of color created a stunning illusion. "The color choices are so striking. It's almost like an optical illusion of movement."

Symphony kept looking at the quilt, letting the soft fabric rest between her fingertips. A strange feeling came over her. She grabbed hold of the bedpost in order to steady herself. Her sense of smell caught a whiff of a musty odor.

"Perhaps this quilt has been in storage for a while. My allergies must be riled up again." She suddenly sneezed several times in a row. "Too much old dust."

Symphony shook it off and reverted her attention to the suitcase. Its vintage look harkened to another time. A cream white leather with brown straps encircled the case's design. Symphony picked it up and looked at it from all angles. It was well preserved, but from the wear, and what Symphony imagined was the time period of its design, it was probably a hundred years old.

"If this belonged to my mother, I wonder where it came from." Psycho moved in his bed like he was turning to listen. "I don't suppose you know the answer to that, do you, boy?"

Sitting on the bed, Symphony gently opened the suitcase by sliding the metal buttons beside the two latches making each release with a click. It reminded her of a little blue suitcase she owned as a child and a laugh escaped her. She heard a noise.

The creak of time announced itself as she carefully lifted the lid. Inside she found a stack of letters and newspaper clippings as well as what, on first glance, appeared to be an old dress.

On the top of the dress was a pale lavender envelope. Nothing was written on the front. Symphony picked it up and turned it over, noticing that it was sealed with a dark colored wax. A flower imprint was visible within the seal. A tingle passed through her body as she touched the waxy impression. Her hand began to tremble with excitement and fear. Part of her did not wish to break the seal and open it. A stronger desire grew inside her that there was no way she could resist.

With a flick of her finger under an open part of the flap, the seal lifted off, and the envelope was open. Taking a deep breath of courage, she pulled out a piece of stationary that matched the lavender envelope. It had a fine linen look. Opening the folded paper, Symphony could see beautifully scripted handwriting waiting to be read. A little thrill of excitement passed over her. She began to read.

If your name is Symphony and you are reading this note, then my dream has come true. I do not expect you to understand why I made the decisions about your life that I did. You cannot get inside my heart and feel the reasons I had. It is my hope of hopes that you have grown into the wonderful young woman I imagined you would be, surrounded in a loving home by devoted parents. My heart breaks as I write these words as I realize that our brief time together is almost over. We must physically part. I will always hold you in my heart like my arms are doing at this moment. I shall leave with you a few items to help you to one day learn more, if you so wish. In my heart, I know that an adventurous spirit and desire to know more will course through your veins as it has through mine. It is in our genes. We have no choice.

If you want to know who you are, you are going to have to go where you have never been. You will meet some people along the way who will help you on your journey. Listen to them with an ear of discernment. Your heart and instinct is your best guide. It is through them that I will communicate with you. Study the contents of this case and prepare yourself. All shall be revealed in time. If you are brave enough to make a journey to find out, you will one day know how my Symphony came to be. Do you feel a tear on your face? It is falling from my eye to your cheek. I shall not wipe it away. No words are more important than these—I love you.

Reaching to her cheek, Symphony felt the tear there. A cold chill tingled her skin. She turned the sheet over. The other side was blank.

"I wanted to find her. I prayed for it. I wanted to know about my heritage, to learn who I was. I never imagined that so much would come along with it." Symphony spoke while she continued to look at the contents of the suitcase.

"Psycho, I am probably the crazy one. I should just stop right here and be satisfied to have found a connection to the woman who gave birth to me." The dog stood up when his name was called. He sat back down after a few moments. "Who I am trying to kid? I already made my decision before I ever set foot in this town."

Symphony kicked off her shoes and stood up beside the bed. She reached for the dress in the case and looked at the design more closely. With a scoop neckline, the deep lavender garment had a wide white collar. Pulling it out of the case, Symphony noticed that the long dress was made of a cotton material and its length would easily stop at her ankles. The design was fitted in the bodice, and then flowed out in an A-line. There were eight small buttons in a straight line down the front of the dress. The button color matched the dress perfectly. The long sleeves had wide white cuffs at the wrists. Turning it over, she saw that the wide white collar continued around the back of the dress to create the look of points. Otherwise, the back was plain.

Going over to Nadia's closet, she opened the door and peaked inside to find an empty hanger. She found one in the large walk-in space, marveling at her grandmother's collection of clothing. Putting the dress on the hanger, Symphony hung it on a hook that was on the inside of one of the closet's doors.

"This looks like it would be about my size. The color is beautiful. It reminds me of a dress straight out of a History Channel series. Why in the world would Amburgey want me to have it?" She looked at Psycho to see what he thought. With all of the strangeness that had recently occurred, it did not surprise Symphony that the phone rang.

"Hello." Symphony picked up a cordless phone on Nadia's nightstand.

"Hey, Symphony. I hope it was okay for me to call on Nadia's line. I tried to call you on your cell, but there was no answer to that or to my texts."

Symphony felt her pants pocket and realized that she must have left her phone downstairs. Jason's voice made his handsome face appear in her mind.

"Oh, I'm sorry. I must have left it downstairs. What time is it?" Symphony turned around and looked for Nadia's alarm clock. Not seeing it, she wondered if the woman had taken it with her. "I think I have lost all track of time. I was just hanging out upstairs having a nice chat with myself."

"Chat with yourself?" Symphony could hear the confusion in Jason's voice.

"Yes, it's a habit us only children develop. Imaginary friends and such, you know."

"Well, I wouldn't know anything about that. I have four brothers. I would have liked for them to be imaginary a time or two though."

"That sounds like a full house."

"It was. I like being on my own now."

"The bachelor life." When her ears heard what her mouth had said, Symphony thought she might hyperventilate.

"Well, contrary to what the local rumor mill would tell you, I am not a bachelor in the truest sense." A feeling of fear came over her. The first thought being that there might be someone else whom he had failed to mention. She was silent, awaiting his reply. "I don't live alone. I have a roommate. He is a slob bachelor. I'm the neat one."

"You are the Felix to his Oscar." Symphony breathed a sigh of relief.

"What? I don't understand what you mean."

"The Odd Couple. It was a play, a movie, a television show, and I actually think it was even a cartoon. It is about two roommates. Oscar is a slob and Felix is a neat freak."

"I remember that. I guess you would be right. Although, I wouldn't use the word 'freak' to describe my neatness. I just had a mother who wouldn't allow her sons to be sloppy. We picked up after ourselves or else."

"With five sons, I can't say that I blame her. I guess she had to run a tight ship."

"Anyway, I wanted to give you a call since I mentioned I would. Did you manage to get all that dust off of you yet?"

"Actually, after I saw you I got even more dust on myself. Since I still have a few clothes at the Rock House, I decided to take a shower there before I came back to Nadia's. I didn't want to go into Peking to pick up my dinner looking like a ghost. It might not be good for their business."

"Peking. I have not had that in way too long. I might have to stop by there on my way home, if they are still open."

"Oh, you are not home yet?"

Not paying attention to what she was doing, Symphony sat down on the bed, on the edge of the quilt. A dizzy feeling began to come over her. She took hold of the bedpost and stood back up. The feeling left her as quickly as it came.

"No, it's after nine and I knew you would be tired, so I thought I would give you a quick call while driving back. Total hands free call, I'm being safe."

"That's good to hear. Are you getting close to Wytheville?"

"As a matter of fact, Exit 73 is within view. I guess I should let you go. Maybe we can get together sometime this weekend. I have to go into the office tomorrow afternoon and work most of the evening. We are having a major software upgrade for our CAD system. But, I should be free on Sunday, if you are available."

"Sounds good. Text me and we can make plans. Hope you enjoy your takeout."

"I'm thinking shredded pork with garlic sauce, extra hot, and some wonton soup."

"That's rather close to what I had this evening." Symphony chuckled thinking that the only difference was the degree of spice she had requested for her meal. "Maybe I should call in your order."

"That's funny. We were meant to be friends, Symphony. I'm enjoying having you in my life.'

Symphony felt a little tingle of excitement pass through her. She could not deny that Jason was growing on her, quicker than she expected.

"I'm grateful for your friendship. I never imagined I would make friends so quickly when I moved here." Symphony paused for a moment and decided to change the subject. "Hey, before you go, how come you have Nadia's private line?"

"I was wondering when you were going to ask that. When she conned me, I mean convinced me, to create those plans for one of the Historical Society projects, Nadia always called me late at night using this number. She said it was when she had her best ideas. Okay. I'm exiting now. You get some rest and I will talk to you later. Good night, Symphony."

"Goodnight." Symphony pushed the button to turn off the phone and looked down at Psycho. His head was tilted to the side as if he was waiting for her to speak to him. "I'm grateful for your friendship." Symphony smacked herself in the forehead with the palm of her hand. "Could I have sounded just a little more formal and unfeeling? Good grief. I need to get myself some sort of apparatus that will stop me from saying stupid things."

Symphony looked back at the quilt. She reached out and let her fingertips gently pass over it. While not the same dizzy feeling she had before, she did feel something when she touched the material.

"It's probably static electricity." Symphony looked down for Psycho and saw that he had left his bed and was walking toward the doorway. "Maybe it is because of this heavy wool rug that Nadia has next to her bed." She looked back at the suitcase and the letter she had left on top of it. "As much as I would love to dive into this suitcase, my eyes are starting to close. It's been here all this time, it can wait one more day."

Symphony turned to walk out of the room toward where Psycho was waiting in the hallway. She was almost to the doorframe when she stopped and turned around. Looking back at the suitcase, she spied the letter and envelope. She returned to the bed and picked the lavender items up. Pulling it toward her chest, Symphony smiled to herself.

"This is from Amburgey. This is from my mother." Symphony paused and let the knowledge sink in. "There's a mystery in this letter. I've got to solve it. She must want to be found after all." She took in a deep breath and exhaled. "I hope that is still possible. I hope she is out there somewhere waiting for me."

WORDS OF THE GRANNY WITCH

"You can't hide a secret that is not completely yours. I've wondered many times throughout my life if that is true. The secret I'm keeping is shared with another. I've waited patiently for the revealing of it, but I'm not sure that it ever was a secret in the truest sense of the word.

"My Granny Witch mentor taught me the talk of the flowers. Every flower or plant symbolizes something; some have multiple meanings. One of the attributes that the white rose symbolizes is secrecy. A white rose is a strange one. It loses its color almost instantly. White roses will turn brown quicker than a young girl's heart will turn her fancy to another. I wonder if that means that secrecy is really an illusion. Do we ever hold a secret? Because if even one other person knows, it's not a secret, is it?

"This girl who is coming. I know secrets about how she came to be. I've kept them for most of her existence. It's not clear to me if I am really the secret keeper or the carrier. Does the secret belong to the one who creates it or the one who exists because of it? My heart is full for this young one. I've bore the load and it has worn on me. She will bear the revelation of it. It's a mystery that she can only solve one way. She'll have to dip deep into her bravery to find the strength to go where her mother went. The reasons might just be the same."

Chapter Ten

"SYMPHONY, I AM SO SORRY that Allison had to call you in." Marcella offered Symphony a doughnut before Symphony even had a chance to take off her jacket. "Drew sounded pretty sick on the phone this morning. I think he has been throwing up."

"It's no problem. He cannot help being sick." Symphony surveyed the box of doughnuts trying to make a choice. "These are some unusual looking flavors. What's that one?" Symphony pointed at an orange one.

"Dreamsicle. It's quite tasty."

"Are these from the doughnut shop down the street?" Taking the first bite, Symphony let out a moan. "Oh, my, that is wonderful. I think I just felt a pound take up residence on my butt."

"Well, there are more pounds where that came from." Marcella waved the box in front of Symphony before she closed it and placed it on a table near her desk. "We may need another jolt of energy after this group tour leaves later."

"Yes, I remember now. There's a big group of people who are touring all of the museums today."

"They are having quite an extensive historic tour. They started at the Edith Bolling Wilson Birthplace Museum about an hour ago. Their guide should now be giving them a brief driving tour of the historic district before they come here. You and I are going to be busy. I thought that I would take care of the guided tour of the Rock House and you could stay at the Boyd Museum since it is more of a self-guided tour. You really haven't had that much opportunity to commit the tours to memory. Does that sound okay with you?"

"Absolutely. That will also give me some time to brush up on the polio exhibit information. Allison mentioned something last week about planning to do another special exhibit for the summer that was related to polio. I think she wants me to do additional research."

"She does have that in her plan for this year. It's something about some of the natural health remedies that are being used today for post-polio syndrome. I think she is thinking about maybe having a special exhibit with some sort of speakers' forum kicking it off."

"Interesting stuff. That's what I'm here for." Symphony glanced at the clock. "I guess I better go make sure that I don't have any doughnut sugar on my face and head to the Boyd."

"It's going to be an eventful morning. We better get a move on."

"I REMEMBER THE fear that polio created. I was a little boy myself and my mother was terrified that my siblings and I would catch it."

Symphony listened intently to the older man. She noticed that it was the second time he had toured the portion of the museum that held a permanent exhibit about polio's impact on Wytheville. When she first viewed the images contained in the exhibit, she found them haunting. She could see that the man was having the same reaction, only it sounded like for a different reason.

"I live in Raleigh now, but I grew up in a small North Carolina town that is about a hundred miles from here. I remember my family driving through this area in the summer of 1950 and seeing that billboard on the road." The man pointed to a small replica of the billboard that was part of the exhibit. "We saw it as we travelled in both directions. I remember noticing it on our way back. My parents had talked about it extensively. Even then, Wytheville was known to be a good place to stop on a trip. We didn't stop on that trip. This billboard was the reason why."

Symphony studied the billboard more closely. The bottom of it indicated that the health message came from three local government agencies of the time: the town council, the board of supervisors, and the health department. The bold black letters on the plain white background lacked the creative colorful flair that billboards, then and now, were known for. It was a simple somber message:

INFORMATION FOR TOURISTS
POLIO OUTBREAK
IN WYTHEVILLE AND WYTHE COUNTY
IF YOU DO NOT STOP WITH US THIS TRIP
WE INVITE YOU TO VISIT US ON YOUR NEXT
VACATION

"It was quite a bold statement for the local government to post such a message." Symphony commented while the man lingered in front of the placard.

"It was indeed. Unfortunately, during that timeframe, the news spread quickly that Wytheville had an unusual number of cases of polio. People drove through the town with their windows rolled up and masks on their faces."

"I am new to the area and this position, but I have read a lot about this time period in local history. It seems that in 1950, the area had the largest per capita cases of the disease in the United States. There were over 180 cases including seventeen deaths."

"I was not aware of those numbers. Polio was taking hold of the health of our nation. Thankfully, there were doctors working on a vaccine to help eradicate it." The man paused and moved to another area of the exhibit. Symphony followed him, thinking that he was not finished talking. "It's funny though, young lady, despite all of the fear about the disease and how widespread it was in the 1950s, I learned later that people did not run out to get the vaccine when it was released. Perhaps, there was a little fear in the cure, as well. Do you know what turned that around?"

"No, sir. I don't. Was there some sort of public relations campaign?"

"Something better than that." The man chuckled. "The King

of Rock 'n' Roll took the vaccine on national television. I saw it myself. They gave Elvis Presley the shot right there on the Ed Sullivan Show. I believe it was in 1956. The vaccination rate shot up to eighty percent after that. It's hard to tell how many lives were saved because of his public vaccination."

"What an interesting story! Thank you for sharing that. I hope you enjoy the rest of your touring today."

The man smiled and nodded as Symphony walked away. Later, she stood to the side while the group left the building. She noticed that the man had a slight limp to his gait. She wondered if that hesitance in his step had come from his own bout with the disease decades ago. She wondered about the scars that were left on all those children who had endured the disease and survived.

Tired of takeout food, Symphony stopped at a grocery store to pick up some fresh food items for the next few days. Earlier that morning, she had surveyed the contents of the refrigerator and disposed of those that had already spoiled. After putting her groceries away, she was happy to find a wok in Nadia's cabinets and was busy making a quick stir fry when the phone rang.

"Symphony, darling, this is Nadia." Symphony had to hold the phone away from her ear. "Am I talking too loudly? I feel like I can't hear you."

"That's probably because you haven't given me a chance to say anything."

"Oh, I'm sorry. I act so silly when I am on vacation. I guess it is all of the relaxation affecting me." Nadia's tone grew softer. "Is everything okay at home? How's Psycho?"

"He's as crazy as ever." The dog was hovering at Symphony's feet. He smelled the chicken cooking. "He's keeping good guard of the place."

"Good. Everything okay with your work?"

"Busy as ever. Allison is handing me more to do each day. Someone was sick this morning, so she called me in to help with a big tour."

"Oh, that's a shame on your Saturday. I'm sure she appreciated your help though."

"I didn't mind. We had lots of people on a pre-planned tour. I met a man who knew quite a bit about the polio epidemic."

"Horrible disease. So life changing for so many children and adults. That exhibit at the Boyd paints an interesting picture of what it was like to deal with it in a small town."

"So, what are you up to, Miss World Traveler?"

"We are having a wonderful time. That's one of the reasons I am calling you. We've decided to take a two-week cruise before we return. It's going to be filled with snorkeling and cooking classes. It's too good of an opportunity to pass up."

"That's great. I'm happy for you."

"I know my timing is horrible. We were just starting to get to know each other. But, there's plenty of time for that later. I know that you are busy with work. And, busy with Jason, I hope."

"He's busy. We haven't spent too much time together since you have been gone. We are planning to get together tomorrow though."

"Symphony, he is a wonderful young man. I know from my experience that you don't find wonderful men often."

"I know. I don't want to rush the relationship either. It needs to progress naturally."

"Progress naturally. When you learn more about Amburgey, you will realize that the patience gene you appear to possess must have come from your father." Through the phone, Symphony could hear someone talking to Nadia. The woman laughed. "Symphony, I am going to have to go. Did you get my postcard and find the suitcase?"

"Yes. The postcard came yesterday. I've just barely gotten into the contents of the suitcase. Where did that quilt come from?"

"What did you say, dear? The band just started playing and I am standing too close to them."

"Where did the quilt come from?" Psycho appeared startled when he heard Symphony shouting.

"When Amburgey returned from one of her trips, she came walking through my front door wrapped in that quilt. She never spoke about where it came from." The music got louder. "Got to run, my love. Have fun. We will talk soon." With a click, she was gone.

"Bye."

Symphony looked at the phone for a moment after the connection had ended. Nadia was an adventurer. From what she was beginning to learn, Amburgey seemed to have been one as well.

"Nadia said Amburgey came home wrapped in that quilt." Symphony talked to Psycho as she poured the contents of the wok onto a plate. "If what others have speculated is true, could that quilt be from another time? Would that explain the strange feeling that came over me?"

Symphony put a few bites of her chicken on a paper plate for Psycho. After sniffing a moment, the large pooch almost inhaled the sample. Symphony stood in the kitchen and ate her meal, allowing her mind to drift over all she had learned about Amburgey. Symphony being lost in thought was a benefit to the dog because she absentmindedly took pieces of chicken and fed him by hand. He showed his gratitude through huge wags of his tail, which knocked Symphony on the leg.

After cleaning up the kitchen and letting Psycho out for a few minutes, Symphony went upstairs to retrieve the letter and the suitcase. She glanced at the quilt still laying on the bed as well as the dress she had hung in the closet. There was no need for her to be in a hurry to move the items since it would be even longer before Nadia returned.

Snapping the suitcase shut, Symphony avoided looking inside. Combing through the contents and trying to decipher the letter would consume the rest of her evening. She did not need to be distracted by additional mysterious items that might lie within. A quick stop in her room, allowed her to change into her lounge clothes and pick up the letter. She had placed it within a book of poetry her father gave her before she left. The antique book's aged binding caused Symphony to think it was an appropriate location to keep the letter. Although, Symphony imagined the letter was no older than she was, it had a mystical quality that made it feel much different.

Returning to the cozy den, she found that Psycho had made himself comfortable in one of two oversized recliners that sat in opposite corners of the room. The rich brown leather of the chairs gave the room a masculine feel. Symphony wondered if this might have been the domain of Nadia's husband, Mr. French. She giggled to herself. The name reminded her of an old television show her mother had watched with her on cold afternoons after school.

"Alright, Psycho, there's something about one of the sentences in this letter that keeps haunting me." Symphony reread portions of it to herself. "If you want to know who you are, you are going to have to go where you have never been." Symphony stopped and pondered a moment. "I have sort of already done that. I have moved to a town where I had not been before. Well, if you don't count when I was born. And, I've moved here because I want to know who I am. Wonder if that counts." Symphony took in a deep breath, holding it for a moment before releasing. "I was never good at riddles. I wonder if that is what Amburgey intended this to be. Maybe I am reading too much into it."

The crackle of the fire she had lit earlier drew Symphony's attention for a moment. Fire had always intrigued her. It was amazing how the destruction of something could offer such comfort at the same time. She thought about the letter she was holding. Her mother must have been filled with anguish when she wrote it. By that point, Symphony assumed from its contents, Amburgey had made the decision to give her child up. She destroyed one relationship to make way for another. Symphony could not imagine being more loved than by the two parents who raised her. For that, she was immensely thankful to Amburgey. Symphony could not help but wonder though what might have been, if those who conceived her had raised her.

During discussions regarding Symphony's plan of work for the first six months of her job, Allison told Symphony that a distinguished gentleman would be volunteering to help her evaluate some of the jewelry items that were in the museums' collections.

Allison never mentioned that the 'distinguished gentleman' was a former movie star.

By their mid-80s, most men his age, if they had not already made their wives into widows, would either spend their afternoons riding around on a golf cart or sitting in a recliner snoozing. Most men were not like Garon Fitzgerald. The summer after polio devastated his hometown, Gary Moore took a one-way train ride to Hollywood. He was eighteen. After a year of barely getting by, Gary met a talent scout who thought his striking good looks and southern charm would shine on a movie screen. Gary Moore became Garon Fitzgerald and the rest was movie history. Sixty-two movies and countless awards, including two Oscars, later, Garon retired back to his hometown. His passion was history.

Symphony was not prepared to have a movie star as an archiving assistant. She would not have said she was ever star crazy. There were certainly performers that she enjoyed more than others in music, television, and the movies. She had never gone and sought one out or even asked to have her photo made with the few whom she had come in contact. But, she had never met Garon Fitzgerald. Her Grammie Wallace had owned every movie the man made, which meant that Symphony had watched all of them at least twice. His classic tall, dark, and handsome good looks and charming personality were legendary. A long line of actors, who emerged in the decades since, modeled their style and career after the icon.

And, there he stood in the storage room in front of Symphony—still tall, still dark, although Symphony suspected that hair dye and tanning were involved, and still handsome, in a senior citizen kind of way. Grammie Wallace would definitely say this was a sign.

She was not sure if she was having a case of star struck or

her Grammie had taken over her body from the great beyond. But, Symphony's heart was racing as fast as her mind was trying to figure out what to say to him.

"It's a little hot in here, don't you think?"

Walking backwards, Symphony began to pretend to fan herself. She could not imagine why she was feeling so nervous and awkward. If she had not seen him in the movies, she was sure she would be offering him a chair and asking him to tell her some historical tidbit about his youth in Wytheville. But, that Symphony seemed to be missing, and this one was acting like a crazy person.

Before she knew it, her leg was hitting a couple of the boxes and she was falling backwards. She felt Garon grab her arm to try and break her fall about the time that she turned her head and hit his.

"Oh, my goodness, I'm so sorry." Symphony could feel Garon's breath on her face; it smelled like Altoids and scotch. "I am such a klutz."

"I wouldn't say that. Your head is pretty hard though." Garon frowned, rubbing his temple. "It's a heck of a way to meet."

Symphony broke into a laugh as she saw the corners of Garon's mouth twitching. A feeling of relaxed comfort washed over her.

"I was probably dropped on my head as a child."

"That would explain a lot, my dear."

Garon looked her straight in the eye and smiled. It was the same smile Symphony saw in his many movies. She could almost feel her Grammie standing beside her, punching her in the ribs to speak.

"Mr. Fitzgerald, I have totally lost my manners." Symphony held out her hand. "My name is Symphony Wallace. It is a pleasure to meet you, sir."

"No. No. None of that 'Mr.' stuff. Mr. Fitzgerald was my dance teacher. You will call me Garon." The man made a little bow in front of her. "I have been led to believe that you are quite a talented archivist. I understand that you might also have an interest in time travel."

The man certainly did not have any trouble getting to the point. Symphony gave him a questioning look. The time travel comment gave a clear indication that he had discussed her in preparation for working with her.

"I am young in archiving experience, but I have endeavored to work hard and learn in my previous positions. Time travel?"

"Allison told me that you were researching the legends associated with Amburgey Gibboney. That little mystery would sizzle on the screen."

"You are familiar with Amburgey's history?" Symphony phrased the question cautiously.

"I am the resident expert. People can ridicule me all they want. I worked in Hollywood, I *know* time travel is possible."

Symphony was not sure that she understood Garon's last statement.

"Show me any A-list celebrity, and I can find you a photo from a hundred years ago that shows someone who is a dead ringer for him or her."

"Doppelgangers are not unheard of in any culture."

"But, a true doppelganger is the double of a living person. I'm referring to a lookalike from another time. There's something to be said for the immortality of some celebrities. It transcends time."

"What about you then? Are you a time traveling celebrity?"

"Sadly, no. That's why I had to retire back to this little town. You can't get old in Los Angeles. They have ordinances against it.

I don't want to turn into a plastic person like many of my fellow actors. I needed to come home." Garon had a far off look in his eyes. Symphony wondered where his thoughts were taking him. In a split second, he was focused back on her. A smile crossed his face. "I needed to meet you."

"I am simply delighted that you have. My Grammie Wallace was a huge fan. I watched all of your movies with her, many times."

"I'm sorry you were forced to endure those movies." Garon winked. "I heard a 'was' in reference to your grandmother. I am sorry to hear that. So many of my fans are now in that category."

"I loved your movies, sir. They are classics." Symphony thought about what she had just said. "And, not just because they are old." She shook her head and rolled her eyes. "I need to quit putting my foot in my mouth."

"No worries at all. My movies are old. I am old. They are classics, just like me. I am proud of my work in film, most of it. Even Meryl has a few performances that weren't exactly Oscar-worthy."

"Yes," Symphony nodded in agreement. "Even Meryl." She recognized the irony of casually talking about her favorite actress with a Hollywood peer who had probably been entertained in the actress' home. Forget a time travelling ancestor, Symphony was in her own version of *The Twilight Zone*. A message notice caused Symphony's phone to beep, and she noted that it was almost nine. "I guess I better get back to work. You are here to work with me today?"

"I am, my dear. I am really surprised that the conversation deviated to me and didn't go deeper into Amburgey."

Symphony noticed a gleam in Garon's eyes. It was a classic expression that she had seen him use with many of the characters he portrayed. It made him look mischievous.

"That particular conversation is not over by any means. I thought we might need to have a little small talk before we got deep into, what I suspect is, the real reason I have finally met you."

"Sharp. Savvy. Sassy. That is a dangerous trifecta. I love it." Garon picked up a pair of archival gloves from a nearby box and carefully placed one on each of his hands. Holding his hands up in a manner similar to a surgeon who was preparing for surgery, he turned to Symphony. "I am ready to work. Allison said that you are delving into the jewels in this collection. That would be my specialty."

"Yes. It is on our agenda for today. I was told that you are quite the expert. Did you gain your knowledge of antique jewelry during your years in California?"

Motioning to a corner on the other side of the room, Symphony and Garon walked in that direction. She spent a great deal of time archiving and logging details about the larger items in the collection. Symphony reasoned that the time already spent was small considering all the boxes of smaller items that still needed to be catalogued.

"I did. One of my first jobs when I moved to Southern California was at one of the most successful jewelers in LA. This is a story you will enjoy. Let's open up one of the boxes and I will tell you about that incredible experience."

Searching her pockets, she found the ring of keys Marcella had given her. Symphony tried several keys before unlocking the first small cabinet where some of the oldest pieces in the collection were stored. She smiled when she saw all of the little boxes that were sitting in neat little rows. The little girl in her could not wait to look at all of the pieces of jewelry.

"Allison and I have been meaning to delve into these boxes for quite some time." Garon picked up a small black-hinged box and turned it over to examine the bottom. "I've spent a great deal of time recently helping her with fundraising for the hearth kitchen so we haven't been able to get to this yet."

"Do you think that you will find any pieces that harken back to your days working in jewelry?" Garon gave a shocked look that caused Symphony to continue. "I did not mean that there would be any celebrity pieces that were donated."

"Symphony, you obviously have not read my biography."

"No, sir. My Grammie had a copy. I was away at college when she read it and didn't have much time for books outside of my studies." Symphony took a deep breath and hoped her answer would suffice. "I do have her copy in my library at my parents' home."

"Darling, you must stop apologizing. I am thrilled that a young woman, such as yourself, even knows who I am." Garon carefully opened up the small box he was holding. "Although, if we are going to be working some together, I probably should make it required reading."

"If you are going to give me required reading, I might have to start calling you professor." Symphony tilted her head and raised her eyebrows. "That is pretty." Symphony peered into the open box Garon was holding. A cameo broach was hidden inside. While the image was the traditional profile of a woman, the face on the broach was dimpled with a slight smile. "That's a little unusual for a cameo, don't you think?"

"Indeed. She looks like she is laughing. The color of the ivory is what is most striking. It has a rust hue to it, almost like a smoky tone."

"Do you think that was its natural look or could the color have changed with age?" Symphony watched Garon carefully take the broach out of the box and examine it with the jeweler's eye loupe that magically appeared in his hand. His movement was so quick and seamless; Symphony would have sworn that Garon made his living as a magician rather than an actor. "You are a sly one."

"My dear, I graduated past sly before you were even born." Garon winked before returning his attention to the broach. "It's hard to say about the color. I would imagine that it was created from some sort of shell, as it obviously is not ivory. The small pearls around the circumference of the piece are another distinctive touch. It is the detailed gold filigree that completes the piece."

"So, what do you know about Amburgey Gibboney?" Symphony thought that her sudden blunt statement would surprise Garon. She was wrong.

"I know more than most people. Maybe even more than Nadia, in some respects." Garon glanced at Symphony with a raised eyebrow.

"I can already tell that you know more by that one statement alone. No one else whom I have met has made any connection between Amburgey and Nadia."

"Most of those who know that Amburgey is Nadia's daughter, don't know about the girl's adventures. Most of those who know about Amburgey's adventures, don't know about her connection to Nadia."

"And why do you know both?"

"Because I am a man of detail, my dear girl. If you know details and have a mind that enjoys puzzles, you can put a world of information together. You see, I also already know that you are Nadia's newly found granddaughter. Unlike many, I knew she had a daughter. So that would lead me to only one conclusion."

"That I am Amburgey's daughter?"

"Well, based on what I said that is really too obvious. The conclusion I was referring to was that you have time travel in your blood. That is the most interesting deduction. I am intrigued to know how you are going to put that 'travel gene' to work."

"First of all, I am not totally convinced that she time travelled. I don't know if I even believe that it is possible."

Garon returned the broach to the box and closed it. Symphony noticed that again the jeweler's loupe had disappeared.

"I have found no other logical conclusion. There were not four Amburgey Gibboneys. There was one and she accumulated quite a few frequent traveler miles."

"Let's assume for a moment that I believe that. Why did she travel back in time? What was her purpose?"

"A reason as old as time."

"Adventure? Money? In search of something?"

"The ultimate motivator of all mankind—love."

"Love? She travelled back in time for love? I don't understand."

"Oh, but you will, my dear. I know someone who can help you."

WORDS OF THE GRANNY WITCH

"Gary Moore cultivated his good looks to his advantage. He kept his body trim with just a hint of the muscular prowess that made women even his mother's age turn and watch him walk by. He took voice lessons with Mrs. Garon and dance lessons from Mr. Fitzgerald. He cut wood and mowed lawns to squirrel away all the money he could. Birthday and Christmas money from his rich Aunt Mildred went to buying the stylish clothes that no one else was wearing.

"The time finally came for his school days to be over. Gary walked across a stage and was handed a diploma with his parents beaming from the third row. His friends were joining the military, carrying a ball to college, or joining the workforce and getting married. None of those things interested him. For as long as he could remember, he dreamed of spending his life pretending he was someone else. Call it illusion. Call it escape. Call it foolish—that's what his father called it. Gary Moore called it a dream and he was going to pursue it.

"It didn't surprise the Granny Witch when he came knocking on the cabin's door as the sun was setting a few days after graduation. She knew he was coming before he even learned she existed. It was only a matter of time and time was something she had by the bushel.

"She smiled when he took a wad of carefully folded bills out of his shirt pocket. The perspiration on his upper lip accented the thin lines of hair that were growing there. He was nervous—petrified. His fear was not of her. She was a kindred spirit. Even in his youth, his awareness of this was keen. His fear stemmed from the knowledge that if he did not have the magic within him, she could not conjure it to come out. His dream could turn to dust before it ever began. His wisdom was vast in this regard. A nervous banter of carefully chosen words that were precisely spoken revealed this intoxicating combination—youth, magic, fire.

"A Granny Witch can see auras. They shine around each person like a light bulb or a dark shadow. She had seen them all, or so she thought. On that late May evening as the sun was setting after the first hot day of an early summer, Gary Moore walked into her cabin and the rays of light from his aura almost blinded her. After it was over, when the magic had been kindled and the vision spoken, she slipped the wad of folded presidents back into his carefully ironed shirt. Granny Witches never rob another human. Taking the child's money was like giving a Bible to the Son of God. Gary walked through the door with everything he needed. She just acknowledged that it was there."

Chapter Eleven

"D O YOU KNOW ABOUT Garon Fitzgerald's experience with jewelry?" Symphony stopped at Marcella's desk at the end of the day to bring her some papers. "I only knew about his acting career."

"Yes, he worked at Harry Winston's when he first moved to California to become an actor."

"Harry Winston's? As in the jeweler of the stars? Beverly Hills?"

"Rodeo Drive, baby." Marcella added a deep seductive lilt to her voice.

"You've watched *Pretty Woman* too many times."

"Guilty." Marcella turned off her computer. "It's been some kind of a day. I need a little dose of sarcasm."

"How did you know that Garon worked at Harry Winston's?

Has he told you stories? He mentioned his experience in the jewelry business today, but we never quite got to the part about where he worked."

"I've read his book. It's delightful. He worked and was friends with a lot of big name folks. Working at Harry Winston's is what helped get him his big break in acting."

"When did he come back to Wytheville?"

"Hmmm, I would say it was about six or seven years ago. Apparently, after he retired, Garon stayed in California for a while and also travelled extensively. He told me once that it wasn't satisfying for him anymore. He said he longed to go back to his small town roots. He had visited here occasionally through the years and maintained contact with a few friends and relatives."

"You can go home again."

"Yes, I suppose you can."

"I almost forgot to tell you. Jason came by to see you. He wanted to know if you were free for dinner." Marcella gave her a raised eyebrow. "I told him that you were working in the archives with Garon Fitzgerald. He asked if he should be worried that Garon might try to steal you away from him."

"Steal me away from him?"

"Yes, those were his exact words. I am telling you, you have snagged the most eligible bachelor in town."

"Ha, I'm sure that Jason was joking. I wonder why he didn't try to call me instead of stopping by. I don't have any messages from him on my phone."

"He said he left his phone at home and was on his way to get it when he stopped. He said you could answer him via text. I told him that you had a date with someone else and that he should get on your schedule sooner." Marcella put on her coat and gathered her belongings.

"You didn't?" There was a little hesitation in Symphony's voice.

"Of course, I didn't. I wouldn't have said that even if I knew it was true. What kind of friend do you think I am?" Marcella shook her head and shooed Symphony out of her office before turning off the light. "If we are going to be friends, and I am thinking we are, you are going to have to start getting used to my sarcasm. There's no way around it. I told him that I would give you the message and ask you to contact him."

"I'm sorry. I should have known better. My time with Garon today has me a little rattled."

"He is still quite handsome to be in his early eighties."

"That's not what I meant. But, you are right. My Grammie would have been drooling all over him today. Do you think he has had some plastic surgery?"

"He was a Hollywood star. Of course, he has." Marcella kept leading Symphony toward the door. "I will say that I don't think he has had much done. I think he took good care of his health and stayed out of the California sun."

"And, there's the good upbringing he had in this clean Virginia air." Symphony laughed as she saw Marcella roll her eyes.

"I suppose that might be correct. He did live here before the interstates came through."

Symphony went out first so Marcella could set the security system alarm panel and then lock the door.

"Are you going to call Jason back?"

"Hmmm, maybe." Symphony walked to her vehicle.

"Maybe?"

"Maybe, I will let him think I'm out with Garon. He's been working a lot lately. I don't want to appear too available."

"When did a guy being a worker become a bad thing?" Marcella opened her car door and continued to talk to Symphony over the top. "He has ambition."

"I know. I want to keep him on his toes."

"Don't make him work too hard, Symphony. His life is full. You don't want him to feel that the relationship is difficult in his already stress-filled life. Jason has been supportive of your interesting circumstances. That's a very positive sign. Remember what your grandmother said about signs."

"They need to be heeded. You are a wise friend, Marcella."

"I know." The woman grinned as she got into her car. "Have a good evening."

"I'M NOT SURE that I have ever been this full in my life." Jason pushed himself away from the table and groaned. "That was delicious."

"Four bowls of taco soup in one sitting is quite a bit, especially with four Mexican cornbread muffins. I didn't know you could eat like that."

"I had a banana for breakfast and a candy bar sometime mid-afternoon. My hunger caught up with me."

Jason slowly got up from the table. Symphony laughed to herself as she watched his pained movements. Heavy dark eyebrows coupled with his violet eyes gave him a smoldering look. She thought that his eyes always seem to have a far-away look in them, like he was thinking something mysterious. There was no hiding what he was thinking at the moment. He looked sleepy.

"That last helping was a bad idea. I'm going to have weird dreams tonight." Jason gave his body a big stretch while he walked around Nadia's kitchen. "When you asked me to come over, I never expected that you were trying to put me to sleep."

Symphony frowned at his statement. Jason had begun pacing back and forth as she put the food away and loaded the dishwasher.

"I'm not taking the blame for your eating habits." Her expression lightened. "But I am glad that you enjoyed it. When I was in grad school, it was mine and my roommate's favorite meal to cook during tough weeks. There are so many things you can do with it."

"Besides eat it?" Jason yawned.

"Ways to eat it." Symphony shook her head. "You can eat it as a soup. You can use it on taco salad, or make nachos with it."

"I get it. Versatile. Like something on one of those cooking channels."

Jason moved closer to Symphony and pulled her into an embrace. Despite the fact that they have dated for a couple of months, the physical aspect of the relationship was moving slowly. This expression of affection caught her off guard.

"Thank you for the great dinner. My ability to have an alert conversation is gone. I think I better head home while I still can."

"Okay. I understand." Jason's arms were around her, blocking her movement. He seemed to be waiting for her to say something. "Would you like to take some dessert home?"

"What I would like is for you to be a little more comfortable around me." Jason released her and backed away. "I like you, Symphony. I like you a lot. Really, more than I've ever liked anyone.

Symphony's mind raced thinking how she should respond. It was not a conversation she expected to be having with Jason that evening.

"I feel comfortable with you."

"It doesn't feel that way to me. I understand that you are still getting used to living here and a new job. I realize that everything that has happened with meeting Nadia and finding out who she is to you is overwhelming. I'm happy that you felt like you could share that with me."

"See. That's a sign that I am comfortable."

"In some ways. Each time I try to talk about our relationship or try to move closer to you physically, you back away." Jason took a deep breath and ran his fingers through his hair. In the short time she had known him, Symphony had begun to recognize the movement as a sign of frustration. "I am beginning to think that perhaps you are interested in us being friends only, platonic friends."

A sad and scared feeling came over Symphony. She wondered if her uncertainty regarding things she was learning about her mother was spilling over into this relationship with Jason. She did not want that. She knew she could have feelings for him if she allowed herself.

"Okay. I guess I need to communicate better. Why don't you go sit down in the living room and I will get you some dessert?" Jason rubbed his stomach and sighed. "I'll make some coffee."

Jason nodded and moved toward the living room. Symphony heard his cell phone ring. She began to fill the coffee pot with water. He came back into the kitchen when the call was over.

"That was work. Something is wrong with the robotics system. It's holding up second shifts progress and will basically shut down third shift if it isn't fixed. I've got to go in."

"Bummer, I didn't realize you had anything to do with robotics."

"I don't normally. The guy in charge is out on medical leave. I'm the backup. So I got to get my butt back up to work." Jason gave her a slight grin. "I'm sorry. Thank you for a wonderful dinner."

Jason picked up his jacket and started walking toward the door. Symphony looked at the pot of coffee that had just finished brewing.

"Would you like to take some coffee with you?"

"You know, after that dinner and the hours I probably have ahead of me, it would be a good idea."

"Okay. Let me look through the cabinets. Nadia must have some sort of travel mug here somewhere. Everyone has those in their cabinets, don't they?" Symphony let a nervous laugh escape. She cringed. She sounded like a teenager.

"Symphony, I want us to continue this conversation. I want to hear what you have to say."

"Found one." Symphony closed the cabinet and showed Jason the tall coffee mug. "Do you want cream or sugar?"

"No, I drink it black." Symphony filled up the mug and put the lid on before handing it to him. He took hold of her hand after she released the mug. "We are going to talk about this. Think about what you want to tell me. I want you to be honest."

Symphony shook her head affirmatively and gave Jason an understanding smile. She followed him to the door. The brief casual kiss that she had grown to expect after an evening with him was missing. It was replaced by a wave and goodnight.

Standing at the door, watching him drive away, she could feel Psycho's tail hitting the back of her leg.

"Where have you been hiding?" Symphony gave the dog a scratch behind the ears. "You are not a fan of men visiting, are you?" Psycho tilted his head like he did not understand. Symphony knew better. "You want to go outside now." She saw the last of the taillights of Jason's Corvette before she opened the door to let

Psycho out. "You've got to show me a sign, Grammie. Help me figure out what to say to Jason."

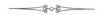

SYMPHONY KNEW SLEEP would not come easy. Her mind was troubled with how the evening with Jason ended. She needed to consider how she would convey her feelings. After letting Psycho back in and cleaning up the kitchen, she led her companion upstairs, where she changed into her nightclothes and returned to the suitcase that Nadia left her.

"I wish Nadia was here so I could ask her what she knew about these items." Symphony was talking to Psycho, but he was interested in a large rawhide bone in his big pillow bed. "Although, these might be items that Amburgey didn't tell her mother about if they are from her travels." Symphony shook her head and rolled her eyes. "Listen to me; I am talking about this time travel stuff like it is possible." Psycho's ears perked up at the word 'listen,' but he quickly went back to his chewing attack on the bone.

The lavender letter was a mystery to her, but Symphony chose to bypass it for the time being to look at the contents of the case. Examining the suitcase again, she looked closely at the vintage cream white leather and brown straps that encircled the case's design. A small gold engraved plate on the bottom confirmed what she had suspected before, that the case was made in 1924, close to one hundred years earlier. She noticed something on the bottom that she did not see at first glance, there was a singed mark, indicating that the case might have passed through flames. Symphony imagined that there was probably a story to go with that mark.

Setting the case on the bed in order to open it, Symphony began looking at the two latches that secured the contents. Each of the two old-style brass latches had a small button beside it that could be slid to one side, releasing the latch. It was a function that was not only heard, but also felt. She remembered with delight having a similar suitcase with the same type of latch when she was a child.

Symphony glanced at the dress that now hung on a door of Nadia's closet. The deep lavender color was accented by a wide white collar.

"Psycho, the dress reminds me of one I wore for a re-enactment I was in during college. It's hard to tell what time period the dress comes from, but I would think around the mid-1800s."

Symphony returned her attention to the contents of the case. Down near the bottom of the case, she saw a sliver of powder blue fabric. As her fingers grabbed hold of it, she noticed that the material was soft and lightweight. Carefully, moving the items on top of it to the side, Symphony gripped the blue material and lifted it out. She stood up to let gravity do its work without pulling on the material. Holding it toward her body, she smiled as she realized that it was a pair of Capris. The powder blue pants had a stripe of white down each outer side that led to a couple of small daisies embroidered at the hem. Looking back into the case, she saw more of the fabric. She pulled out a matching blouse with short sleeves. The daisies were on the sleeve cuffs and a mock front pocket.

"This is really cute in a Lucy Ricardo kind of way." Symphony took the two pieces to a full-length mirror in the corner and held them up in front of her. "I think this would fit me." Walking back toward the bed, she laid the outfit down. "Allison has been talking about us dressing up in vintage clothing when we hold the post-polio syndrome forum. This might be the perfect outfit for me to wear."

Glancing at the clock, Symphony saw that it was after ten. She carefully placed the outfit on the bed and picked up a stack of letters from the suitcase.

"I'm heading to bed, Psycho. Are you going to stay in here or come and bunk with me?"

The dog gave her a blank stare, so Symphony turned out the light and left the room. A few minutes later, Symphony was snug in her bed when she untied what appeared to be an old hair ribbon from around the stack of letters. Flipping quickly through the stack, she noticed that all of the letters were from different time periods and were all addressed to a person named 'O. Helvey.' The address was simply Old Mountain Road, Bland, Virginia.

The letter on the top of the stack appeared to be the most recent. Dated July 15, 1950, it began without a salutation.

I'm not for certain that you will receive this. You told me it was possible and I did not believe you. But, you also told me that it was possible to travel in time. Now, I know that to be true. I would never have imagined that your magic could work so precisely. I know you said that it would all come from my ability, that I just needed a token, a portal, and a reason. I suppose that you proved that true as well. You opened the door though and I thank you.

Let me start off by saying, I have not found him. You said it was a long shot that he would be in this time. I shall try a little while longer before I attempt to return. There is work to do here and I must be a part of it.

We knew it was risky for me to travel to this particular time period. What I read in history books and newspaper accounts only scratched the surface to what it was really like. Fear hangs over Wytheville like a dark cloud. Every day, there are reports of new cases of polio. Every week, you hear of someone passing from it. It is frightening. I could not have imagined where I would end up when I journeyed back to 1950. As it turned out, I became a nurses assistant at the clinic on Main Street. There is so much help needed and not enough medical personnel. I certainly don't have the experience that would be the most useful. Yet, I am willing to work hard and want so desperately to help these people. It is so excruciating not being able to tell them that soon there will be a cure—a way to prevent this horrible disease. I am listening to your wise caution. I do not want to be imprisoned in this time.

It just occurred to me that if you receive this letter, you might actually do so in what is my current time. You told me that is how it would be and that my words now would help you guide me later. It makes me wonder though, if that is true, why you didn't stop me from coming to this time. Oh, that is a jumble of confusion, isn't it? If you told me not to come, there wouldn't be a letter to guide you. It had to be, as you say. It had to be.

Symphony turned the paper over to finish reading. The page was blank. She looked back inside the envelope and nothing else remained. She wondered if the letter really ended that abruptly or if the recipient or someone since chose to remove part of its contents. As she folded the paper and returned it to the envelope, Psycho jumped on the bed and startled her.

"So, you decided to bunk with me tonight. I could use the company." Symphony glanced at the clock on the nightstand. "I could also use the sleep. I better save the rest of these letters from the past for another time and concentrate on dreaming in the present."

SYMPHONY WAS REACHING a meticulous stage in the archiving process with the photographs and information she gathered about each item. While the computer software would make the information easier to find later, logging in the information properly for each item took longer than most people would imagine.

"You are discovering one of the reasons why many museums are slow to complete this process." Allison joined her in one of the storage rooms while Symphony worked on inputting data into the computer program. "It takes a great deal of time. Most museums barely have enough staff to keep their doors open, much less do this behind-the-scenes work. We were fortunate to get some extra grant funding for this work."

"Does that mean that my position is gone when the money is used up?" The question had crossed Symphony's mind long before. She was beginning to feel comfortable enough with her supervisor to ask. "I know this is a reality of museum work. I hope to not become a victim of it." Symphony took a deep breath and gave Allison a weak smile. The question had weighed on her mind.

"No, Symphony. No fears for you at the present time. I had secured funding for your position. We are using this grant funding to help pay for these archiving duties. It was a rare find. It will only help to extend your time and responsibilities with us." Allison sat down next to Symphony at the large table where she was working. "I understand your concern. Please understand, if I had thought this was only going to be a temporary or limited time position, I would have advertised it that way. I had approval from town council to create this position. For several years, I had tried to do so, and things finally worked out for our department to get additional funding. We are growing and the new aspects of our museum system are going to offer more attractions for visitors to experience, especially those who are interested in the downtown area. It is good. My hope is that you will be here long after I retire."

"Only if that is a long way off." Symphony watched Allison look at some of the items she had recently photographed. "I've spent quite a bit of time this week with Garon Fitzgerald." Symphony saw Allison trying to hide a little smirk that had crossed her face. "His presence here this week has been about more than his knowledge of jewelry, hasn't it?"

"Everyone knows about his acting, but few people realize what an expert he is in antique jewelry. I think he really enjoys it. He's been dying to dig into our collections and see if there are any pieces of real value. I've told him that I think most of the items are probably only in the costume category. He will be able to confirm or deny that."

Symphony shook her head while Allison chatted away. Her boss rose from where she was sitting and walked around the room peeking into various drawers and boxes. Symphony followed Allison to where she was standing and tapped her on the shoulder. When Allison turned to face her, Symphony held out a pair of archiving gloves.

"Goodness. I forgot. See, this is why we needed to have someone in charge of this who is more competent at remembering these details." Allison took the gloves and slipped them on. "I'm ready to do a white glove test now." Allison made a silly face as she pretended to pass a fingered glove over a tall filing cabinet that stood nearby.

"Sometimes, you remind me of one of those comedic actresses from early television. Someone like Carol Burnett."

"What a compliment! She was fabulous." Allison paused and

furrowed her brow. "I guess she is fabulous. I don't believe she has passed on. Some of those stars live to be quite old. I think there must be Hollywood secrets to longevity. For some of them, I'm sure it must be connected to money."

"Money?" Symphony gave Allison a surprised look.

"It can't buy happiness, but it can buy good medical care, good food, and pampering luxuries. I read an article once that said Bob Hope had a massage every day for over sixty years. He thought having a daily massage contributed to his overall health. He lived to be 100. There must be something to it."

"You might be right. Since we have taken a strange detour in our conversation, will you answer my question now?"

"What question? Did you ask me a question?" Allison turned away from Symphony and was looking at a file on a nearby table.

"My question about sending Garon to work with me."

"Well, like I said before, few realize that he is an expert in antique jewelry—"

"Allison, you're stalling. We can play this game all afternoon. You are the boss. I'm going to keep asking though because we both know that it has more to do with Amburgey than it does with these archives. You could have gotten his opinions at any point. You can go ahead and tell me. He's already revealed that he knows a lot about my mother."

"I surrender. Even when I was a child, I could not keep a secret." A little smile crossed Allison's face giving Symphony a glimpse of the child still inside of the adult. "Garon probably knows more about Amburgey's time travel journeys than anyone."

"You both speak of time travel like it is a given. Like there is no doubt that the phenomena exists."

Allison took a deep breath. Symphony had begun to recognize

the mannerism she exhibited while pondering. She watched Allison close her mouth tightly causing her lips to almost turn white from the pressure. Marcella called it her 'deep thought' look.

"It is not in my nature to believe in the unexplainable. I would scoff at ghosts and visitors from other galaxies. I've read the research and talked extensively to those who have studied her. There is no other plausible explanation for Amburgey Gibboney. Now that I know that Nadia is her mother, it even makes more sense to me." Allison sat down at the table where their discussion began. She motioned for Symphony to do the same. "Garon is one of the reasons I now believe. He has been quite serious about this topic for some time. I think he will help you."

"I guess I am too sensitive to this subject. I did not expect to discover as much as I have so quickly. It's a whirlwind of information." Symphony's mind raced with everything she had learned since arriving in Wytheville. "It's overwhelming."

"You're right. Too much information on that topic. I can help you focus on something else. We need to kick our work on the symposium into overdrive. This is going to require some extensive research on your part. Interestingly, there is someone locally who has worked on natural treatment of post-polio syndrome." Allison paused and laughed under her breath. "This is another controversy of its own making. It makes a lot of sense though and I think it has merit to be included."

"Did I miss something? I don't see the humor."

"There is a woman over in Bland County who is known for creating medicines from herbs and other plants. Her practice is steeped in Appalachian tradition. Have you heard of the term 'granny witch'?"

"Certainly. I minored in Appalachian Culture Studies. Granny witches are the sacred women of the culture. Though, I did not expect to find any of them in the mountains around Wytheville."

"Don't let the interstates fool you. The hustle-bustle of the traffic seems like a different world when you get a few back roads away from it. Cybelee is a good example of that."

"Cybelee? Is that the woman's name? How unusual."

"The name is fitting for the woman who bears it. Many call her a modern recluse. She lives in a tiny cabin at the end of a secluded, wooded, dirt road. Cybelee rarely leaves her home. Yet, she has all of the modern conveniences, including a hot tub in her backyard and a satellite dish to insure she has internet service. Her income is made through the selling of her natural remedies and her equally unique jewelry. I noticed the other day that you were already introduced to her beautiful pendants."

While Allison was talking, Symphony resumed logging some of the archive items into the software program. The last comment Allison made caused her to stop typing and look up.

"What do you mean?"

"The pendant you have on. I noticed you wear it every day. It appears to be one of Cybelee's creations—a BloomSpoons pendant." Allison pointed at the pendant that hung from Symphony's neck. "It's one of the larger ones I have seen. It's quite unusual. May I?" Allison reached over to Symphony and took the pendant in her hand. "I've seen many with a mixture of flowers as yours has. I've never seen one with so many other components that are uniquely interesting. That tiny gear within it is so whimsical. What shop did you find it in?"

"It was a gift." Symphony tried to focus on what Allison was saying. "I don't know where it came from."

Something inside her told Symphony that it was not the time

to reveal who gave her the pendant. She needed to digest the new information from Allison. This woman, Cybelee, had to have once had a connection to Amburgey. Perhaps, Cybelee would know something about how her mother travelled to another time.

"Marcella has Cybelee's email address. I would like for you to contact and visit her, if she will allow it. It would be wonderful for her to be a part of our symposium. It's a long shot that she would come. But, at the minimum, perhaps we can share information about her regimen for post-polio syndrome. She has an extensive section about it on her website."

"Her website?"

"Yes. She ships not only her jewelry, but also her natural remedies internationally. It's hard to tell what that woman is worth. She has a jaw-dropping internet following."

"How does she ship things if she rarely leaves her home?"

"One of the rural mail carriers takes care of all of her shipping. Sweet lady, her name is Kim. She's also a writer. Marcella can tell you about her books. Something about people turning into animals. It begins with an 'S.'"

"Shifters?"

"That's it. I don't quite understand it. Marcella has read the books. She wonders if Cybelee was an influence on Kim's stories in some way. It's a complicated saga."

"Interesting. I guess I will have to get Marcella to fill me in."

"I have an outline of questions that I think would be good for you to cover with her, especially if she turns down our invitation to be a part of the symposium."

"She's really so reclusive that she would turn down the opportunity for the exposure?"

"Cybelee has had plenty of exposure. She doesn't like to be

exposed." Allison rose from the table. "You think you have met some eccentric people since you have been here. Just wait until you meet *the* Granny Witch of Southwest Virginia."

WORDS OF THE GRANNY WITCH

"As long as there have been people walking on this Earth, they have carried tokens to remind them of their life. The modern world uses jewelry to draw attention. The meaning of it goes far deeper.

"You wear a gold band on the ring finger of your left hand to link you to another human. An antique ring on your other hand signifies that grandmother whose hand it once adorned, who you came from but never met. A locket holds a love from a time long gone or the sweet face of a child who now has a child of his own.

"The jewelry made in this cabin comes from the soil of these ancient mountains. But, the petals and leaves that give color to the pieces are only the specks of the specialness. It's the magic of the spell quietly spoken as the resin seals in the color of the life of the flower. It's the generations of granny witches who dug in the ground to feed their children and cure their neighbors.

"They come to me from all over the globe seeking a ticket to something wonderful. I shake my head every time I wrap a package. The special comes from the wearer and the spirit that makes their personal piece glow. These pieces of adornment would turn black when hung over a cold heart. That never happens. My pretties don't go to those who have the darkness in them. Never even by accident. These living tokens of magic choose who shall wear them. No one with darkness needs to even try.

"She does not know that she wears the original. It never lay in a box on a store counter. It never travelled around the world in a padded bag. It was for her and her alone. It was created before she breathed her first breath all alone in this world."

Chapter Twelve

"YOU'VE BEEN WORKING EVEN longer hours than I have."
Symphony jumped as she leaned into the back of her Jeep
to retrieve the box of work she had taken home the night before.
The sun had risen a few minutes before she parked her vehicle in
the lot across the street from the Rock House. Still in her sleepy
state, Symphony had not paid attention to her surroundings or she
would have seen a familiar red Corvette parked nearby.

"I'm awake now." Symphony accepted a paper cup of coffee
from Jason. "I don't know how I missed seeing your car when I
drove in."

"I just arrived. You've been looking through that box for
several minutes. I didn't mean to sneak up on you. Our schedules
seem to be off lately. I've seen your Jeep here early every morning
this week. I took a chance and got up earlier myself this morning

and picked you up some breakfast hoping that you might take a few minutes and eat with me over at the shelter in Withers Park."

The tension of a long hard week and the tired feeling that had taken up residency left Symphony. Her whole being was warmed and relaxed by the smile in Jason's eyes. She nodded before turning to close the hatch of her Jeep. It only took him a few steps to return to his car and retrieve a large bag of food.

There was a crispness to the air as they walked down the sidewalk on Monroe Street toward the shelter in front of one of the municipal parks. Symphony learned that Withers Park was named for a local family and that the land had a history that included baseball.

"I hope you like the breakfast I chose for you. It's one of the shop's specialties."

Emotion welled up inside Symphony when she opened up the container lid and glimpsed her breakfast.

"It's orange French toast. I took a chance that you would like it. It's my favorite." Symphony stared at Jason in awe. He took out the contents of the bag and placed them in front of her. Little containers of butter and maple syrup surrounded her plate. "You're not saying anything. Maybe I should have asked you first." Jason's smile turned to a frown. "I'll go get you something else."

Symphony reached across the table. Taking hold of his arm to stop him, she also stood up. In the awkward stance of straddling the seat of the picnic table, Symphony took Jason's face in her hands.

"You are such a good man. You looked inside my heart and found this memory and you didn't even know what you were looking for." Tears began to stream down Symphony's face as a mixture of emotion came to the surface. "My Grammie Wallace always made me French toast, orange French toast. I've never seen it in a restaurant. It's incredible that you chose it."

It was the sign she had been waiting for. With his face still in her hands, Symphony leaned over and kissed him. Closing her eyes, she could feel one of her teardrops escape onto his face as his arms encircled her. After holding there for a moment, they began to teeter causing them both to break away and catch themselves.

"That could have been messy." Jason adjusted his stance.

"I would hate to have lost this delicious breakfast."

Symphony sat back down. Now that he was seated, she noticed that the teardrop was lingering on his cheek. She reached up to brush it away. He caught her hand and held it.

"No, let it stay there. I will take it with me today."

For the second time in those brief moments, a pool of emotion smoldered just below the surface as his words sunk in. He was still holding her hand across the table when she began to eat.

"Oh, this is so delicious." Symphony eagerly took another bite. "It's almost as good as my Grammie's."

"What are the chances of me finding a girl who likes this as much as I do?"

"About the same chance of me being passed by a red Corvette while I was listening to the song on the radio." Symphony watched Jason roll his eyes. "I am one lucky girl. I hope this is just the beginning of my good fortune."

Jason stopped eating and looked her straight in the eyes. The feeling of nervousness that she had once felt under his gaze was gone, replaced by one of comfort and ease.

"I've been waiting to hear you say that for weeks."

"It's the French toast talking." Symphony winked and let out a hearty laugh. "It's the way to this girl's heart."

"HE BROUGHT YOU breakfast. That's a nice gesture." Marcella commented. Symphony had finished telling her about the breakfast visit from Jason that morning. "I told you he was a keeper. I hope you have told him that."

"I think he got the message this morning." Symphony sat at the edge of Marcella's desk while she checked her email on the laptop. "Oh, I've got a response from Cybelee. Do you have any idea what her last name is?"

"I've never heard a last name mentioned, even in magazine articles that have been written about her."

"Just Cybelee."

"Yes, you know, like Cher or Madonna. When you reach a certain level of famous, you don't need a last name, I guess."

Symphony opened the email and began to read while Marcella continued talking.

"So, what does she say?"

"Believe it or not, she wants me to come see her today. She said to bring you with me." Symphony gave Marcella a raised eyebrow look.

"Lovely. I've talked to her many times. I must have made an impression on her." Marcella chuckled. "What time does she want us to come?"

"At three o'clock. I'll have to call Garon and postpone our work in the archives."

"I bet he would like to go, too. Going to see a granny witch would be right up his alley."

"Hmm, I wonder what Cybelee would think if we brought him along?"

"Who knows? Maybe she is a fan."

"Somehow, from what you and others have told me about this woman, I cannot imagine her being a fan of anyone. She seems too reclusive for such."

"Well, you never know. I understand that she has a quite powerful satellite and the fastest internet speed of anyone in Bland County. Her reclusiveness appears to have more to do with her face-to-face interaction with people than her overall communication skills."

"Maybe I should take some time over lunch to read up on her."

"That might be a good idea. Be warned though, all those articles only have the information that she allowed to be included. Cybelee is a mystery yet to be solved. Maybe, we will discover something important today."

After leaving Marcella's office to walk to the Rock House, Symphony pondered the idea of meeting the mysterious Cybelee. She found Garon Fitzgerald waiting on the porch in a rocking chair.

"Don't even think about going to see her without me." Arms folded in front of him, Garon looked more like he should be waiting to film his next movie scene than journey to the rural portions of an Appalachian county. "But, before we go, I'm going to trust you with a secret."

Symphony raised her eyebrows at Garon's last comment as he rose to follow her inside. While they had only become recently acquainted, Symphony had decided that the man did not know how to dress casually. Despite the years he had been away from the spotlight, he still had that movie star look with his fashionable clothes and impeccable tailoring.

"How did you know?"

"Allison, of course. She called me about thirty minutes ago

regarding the refreshments for the symposium and mentioned that you would probably be calling me to reschedule our afternoon of archiving work. I asked why."

"How in the world did she know? I just found out myself."

"Cybelee is nothing if not thorough. She confirmed who you were with Allison." Garon closed the screen door behind them after they entered the foyer of the Rock House. "There was a time that you could travel to Kimberick Holler and walk right up to the front door of that cabin unannounced. Times have changed."

"That sounds like experience talking." Symphony set down her laptop and headed toward the kitchen. Garon kept talking while following her.

"That's the secret I want to share with you before we go. And, I am sharing it with only you."

"I appreciate your confidence, Garon. But, I have got to ask, why me?" Symphony started to open the refrigerator, but stopped when she heard Garon's answer.

"Because my secret may help you understand what your mother did in order to be able to travel in time."

"Okay, you've piqued my interest. I was going to Google Cybelee during my lunch hour, but this conversation sounds more interesting. How about I buy you a sandwich and we go sit a spell and chat?" Symphony batted her eyelashes and used her best southern accent.

"Why, my darling, a gentleman always buys lunch." Garon did a sweeping bow and extended his hand for Symphony to lead the way. "Especially one who is living comfortably off of several successful decades in Hollywood."

"In that case, I might order a steak sandwich."

"We must get our food to go and eat in a secluded area. I am serious when I say that I am telling you a secret."

After a brisk walk into the heart of the downtown area and speedy service from a corner café, Symphony and Garon followed the brick sidewalk to a large wooded park that was near the courthouse. Symphony had walked through the park once since moving there. She was told that it was the main location of a large multi-day arts and music festival during the summer.

"This is a beautiful park." Symphony looked at their surroundings. She sat down on a bench near a creek that ran through the park. "It's larger than I imagined."

"It's a great location for outdoor concerts." Garon began to unwrap his sandwich. "There are lights in the trees that make it a gorgeous spot for an evening wedding. Perhaps, you will have a need for such a location in the future."

"I hope that is the case one day. What are you alluding to, Mr. Fitzgerald?"

"It's a small town, my dear. You are dating a beloved young Wytheville bachelor. It's news. Once the cat is fully out of the bag regarding who your grandmother is, the wedding date lottery will begin."

"Thanks for the warning. Jason and I are at the beginning of our relationship." Symphony smiled as her thoughts returned to their early morning breakfast. "He is a wonderful guy and I hope to have the opportunity to get to know him better. It is quite premature to be talking about anything more than that."

"Point taken. Just realize that the rumors are out there. Be prepared for the questions."

"My immediate questions are all for you, kind sir. I'm ready to hear this deep dark secret you seem intent on telling me."

"You jest, but you hit the nail on the head. This secret is deep and dark. It's the kind that they make movies about. Thankfully, no one in LA knew it or they certainly would have."

Garon set his sandwich down on the paper it was wrapped in and looked out at the large lawn area in front of them. He seemed lost in thought. Symphony chose not to disturb him and remained quiet.

"I am an old man now, and I look back on a life that has been incredible. It has surpassed the wildest dreams I had as a boy living in an old drafty house on Withers Road." Garon paused again, this time turning to face Symphony. "From a young age, I had a burning desire to be a performer. There was nothing else that I ever wanted to be. I would sit in that old movie theater downtown with my eyes glued to the big screen. The glow of the life coming from it was mesmerizing. I wanted to be in it. Not as a character in the movie, but as the person making that slice of fiction come to life. My dream was that clear to me. Growing up in a tiny town in rural America made that dream seem impossible. I knew that my young handsome face and propensity for the dramatic was not enough. I needed help from a source bigger than my limited experience could imagine."

"Garon, I do not think anyone would doubt your talent. You have many awards that laud your acting ability. Your success wasn't a fluke. The longevity of your career and diversity of roles proved that."

"Symphony, I have grown quite fond of you in our short friendship. But, my dear, just be quiet and listen."

"Yes, sir. My lips are sealed." Symphony put her lips together.

"That will make it too difficult for you to eat your delicious sandwich." Garon winked. "Just don't interrupt me. This secret has been held in so long that it will be painful to come out.'

Symphony controlled her strong desire to question by taking another bite of her sandwich.

"By the time I graduated high school, I had saved every nickel I could for a train ticket to California. I never said the words to anyone, yet, everyone in my life knew it just the same. In that time, an actor who was earning any kind of living in Hollywood was not just a speaker of words. You had to be a good dancer and a decent singer as well. I had studied and practiced with the best teachers here that I could find. I knew complicated dance routines as well as I knew multiplication tables. I toned my body to be lean and strong. Lifting a girl in a dance routine is not like hoisting a sack of potatoes. You have to be careful not to hurt her or yourself while looking fluid and agile. I avoided anything that had the potential to scar my face or damage my looks in any way. All of this effort was a full-time job. I knew it was not enough."

Garon rose from his spot on the bench. Walking toward a trashcan, he threw his half-eaten sandwich away and looked out over the same area that Symphony gazed upon moments earlier. Symphony sensed that his view was entirely different.

"One of my many jobs was washing dishes at the Greyhound bus station. It was a busy place. I got lots of hours as it was always open to serve the travelers who arrived at all hours of the day and night. There was a woman who worked there named Hazel. The people of the time would have called her colored. I never cared for the term, even before I knew it was a wrong one."

Garon returned to his spot on the bench beside Symphony. She noticed that he had a slight, almost invisible, limp. She wondered if there was a story behind it.

"Hazel was a character. She was a waitress on the overnight shift. No matter how late or early the hour, Hazel had a greeting for every person who walked through the door. It was a hearty 'Good morning, good morning. How are you this morning? Good morning.' It was like a chant to uplift the person who had spent too many hours in the confines of a crowded bus."

Garon's description reminded Symphony of a woman who worked in the cafeteria at her undergraduate college.

"Her friendly attitude hid a life that had been anything but pleasant. She had endured more heartache and tragedy than a dozen people ought to experience. I learned that when we would drink coffee in the wee hours of the night between buses. I also learned that Hazel knew things. She knew secrets. She had lived and worked in this community long enough to know the things people don't talk about. She kept other people's skeletons tight inside, safe with her own. The wisdom she gained from knowing was right there at the surface though. If she liked you, she would tell you. One night, she told me about a woman who could help me become a movie star."

"Hold on, Garon. I know you want me to be quiet, but I don't understand. How could a waitress in a small town on the opposite coast know someone who could help you with your dream? That seems rather far-fetched, like a fiction story."

"Indeed. But, sometimes it's in the fiction that you find the strongest truths. It's those stories that are on the edge of being ridiculous that turn out to be the truest. Hazel was one of the few people with whom I shared my dreams. She would never have told me about Orenda if she didn't think she could have helped me."

"Orenda. That's an unusual name. Yet, for some reason, it sounds familiar to me."

"Orenda was a mountain woman, a granny witch as Appalachian culture names it now. She lived in the same cabin where we will sit with Cybelee today. She's the reason you recognize my face. She made me a movie star."

Symphony rose from the bench and threw her trash away. Glancing down at him, she thought she glimpsed a look of amusement on his face.

"Is this some kind of joke? You do know I have a serious assignment that Allison has given me to find out about the medicines that Cybelee creates for those who were afflicted with polio. This afternoon isn't about some big tall tale you want to try to make me believe."

"Amburgey would not be pleased with your scoffing. Your attitude is obviously a product of your nurturing, not your nature. One person's fiction is another's truth. It may sound like fiction, but it is not false. Perhaps, I overestimated your desire to know the truth about your mother."

"What does my mother have to do with this? You are talking like you knew her."

"I did. We crossed paths once. If you want to know the truth behind your mother's story—the truth behind your existence— you've got to look past the truth of the matter. What everyone thinks is the fiction of your mother's complicated life is the real truth of her story. But, in order for you to understand, you have to accept that certain things are possible. You've got to know the secrets that no one wants to tell."

Abruptly, Garon ended the conversation and began walking toward the parking lot, leaving Symphony standing alone in the large park. Despite the warmth of the spring day, she felt a cold breeze encircle her. It made her reach for her arms to warm herself. It left her feeling that something had occurred that she would never be able to explain. It was a sign.

"Mr. Fitzgerald, it's nice that you could join us today." Marcella's eyes communicated her amusement in being right about Garon accompanying them on their visit to interview Cybelee. "You sit in the front seat so that you and Symphony can chat."

"You are another one who insists on calling me mister despite my repeated instructions to the contrary."

Symphony noticed that since their abrupt parting during lunch, Garon had changed into the most casual look she had seen him wear. The plain sports shirt and khaki slacks he was wearing made him look like he was dressed in some sort of uniform. On his head was a straw hat like older men wore while they were gardening. Glancing at his feet, she noticed that he had on exercise shoes. His sunglasses were the only evidence of his normal attire.

"Are you trying to go incognito?"

"Marcella, how are those lovely grandchildren you have photographs of on your desk? Will I get to see them again this year at Chautauqua?" Garon ignored Symphony's question. "I bet they are growing like weeds."

"Yes, they are growing. They are looking forward to the theater workshop that you and George are putting on again this year. All three of them have been bitten by the acting bug."

"Children are naturals. They have not been brainwashed yet with the limiting views of society regarding normal behavior. They are free spirits and delight in expressing their creativity. Children are so much more honest than the adults that create them. Conformity poisons creativity. You are about to meet one of the most creative souls that has breathed this mountain air."

"Marcella, do you have directions to where we are going?" Symphony stared at Garon as he got into the passenger seat next to her. They had not spoken since their earlier conversation. The sting of what he said about Amburgey was still fresh. "If Garon is going to ride up front, you might want to pass them to him."

"We don't need directions." Symphony gave Garon a surprised look. "Everyone knows where Cybelee's compound is located.

"Compound?" Symphony shifted her attention to Marcella who was seated behind Garon. "What do you mean 'compound'?"

"I thought you were going to research her on the internet during lunch." Marcella gave Symphony a wide-eyed look.

"I ended up not having time for that type of research." Symphony darted her eyes in Garon's direction. He slid his sunglasses down to look at her. "Something came up."

"Well, then, you are in for a surprise. Make sure you have your driver's license easily accessible."

Symphony started to reply. But, in the rearview mirror, she could see Marcella's hand go up indicating for her to stop. Beside her, an evil sounding snicker came from Garon.

"Let's get this show on the road. It's after two. We do not want to be late. Cybelee would be displeased."

Symphony started the vehicle and proceeded to leave the parking lot. Maneuvering via several streets to the interstate, Garon and Marcella made idle chitchat about aspects of Wytheville life that Symphony had not yet become acquainted. It gave her time to let her mind wander and think about what she had learned that day. It was obvious that Garon had been on the verge of sharing something quite personal with her and that the information, directly or indirectly, related to her mother. She regretted she had not remained quiet, as he had asked. She realized she might have missed an opportunity for him to give her knowledge no one else could.

After getting off the exit that would lead them to Kimberick Holler, Symphony more closely followed the conversation to insure that she was not missing any turn instructions given by Garon. Growing up in West Virginia, Symphony had seen her fair share of back roads and remote locations. As beautiful as her childhood home was, Symphony was amazed that this rural part of Virginia had a beauty all its own. Taking the roads that led to Kimberick Holler, she began to understand that part of the reason Cybelee was reclusive might have to do with the sheer beauty of her surroundings.

"You are coming up on the turn into Kimberick Holler." Garon pointed ahead. "Slow down. I think you will find that the road conditions will drastically change."

Symphony barely slowed the vehicle when she saw the road to the left. Unlike the asphalt pavement she had driven, she was now beginning to travel on gravel, and not a lot of that.

"This looks like what we called a washboard road in West Virginia."

"Now, you know why I insisted that we bring an SUV instead of a regular car." Marcella leaned into the front seat area to get a better look at what was ahead. "I've never been here before, but I've heard stories of people who have gotten their vehicles stuck."

"Cybelee does not want it to be easy to get to her. You have to work for it."

The vehicle rocked back and forth on the rocky and occasional hole-filled road. Garon took off his sunglasses when the tree cover became dense. Symphony felt like she was driving straight into a forest—in every direction all she could see were trees. It was like a tunnel of green with golden slivers of light shimmering every so often.

"I realize that I am driving slowly, but, this wooded area seems endless. How far back are we going?"

"Five miles." Garon's reply was short and quick.

"Five miles!"

"That's just to the gate of the compound."

"You keep using the word compound. I thought this woman lived in a little cabin in the woods."

"She does. It is quite small and in the middle of one hundred acres of land." Garon turned to Symphony and smiled. There was a gleam in his eyes. "There are several buildings on the property where she creates her medicinal products and her jewelry."

"BloomSpoons Inc. has a strict policy of following all regulations administered by the FDA under the Dietary Supplement Health and Education Act of 1994."

"It sounds like you are reading right off of a bottle of something." Symphony looked at Marcella in the rearview mirror.

"I'm reading from the pamphlet. There's a panel on the jewelry brochure about 'natural remedies.'" Symphony could see Marcella making quotation marks in the air. "I thought it would be good to bring it along in case we needed a phone number or something."

"So, you are really telling me that this woman is running a national company all by herself in the woods of Bland County?"

"It's an international company. There are many employees." Garon shook his head. "Watch out for that deer."

Because of their already slow speed, Symphony barely tapped on the brakes to stop for a deer that crossed their path. It did not seem interested in them at all.

"And they come up this road to work each morning?" Symphony could not believe what she was hearing.

"I'm not sure how many people BloomSpoons employs." Marcella continued to answer the question. "Most of them live on the outskirts of the property near where the production buildings are located. They would access that area from a main road on the other side of the property."

"Why didn't we come that way?" Three more deer crossed their path a few feet ahead.

"We are going to see Cybelee at the cabin. Have you not been paying attention at all?" Garon gave Symphony an aggravated look as he turned around to speak to Marcella. "She seems so bright most of the time."

"Are you reciting from a script from one of your old comedies? Because it is not one of your funnier ones."

"Someone is getting a little cranky, Marcella." A break in the overhead tree coverage caused Garon to put his sunglasses back on. "It's a good thing we are coming up to the gate. The guard will be asking you several questions. Try to be polite."

Symphony pulled to a stop at the gate and put the vehicle in park. Taking a deep breath, she rolled down her window and put on a smile for the extremely short woman who came out of the small guard building.

"Good afternoon. Please state your business." The woman's manner was friendly, yet, direct. Symphony noticed her nametag, Brenda Sue.

"Hello, I'm Symphony Wallace, and I have an appointment with Ms. Cybelee."

"May I see your driver's license, please?" Brenda Sue looked around Symphony at Garon and Marcella while she retrieved her license. "What is the purpose of your visit?"

"We are here from the Town of Wytheville Museum

Department. We want to interview Ms. Cybelee regarding a symposium we are planning about post-polio syndrome."

"I suggest that you do not call her that."

"I'm sorry. What?" Symphony handed Brenda Sue the driver's license. "I don't understand."

"Don't call her Ms. Cybelee. She will not like it. She doesn't like titles and she doesn't like last names." Brenda Sue looked down at Symphony's license. "I see that you hail from wild and wonderful West Virginia. But, you said you are coming here today from Wytheville."

"Yes, ma'am. I just moved to Wytheville a few months ago for my job with the Museums. I grew up in West Virginia."

"That's excellent. I'm a native of South Charleston myself. Moved here a few years ago because Cybelee changed my life."

"Changed your life?" Symphony took the license back from Brenda Sue's extended hand.

"I was suffering from a horrendous medical condition. I'd been to doctors all over the East Coast. Every treatment or medicine they prescribed was just a temporary fix. In a few weeks or months, I was back to living in misery. Then, one day, a friend of mine told me about BloomSpoons natural remedies. I figured, since it was all natural, what did I have to lose?" Brenda Sue moved closer to the vehicle and leaned in. "I'll tell you what I lost, a whole heap of pain and misery. I could barely walk. Now, I can run! You hear that music inside my little office? That's Mr. Elvis Presley. He and I spend our days sitting in this little house rocking and rolling. It's a wonderful thing."

"Elvis lives!" Marcella shouted from the back seat.

"I knew him during his days in Hollywood. Always a southern gentleman." Garon chimed in, lowering his sunglasses to wink at Brenda Sue.

"Oh, my! You are Garon Fitzgerald!" Brenda Sue started walking around the vehicle toward Garon's door. He jumped out to meet her.

"I think I'm in the *Twilight Zone*." Symphony turned around and looked at Marcella. "This is not how I thought this afternoon was going to progress."

"Just think, we haven't even gotten through the gate yet. You can imagine what it will be like once we meet Cybelee." Marcella was chuckling as they watched Brenda Sue taking a photo of herself and Garon with her cell phone.

"It's ten till three." Symphony looked at her watch. "We have no idea how long it will take to get to her cabin. Garon, I think you need to get back into the vehicle. We need to get going."

Brenda Sue gave Symphony a stern look while she hugged Garon one last time and whispered to him. Despite her previously fast movement, she walked quite slowly around the front of the vehicle as she headed back to Symphony's side.

"No one has opened up that gate for you, young lady. You don't get to go forward until I say so. I was having a nice visit with Mr. Fitzgerald." Brenda Sue smiled at Garon.

"Call me Garon, love. I swear, if I did not see a gold band on your finger, I would just try to sweep you off your feet."

"Garon, you charmer. It's just like when you played Vince in *Mystery Train*. You were so debonair and charming. You didn't have to do one bit of acting in that role, did you?"

Symphony caught a glimpse of Marcella in the rearview mirror. She was rolling her eyes.

"Brenda Sue, dear, Symphony has an appointment with Cybelee at three o'clock. I would hate for that dear woman to have to wait one second longer."

"Of course not, you are so right. We cannot make Cybelee wait." Brenda Sue turned around and pushed a button, causing the gate to immediately open. "Now, remember what I said, young lady. No titles and don't even think about asking what her last name is." The woman leaned into the window and reached her arm over Symphony toward Garon. "My shift is over at four. So, I suppose this is goodbye, Garon."

"Not goodbye, my dear. Au revoir, until we meet again." Garon took the woman's hand and kissed it.

"Oh, my. Toodles."

As soon as Brenda Sue leaned out of the vehicle, Symphony stepped on the gas. She could see a cloud of dust and the surprised woman's face in the side mirror.

"Really, Symphony. Was that necessary?" Garon turned back around in his seat. "Are you trying to kill us?"

"Did anyone ask that woman how far we have to go yet?" Symphony barely paused before she answered her own question. "No, I don't think so. We don't know how far it is and it is eight minutes till three." Symphony was looking at Garon instead of the road.

"Symphony, slow down." Marcella leaned up toward the seat. "The road is ending."

Symphony turned toward the windshield and slammed on the brakes, barely stopping in front of a log fence that ended the road. She let out a big breath and closed her eyes after putting the vehicle in park.

"We're here with five minutes to spare." Marcella began to open her door.

"We still have to walk to the cabin." Garon beat Marcella out of the vehicle and was opening her door.

Symphony jumped out and opened the back door to quickly retrieve her bag. Within it, she had a notebook with a list of questions as well as a recorder. She hoped that Cybelee would allow her to record their conversation. Looking down at her hand after she closed the door, Symphony saw that she was shaking. Her nerves were shot from the entire day of unusualness. She hoped that she could hold it together during the interview.

"You will be fine."

Symphony almost jumped out of her skin as she felt Garon's arm reach around her from behind.

"You scared me." Moving out of his grasp, she walked straight for the path. Marcella was already waiting there. "Lead the way, Garon."

The man walked around her without meeting her gaze. Despite his almost nine decades of life, he was in fabulous shape. He still had the long agile stride of a younger man.

"It must be his years of dancing." Marcella whispered to her. "I think he walks about five miles a day."

"That must be how he stays so thin. I've seen him eat." Symphony engaged in the banter, hoping to calm her nerves.

"My ears are just fine, young ladies. Less talking, more walking."

Symphony pulled up the rear as they began walking single file up the curvy, steep path. She noticed that the crunch under her shoes appeared to be crushed shells. She made a mental note to ask about that unusual aspect. The path was about as wide as a yardstick and curved like a snake up the hill. Designed to look rustic, there were solar lights that alternated on opposite sides of the path every two feet or so. They looked like small lanterns that might be found on a ship. She wondered if the crushed shells on the path were meant to complement the lights.

"Aren't the flowers beautiful?" Marcella broke the silence. She paused in the path and pointed to large beds of wildflowers on each side of the path. "It's like a multicolored carpet. I've never seen such a variety of colors in one place."

"Oz." Garon stopped a few feet ahead. "It looks like the Land of Oz. You better be careful that no one drops a house on you, Marcella."

"Why, Garon, are you calling me a witch?"

"Never, my pretty. Keep walking and watch for flying monkeys."

"Didn't you play the Scarecrow in that movie, Garon?" Symphony decided to join the banter, hoping to ease the tension between them.

"I'm going to take that as a compliment, instead of how it was intended. What I wouldn't give to get the residuals off that movie."

Garon momentarily turned around. When Symphony and Marcella caught up with him, Symphony looked over his shoulder and gasped, causing both of them to turn and look at what she saw.

"Oh, my goodness. I've never seen anything so beautiful." Marcella's comment mirrored Symphony's thoughts.

The path had opened up to double the former width. Beautiful gardens that mimicked those they had seen on the path surrounded the path on each side. In the middle of the path, standing over ten feet tall was the remains of a tall hollowed-out tree. Within the center of the trunk was an unusual globe that glowed as if being lit from inside. As Symphony slowly walked toward it, she noticed that the glow was an illusion from the hundreds of pieces of cut glass that created the round shape.

"It's all broken glass." Marcella came up behind her. She reached out her hand to touch it but drew back a few inches short,

202 ROSA LEE JUDE

like an unseen force had pulled her hand back. "It looks sharp."

"No. I don't think so."

Garon walked toward Marcella from the other side of the tree. Simultaneously, Symphony walked in the opposite direction. The globe looked like it was suspended in mid-air.

"There aren't any sharp edges." Symphony looked closely at the all of the different colored pieces of glass that completed the design. "It appears that they have been cut and smoothed at different angles to constantly be able to reflect the light, no matter what direction it is coming from."

"The colors are mesmerizing." Marcella took a few steps back and began to walk around the way Symphony had done. "It's like every shade of every color imaginable."

"And, ones we have never imagined." Garon followed Marcella as she paced around. "It's like it puts you under a spell."

Marcella and Garon continued to pace, while Symphony looked above the globe. The object suspended above was clearly visible when you concentrated on it. Yet, when she blinked from the light coming off the globe it disappeared.

"Hey, do you all see—"

"You're late!"

A strong voice startled Symphony. All three of them turned simultaneously and faced where the voice was coming from—the porch of the cabin. A female figure stood just over the doorway onto the porch. She was in a shadow and not clearly visible.

"It is all my fault, dear lady." Garon began to approach the porch. "I spent too long chatting to the delightful woman who guards your estate." Garon paused and looked back toward Symphony and Marcella. "And, this incredible piece of art that adorns your yard. It harkens to the designs of the masters."

"It matters not what was the cause. Time is precious and should not be treated lightly. Come in."

The brightness of the afternoon sun reflecting off of the globe continued to make it difficult to see the woman. She had turned and walked back into the cabin before Symphony got a clear view of her.

Garon immediately walked up the porch steps with Marcella not far behind. Symphony took in the porch while walking toward the steps. The front of the cabin appeared small; yet, something about its appearance made her wonder if the small entrance was hiding a larger structure. There were lichens growing on the wooden shingles giving off the mossy white look of neglect. She imagined it was more about the character of the structure than its upkeep.

Twisted branches of rhododendron made a gentle porch railing that was sturdy and soft simultaneously. Symphony imagined that morning glories might find a home within the branches to whisper hello on a foggy August morning.

Standing on the second step, holding on to the railing, Symphony noticed that holly bushes guarded both sides of the stairs. Grammie Wallace would say that was for luck and to keep any mischievous spirits from entering. The bluebells and foxgloves surrounding them made a welcoming call to the fairies.

Symphony could hear Garon chatting from where she lingered on the porch. The floor space was larger than might be imagined with an assortment of eclectic furnishings on each side of the door. It looked comfortable and inviting with a sense that it had been a place of rest and reflection for a long time.

"I invite all of you to be seated."

As Symphony entered the cabin, it appeared that Cybelee was

endeavoring to regain some control while Garon wandered around the room. Symphony tried to focus on their host, despite her desire to take in the surroundings.

"Please accept my sincere apologies for our tardiness. We are so honored that you have allowed us some of your valuable time. We will make this as brief as possible." Symphony walked toward Cybelee with her hand extended. However, the woman remained with her back to Symphony and appeared to be preparing tea on a stove in the far corner of the room.

"Be seated while I prepare a special brew of my tea. It will calm our nerves and slow our time."

Symphony sat down in a straight back chair near the room's fireplace. She caught Marcella's eye, from where she was seated a few feet away. Marcella shrugged her shoulders and shook her head at Cybelee's statement. Garon finally landed from his exploration of the small room at the closest chair to where their hostess now stood.

"May I help you with that?"

Garon rose again as Cybelee turned around with a small tray in her hands. The distraction gave Symphony a chance to have her first real view of the woman. Standing at an average height, Cybelee was overall a small woman. Long dark amber hair hung way past her shoulders with a slight wave in its style. Her complexion was dark from the sun. Between her long hair and a large pair of glasses with tinted lenses, her facial features were obscured. It was difficult to estimate the woman's age. Everything about what was visible appeared ageless.

Cybelee allowed Garon to take the tray. While he stood in front of Symphony and offered her a cup of tea, the woman was seated in a large wooden rocking chair. After taking a cup of tea,

Garon moved out of Symphony's line of sight. She remained quiet watching Garon serve Marcella, before he returned the tray to a nearby counter and took a cup to his seat.

"You have questions for me, I presume."

As the woman spoke, Symphony sipped the tea and noticed Cybelee's attire. The outfit reminded Symphony of something that might have been worn in the 1970s. The blouse and slacks were long and flowing with wide sleeves and pant legs in a non-descript pattern of earth tones.

"Yes, ma'am." Symphony set down her tea on a small table beside her. "We are so appreciative that you have allowed us to talk to you about your treatment system."

"Allison Emerson sends her regards and thanks." Marcella added to Symphony's comments.

"Allison has done great work for historic preservation. It has been her life's work." Cybelee nodded to Marcella. "Please begin your questions."

"Certainly. I was wondering if you would mind if I recorded our conversation." Symphony took her notebook and recorder out of the bag beside her feet. "I want to make sure that we accurately document your responses."

"That will be fine. There are several audio recordings about our remedies on the internet. It is often my voice that is used."

"Great." Symphony turned on the recorder. "Interview regarding natural treatment of post-polio syndrome with Cybelee of BloomSpoons Inc." Taking a deep breath, Symphony looked at her first question. "How did you first become interested in working on treatment ideas for post-polio syndrome?"

"Long before my company took shape, I came in contact with many persons who had contracted polio. These individuals came to this cabin seeking help." Symphony watched Garon's body language react to Cybelee's statement. After repositioning himself in his chair, his eyes met Symphony's. "People have a natural tendency to look to nature for answers. It is wise. All the true answers to life's problems can be found there. I became acquainted with one woman who I met quite accidentally in the mid 1990's who suffered from great pain. She had been to countless doctors and given medicines and other treatments that did little, if anything, to ease her suffering."

Symphony glanced at Marcella. She was taking notes. It reminded Symphony that someone had told her that Marcella had once been a newspaper reporter. Notetaking was no doubt a long-held habit.

"The woman's name was Nell. She was in her late forties. As a child, she had a brief incidence of polio with a high-unexplained fever. It was a scary time to have such a sudden illness. Yet, doctors then gave her parents no reason to believe that she had anything but a mild case of the disease. The woman lived a healthy life. Her only visits to the hospital in her adult life were for the births of her two children. Her medical life was quite normal until she was in a serious car accident in the early 1990s. While she did not suffer any broken bones or internal injuries, shortly thereafter she began to have back pain and difficulty walking. After going to numerous doctors and undergoing dozens of tests, something happened quite accidentally which led her to discover what was wrong."

Cybelee paused and took a drink from a glass of water that had been sitting within a holder in the rocking chair. The action gave Symphony the opportunity to view the chair's unique design. It was made from a light-colored wood and had been left to its natural color. Wider than most rocking chairs, the arms and spindles were carved to look like ivy. So high was the back that Symphony could see almost all of the intricate carving of the headrest. It was one large owl facing forward in the middle and two other ones in profile on each side. Stain was used to highlight the birds' features including the detail of the feathers.

"While at one of the larger city hospitals that Nell went to for tests, her husband happened to be reading a newspaper that told the story of someone with post-polio syndrome. The symptoms described were almost exactly what Nell was experiencing. Through the friend of a friend of a friend, as they say, Nell found her way to this cabin. I listened to her complaints. I studied her symptoms. I had been working with some who had fibromyalgia and chronic fatigue syndrome. There are many similarities between the symptoms of these two ailments and post-polio. Through trial and error, we found some natural combinations that gave Nell dramatic relief. A cure? No. A better, less painful, life? Absolutely."

"That is an amazing story. In the years since, I understand you have worked with many others who had such symptoms. Is that correct?"

"Many."

"Many? Would you care to quantify that?" Symphony thought she saw a small smile cross the woman's face. Up until that point, her storytelling had yielded little sign of emotion.

"I have not kept a count."

"Dozens? Hundreds?"

Both Marcella and Garon chuckled.

"Please forgive her, Cybelee. She did not have much time to research in preparation for this interview. Allison gave her little notice of this particular aspect of the assignment." Marcella smiled at Symphony. "Symphony has recently moved to our area, and I do not believe she had heard of you prior to coming here."

"It is fine. It is how I like it best. Perhaps, Symphony knows more than she realizes. I'm sure she was told many things." Cybelee looked at Garon. "I would say that the number is more correct to say thousands. I have not worked with all of them personally. That number is quite small. But, my staff has been in contact with many of those suffering from these issues. We hope we have made a difference in their lives."

Thirty minutes passed while Cybelee answered the remainder of the questions Allison had listed. Symphony clicked off the recorder and closed her notebook. As Marcella and Garon rose and began to thank Cybelee, Symphony asked one final question.

"How long have you lived in this cabin?"

Symphony saw the shocked look cross Marcella's face. Garon closed his eyes and sighed, whispering under his breath.

"We were so close."

"Did I say something wrong?"

Symphony looked from her friends to Cybelee. The woman's demeanor completely changed. She had such a tight grip on the ends of the chair's arms that her knuckles turned white.

"I am a private person. I prefer to live my life in solitude. It becomes my situation."

"I'm sorry. I didn't realize. I apologize." Symphony slung her bag over her shoulder and rose from where she was seated. "I suppose it is a moot point for me to ask you if I might return." A nervous laugh escaped as she briefly made eye contact with Cybelee as she walked past her on the way to the door where Marcella and Garon were waiting.

"You may return. If you do, I will reward your bravery with the story of how I became a granny witch." Cybelee rose from her chair. She seemed to teeter a moment before she got her bearings. "Close your mouth, Garon. I know you have been waiting for me to say it. You know the truth of that tale."

THE MAIN ROAD WAS in view before any of them spoke. It seemed that each wanted to digest the experience separately before discussing. It was Marcella who broke the silence.

"It's impossible to determine how old she is. From a distance or close up, it's like she is ageless. I wonder if it is because of the color she was wearing."

"I think she had on more makeup than was easily noticed. I've seen the same phenomena in Hollywood. Even those who have not gone under the knife, and there aren't many of them, have a way of hiding their age with makeup application techniques. It's a whole industry in itself."

"I think she's in her late forties or early fifties, but she is aging faster than she would normally." Symphony spoke before she even thought about what she was saying. It just came out.

"That's an unusual statement." Symphony glanced in the rearview mirror at Marcella. "You did not appear to be looking at her that closely."

"Well, it's just a feeling I had. I can't explain it."

"I, for one, am shocked that she invited you back. It must be because she wants to help Allison with this symposium. Did Allison ask her if she would come and speak at it?" Garon pointed to the convenience store they were approaching. "Let's stop and get something to drink. There was something off about that tea."

"It was probably a truth serum. Maybe that's why I keep letting these random thoughts escape." Symphony turned the vehicle into the parking lot.

"Allison asked Cybelee and she declined. She did tell her that she would give us all of the information we needed to adequately explain the principles of her treatment." Marcella opened the vehicle door. "What does everyone want to drink?"

"I'll just take a water. Thanks." Symphony took off her seatbelt and stretched.

"I'm coming with you."

Garon got out. He and Marcella both slammed their doors at the same time. The noise and movement made Symphony jump.

"Are you okay?" Marcella leaned into Garon's open window. "You seem rather jumpy."

"I guess it is just nerves from driving on that road after interviewing Cybelee. It's been a long day."

"You need some chocolate. I'll bring you some." Marcella gave Symphony a wide-eyed look before she turned and walked toward the convenience store.

Symphony leaned back on the headrest and closed her eyes. The day had been a whirlwind of activity, surprises, and emotions. Her hand went to the pendant that was under her shirt. She was probably not willing to admit it, but she would have sworn that she felt some sort of vibration from the pendant as she entered the cabin. There was so much going on at that moment; it could have simply been her imagination. Yet, deep in her heart, she knew that the pendant had a kinship to that place. It had a connection that transcended time.

WORDS OF THE GRANNY WITCH

"What comes first? What comes second? What is real? What's make-believe? The person who dares to ask these questions is the one who learns what is behind the curtain of illusion and the reality that is lurking beyond every piece of accepted truth.

"Most of those who come to the world in which I live only see the flowers in the pots that line the path to my door. What they cannot see with their eyes, they refuse to imagine with their hearts. Deep within the ground is the real life of that flower. The pretty multi-colored petals that I so carefully preserve are at the end of its journey. The magic of the plant happens in the soil—in the root of its life.

"So it will be with the plant called human. People look at the pretty outside and fail to learn what is held within. Sometimes the outside is an illusion shielding the eyes from the evil that is consuming it. More often, the outside does little justice to the beauty of a person's soul.

"One wiser than me wove a spell of confidence for more than one who passed over her doorway. Little did the sad hearts know that the token of magic put into his pocket or her hand was just that—a token. The power was already in the young heart's possession. The spirit of belief and courage of wonder was what made a dream come to life. That, and what is also the essence of everything, big and small—work, determination, and the perception that yes, it could be. Some travel a thousand miles or a hundred years before that becomes understood."

Chapter Thirteen

"T HAT'S GREAT, NADIA. I'M SO GLAD YOU will be back in time for the symposium." Symphony paused, listening to Nadia recount the details of her return trip from the cruise. "I guess I better get packing." Symphony smiled at Psycho. She knew what Nadia was going to say. "Okay, we can talk about that when you get back. Safe travels."

"Your Mom is coming home." Symphony reached down to rub Psycho behind the ears after she hung up the phone. "You better get ready to share that big bed again. I better finish going through that box she left me. I can't believe how little time I have had to go through it. There's some really good stuff in there. Mysterious stuff."

The crazy day that began with a surprise, and game changing, breakfast with Jason was finally over. He left that afternoon for a two-day meeting out of town. As happy as she was with the way things were developing with him, Symphony was content to have a little time to digest it all. With the visit to interview Cybelee fresh on her mind, a million thoughts were racing through her head. She would almost swear that the pendant was keeping time with her heart rate. It felt like it was twitching to get her attention. Since Nadia would be home by the end of the weekend, she was also glad to have a peaceful evening to further explore that suitcase. There had to be some answers contained within it.

"Why don't I make some grilled chicken on that panini press I saw on the shelf in the pantry? We can both be happy with that. Mine on a green salad and yours a la carte." Psycho wagged his tale as soon as Symphony said 'chicken.' "I better fix three pieces so we are sure to have enough."

Having finished grilling the chicken, Symphony began chopping up a salad. She heard the ding of her cell phone indicating that a text message arrived. Glancing at the phone that was near her on the counter, she read a message from Marcella.

"She is becoming a good friend. Have you met Marcella?" Psycho replied by raising his head from the big red pillow Nadia had for him in the corner of the kitchen. "I bet she is a dog person. Let's go outside for a few minutes before we eat."

After making a quick reply to Marcella, Symphony opened the back door and watched Psycho scamper out into the yard. In the distance, she could see a beautiful sunset in the making. Symphony wondered if Amburgey had stood in that same location and watched the summer evening sky. Psycho returned to her side a few minutes later.

"You're ready for some chicken, aren't you, boy?"

Returning to the kitchen, Symphony diced up the chicken

and placed a small plate of it near Psycho's regular food bowl and refilled his water. Adding some poppy seed dressing to her salad, she placed her plate along with a whole grain roll on a tray to take into the den. That was where she had put the suitcase earlier.

Decorated for comfort, Symphony thought that the den was the most masculine room in the house. She imagined that it was a favorite of Nadia's late husband. Less frequently seen in more modern homes, there was an old-fashioned ashtray with a heavy glass tray portion next to one of the big comfy chairs. It reminded Symphony of the one that sat next to her Grandpa Wallace's chair. He did not smoke, but it had belonged to his favorite uncle. So, her Grandpa had used it as a place to store individually wrapped pieces of hard candy. The memory made her smile.

With the news on television as background noise, Symphony finished eating her salad and looked through a small stack of photos that she found in a little satin pocket in the suitcase. During her first visit to the house, Nadia had given Symphony a photo of Amburgey. It was a casual shot of a teenage girl sitting on a bench in Nadia's garden. Symphony saw a slight resemblance to herself in the way her small nose turned up and the expression in her eyes. But, the girl in the photograph was far more beautiful than Symphony thought she was or ever had been.

The photos that she was studying were a mix of formal school shots and casual family situations. One with a big dog that could be a double for Psycho was especially endearing. Amburgey's expression showed her laughing.

"Maybe this is your father, Psycho." Symphony turned the photo so that her couch companion could see it. He sniffed it and laid his head back down. "Or, maybe grandfather is more correct, timewise. Either way, it appears that golden retrievers have been the dog of the house for quite some time."

The last photo in the stack, by the sepia tone to its color, appeared to be a hundred or more years old. It was of a handsome man. Symphony wondered if it could be an ancestor. Flipping the photo over to look at the back, there appeared to be the date of January 17 with the year smudged out, all that was visible was a '1' at the beginning.

"Well, that narrows it down to around a thousand years."

Symphony chuckled to herself. She knew from the work she had done with archives that deciphering smudged dates was one of the Achilles' heels of historic preservation. Having a clear date would make research so much easier.

"The name 'Jasper' is also on the back. He doesn't look like a Jasper to me. I don't think I have ever met someone named Jasper. This guy looks a little familiar though. Don't you think so, Psycho? There's something about his eyes."

Restacking the photos, Symphony decided to leave Jasper on the top. Looking back at the contents of the suitcase, she remembered that she had left the little 1950s looking Capri outfit upstairs on Nadia's bed.

"I really need to see if I can steam that outfit and get the wrinkles out. It actually looks new, considering the age it must be. I would be afraid to have it dry-cleaned. I think it will be just perfect to wear to the symposium. Allison is all into the idea of us being in 'period costumes.'"

Looking back within the satin pocket of the suitcase where she found the photos, Symphony saw there was a folded piece of paper near the bottom. Pulling it out, she noticed the edges were singed like it had been touched by fire. Opening revealed that it was a program from the Wytheville Opera House dated March 7, 1924.

"It seems strange that someone would save a theater program that was burned. I wonder how Amburgey got it and what significance it has." In answer to her question, Psycho got up and turned around in his bed. This time with his back facing her. "I guess you are not interested in this topic. Sorry, but that is not going to make me stop talking to you. I need to ask someone my crazy questions. Since you are the only one here, it's your lucky day."

Symphony started to place the program and photos back where she found them. She lingered on the photo of the young man for a few seconds.

"Jasper was quite handsome. If I am anything like my natural mother, I could imagine going through a box of old photos and finding one of a handsome man I wanted to dream about. He looks mysterious and from a different time."

Symphony smiled at Jasper before she slipped the stack of photos and the program back into the suitcase pocket. As she did, a small, embroidered change purse caught her eye. The vintage look harkened to another era. There were small and large flowers embroidered on the front and back, and multi-colored jewels around the hinged opening. Inside she found several yellow feathers and a newspaper clipping with a photo of a man.

"I think this might be Woodrow Wilson. What do you think?" Psycho let out a snort. "He looks quite presidential."

A quick internet search on Symphony's phone gave her an assortment of photos of President Wilson to compare the clipping.

"Strange contents for a change purse. A photo of a president who wasn't even alive during Amburgey's life and what appears to be canary feathers. Very strange contents indeed."

"BUT, THAT WASN'T the strangest item I found last night." Symphony's morning assignment was a change of pace. She was helping Marcella inventory a large shipment of items for the gift shop. "I saw a little sliver of lace peeping out at the bottom of the suitcase. It was a wedding veil!"

"Oh, my. Do you think it belonged to Amburgey?"

"I have never seen any evidence in my research that she ever married. Nadia hasn't mentioned it either. Of course, she could own a veil without getting married. Maybe it is a family heirloom."

"True. The items in this suitcase were supposed to be important to Amburgey. Is that correct?" Marcella continued counting puzzles in a box while they talked.

"I think so."

"It must have a special meaning. Maybe it belonged to someone who was important to her."

"Or, maybe it was hers for a wedding that never happened."

"No wedding dress?"

"It is a small suitcase." Symphony paused to count the boxes that were still unopened in the front area of the offices. "We've got to go through all of this stuff?"

"Yes. It was a big order. The gift shop needs to be stocked for the summer season." Marcella went back to the list on her clipboard. "I suppose you have a lot of questions to ask Nadia when she returns. When is she coming home?"

"Nadia called yesterday. She is coming home this weekend. I'm glad she will be back in time for the symposium. Speaking of which, I must transcribe the interview with Cybelee. Did she also send Allison some additional information?"

"Yes. Allison wants me to put together a presentation for use during the symposium that covers the basics of her treatment plan."

"It's a shame that she will not come for it. Does she ever go out in public?"

"I can't say that I have ever heard of her doing so." Symphony watched Marcella pause. Her eyes were darting back and forth like she was trying to remember something. "If she does, she must do it quite discreetly. It seems she truly is that private of a person. You saw yesterday, she is by no means shy. While we were sitting there, a thought crossed my mind. I wonder if her reclusiveness has something to do with her appearance. There doesn't seem to be anything obviously wrong. At the same time, there was something, I don't know how to describe it. There was something unnatural about her."

"Unnatural is a strong word." Symphony stopped what she was doing and focused on what Marcella was saying. "I did not notice any disfigurements."

The phone rang and Marcella walked back into her office to answer it. Symphony sat down in a nearby chair and reached for her phone to check her messages. A flash of memory quickly crossed her mind as she looked at her own hands. She remembered that it was Cybelee's hands that caught her attention. She closed her eyes and tried to recall what she had seen.

There were remarkably few visible lines on the woman's face. The large tinted glasses did obstruct some of that view. Symphony might have thought that Cybelee was barely midway through her fourth decade had it not been for the woman's hands. She had been so caught up in asking her questions correctly that she did not allow her mind to think about it. Her hands had the look of an older person than the rest of her body appeared. Being removed from the situation, she realized that a beautiful ring had also caught her attention. It was a piece of antique jewelry with an unusual design. A realization came over her about the similarity to something she had seen before. Symphony rushed into Marcella's office.

"That was an interesting phone call. The person wanted to know what kind of rocks we had on display." Marcella rolled her eyes and shook her head.

"Rocks? Is there a rock exhibit in one of the museums that I have missed?"

"No. I do not believe so. The name confused the person. He thought that the Rock House was really a house for rocks. I explained to him that it was called the Rock House because it was made of rock. He did not seem quite as impressed."

"I hadn't thought about that. Do you get that question often?"

"No. Thankfully, most people are not confused by the name." Symphony moved behind Marcella's desk and stood behind her. "Is there something I can help you with, Symphony? You have entered my personal space area." Marcella rolled her office chair around to face Symphony.

"I'm sorry. I didn't mean to move into your space so suddenly. I just had a flash of memory from our visit with Cybelee, and it made me want to check something on the computer."

"Okay. Be my guest. I will get back to the inventorying." Marcella left her desk.

Symphony sat down and immediately began doing an internet search. With the image of Cybelee's ring lingering in her mind, she quickly stretched her memory for where she had seen such a piece of jewelry before.

"I knew it!" Symphony exclaimed when she finally found what

she was searching for. "It's an Essex crystal. I remember seeing a piece like this on a research trip we took in grad school."

"Are you talking to me?" Marcella returned to her desk. "I thought I heard you say something."

"Actually, I was talking to myself. But, I will tell you." Symphony motioned for Marcella to come closer so she could see the computer screen. "Did you notice that Cybelee had an unusual ring on?"

"Well, I don't recall what the ring looked like. I thought her hands looked rather old for her age though."

"How old is she?" After a few seconds passed, Symphony turned to look at Marcella. She appeared perplexed.

"I don't know. I've never heard anyone discuss her age. Maybe I thought she was younger than she actually is. Cybelee is rather timeless, I suppose."

"Timeless. Another interesting word choice." Symphony took a deep breath before she continued. "After we were talking earlier about Cybelee's appearance, I tried to relax my mind and think about my perceptions of her. A ring she had on sprang to mind. I thought that I remembered seeing a similar piece several years ago. I was right. I think that Cybelee was wearing an Essex crystal or something similar."

"What's an Essex crystal? I'm not familiar with that." Marcella looked over Symphony's shoulder at the computer screen.

"It's a unique design technique that dates back several centuries. I read a passage here that refreshed my memory. I saw an exhibit of some pieces like this one that is pictured here while I was in grad school. It is a long and highly skilled task to make one of these beautiful pieces. It begins with a rock crystal being cut and polished into a cabochon shape. The crystal is then carved from the back to create the design. Lastly, the crystal is painted to depict a miniature. Most of the pieces were created to depict animals and flowers."

"That's beautiful. I've never seen anything like it. Did you see the one Cybelee was wearing close enough to get an idea of what it depicted?"

"I only saw it briefly and my mind was trying to concentrate on what she was saying. But, I think there was a bird with a flower in its beak and flowers around it. I believe there might have been small diamonds encircling the entire round crystal." Symphony paused and read a couple of paragraphs on the screen. "One passage calls it a reverse intaglio in Essex crystal. A design created from the back."

"It's gorgeous. A rare piece of jewelry for a rare woman." Marcella picked her clipboard back up to return to the inventory work. "I think I can finish what is left, if you need to work on transcribing the interview. Are you going to work on that at the Rock House?"

"Yes, I think I will. If you are sure you don't need my help. I will head in that direction. I'll snoop around and see if I can find any hidden rocks lying around, too."

"You're so funny. Maybe you should pursue a career in comedy." A lilt of sarcasm could be heard in Marcella's voice. "You just get on out of my way and into the mysterious world of Cybelee, no last name."

BY THE TIME Symphony finished transcribing the interview, it was past two o'clock and she was starving. She had several more hours of work to get the information ready for the symposium. She needed a real break to rejuvenate her senses to finish the task.

After checking in with Marcella regarding that she was finally going to lunch, Symphony set off for a brisk walk in the downtown area. She had been so busy during her first few months in Wytheville that she had not had a chance to get back to completing the walking tour she had enjoyed during her first few days there. Making a stop at her Jeep, she found the crumpled brochure that Bernie from the Trinkle Mansion had given her and set out to explore a portion she had not walked previously.

One of the newest restaurants in the area had become a fast favorite of Symphony's, in more ways than one. Simply called Food, the restaurant specialized in quick meals that could be held in your hand while eating on the run. Her current favorite dish was a breadstick-like item that was filled with chicken and veggies. It was called Pot Pie on a Stick. She could eat a dozen of them, but settled for the standard serving of four with what they called a Power Smoothie. It was green and delicious and would give her the energy she needed to walk a broad loop through the historic district.

Quickly realizing that both of her hands were occupied with food and could not hold the brochure, Symphony glanced at the loop that went down Church Street and began to walk in that direction.

Having only driven hurriedly down the street, her leisurely walk gave her an entirely different perspective. True to its name, the road was lined with churches on both sides. Large, imposing buildings she imagined were filled with parishioners singing praises on early Sunday mornings. Since the churches were included in the brochure she had just stuffed back into her pocket, Symphony realized that she was walking in the footsteps of many people before her.

"You won't get anywhere quickly by walking slowly."

Symphony stopped to turn around as someone walked briskly by her. It startled her for a moment until she realized that she had met the person before.

"Mr. Boyd. Where are you going in such a hurry? I would love to talk with you." Symphony watched the man stop in his tracks. "I must know if you are indeed a descendant of the Father of Wytheville." She wondered if the surprise question might cause the man to engage in a dialogue. Symphony took a sip of her smoothie, waiting his reply.

"My name is Thomas J. Boyd, young lady." Tom Boyd slowly turned around to face her. "Of course, I am a descendant. I am *the* descendant. My investigation of you revealed that you are a descendant of a local legend yourself."

Symphony choked on her drink and almost dropped the rest of her lunch.

"You aren't the only sly one." A broad smile crossed the man's face. "I like your stealth maneuvers. You would have made a good soldier." The man turned to walk away.

"How do you know that about me?" Symphony regained her composure. "Who have you talked with?"

"No one recently. My theory was all deducted on my own. You just confirmed it." Tom Boyd turned back to face her. This time a sly smile was visible. "In truth, few alive now knew her then. I knew her. You being the daughter of Amburgey Gibboney is as plain as that cute button nose on your face. People can put two and two together and get four. Few see past what they think is the correct answer."

Symphony was not sure if it was the rush of cold to her brain from the drink or the full morning of detailed work. The man's words were making little sense to her.

"I don't understand what you are trying to tell me, sir."

Tom Boyd looked up and down the street. Symphony did the same. There was no one in sight. Despite that fact, he moved closer to Symphony and his voice was barely above a whisper.

"People have heard about the legend of Amburgey Gibboney like it is a paperback novel. She's been gone from this town for so long—your entire life—that they only remember the part about the adventures she might have taken. They don't seem to remember what caused her to take those trips to another time."

"Do you know what that was?" Symphony played along and looked around her as she whispered. "Is it a government secret?"

"Government secret? Why would Amburgey's travelling in time be a government secret?"

Tom's voice became so loud that it made Symphony wonder if someone inside one of the nearby houses could hear him.

"I just thought that since you had a background in the military—"

"Indeed. I see where your mind is going. Nothing I ever did in my years *there* had anything to do with my life *here*. You are a smart one. Amburgey was a smart one."

"Thank you, sir." Symphony watched Tom Boyd turn and quickly begin to walk away. She scurried to catch up with him. "You didn't answer my question. Do you know why she time traveled?"

"Yes, I do." Tom kept walking.

"Do you want to share that information with me?"

"What rules most young fools in this life? Emotions, human emotions. In Amburgey's case, the love of a man."

"The love of a man? What man?"

"He wasn't a what, he was a who. Of course, one who led to another."

"What?"

"No, who. It obviously happened."

"Obviously? I don't understand."

Tom's brisk walking skills had taken them to the corner of Church Street and Withers Road. Tom was crossing from the right hand side of the street to head to the left hand side of the street they were turning on to. Symphony stopped in the middle of street when she heard his answer.

"It obviously happened because you exist."

Symphony was not sure how long she stood in the middle of the street after Tom Boyd continued to walk away. The blaring of a car horn brought her back to reality and caused her to drop the remainder of her food when she turned to look where the sound was coming from.

"Oh, crap." A police car was stopped in the middle of the street and an officer was getting out. "I'm sorry, Officer. I will clean this up." Symphony bent down and began to pick up the remains of her food while the officer walked toward her.

"Are you okay, ma'am? I was driving down the street and saw you just standing there. You looked lost." The officer picked up the smoothie cup that had miraculously hit the ground without breaking.

"No, I'm not lost. I was just talking with someone."

"Talking with someone? I don't see anyone around."

As they both rose from where she had knelt down, Symphony looked around her. Despite the fact that she could see quite a distance in each direction, Tom Boyd was nowhere in sight.

"IT'S NO SECRET that Tom Boyd has the ability to vanish quickly."

At the end of the day, Symphony decided to tell Marcella about her afternoon experience.

"I have been told that before. Actually, I've experienced that before. It's not what has got me addled." Symphony absentmindedly began playing with the little figurines on Marcella's desk. "Something happened to me while I was standing in the street."

"What do you mean?" Marcella turned from where she was locking up a file cabinet and gave Symphony a concerned look. "You weren't hit, were you? You didn't mention anything about another vehicle besides the police car. Did you black out?"

"No, I wasn't hit. I don't think I blacked out. I don't exactly know what happened. It's like I got a flash of something."

"Flash of something? You are going to have to be more descriptive than that."

Symphony was silent. She had known Marcella for a couple of months. She did not want her new friend to think she was crazy.

"You can tell me." Marcella walked around her desk to stand closer to Symphony. "Even if it sounds crazy, you can tell me. I'm your friend. Trust me."

"Do you moonlight as a mind reader?"

"No. Does it pay well? I can always use some extra money for shopping." Marcella smiled and continued to stand in front of Symphony. "I'm not leaving until you tell me. We can save both ourselves some time by you going ahead and spilling it. I'm stubborn and persistent."

"I know you are. I've learned that already. I've also learned that you are a good friend." Symphony took a deep breath. "It's just that what happened is crazy. It's not possible."

"Not possible? Like meeting the grandmother you didn't know you had within the first two days you lived here. Not possible like a little red Corvette driving by you while the song was playing on your radio and that car being driven by the man of your dreams." Marcella held up her hand to stop Symphony. "Don't try to tell me that you are not already in love with him. I see your face every day and your face tells me the truth."

"I don't like this side of you."

"What side?"

"The side that is painfully right."

Marcella smiled as she blew on her fingers, and then made a gesture like she was polishing them on her shoulder.

"Standing in the street after Mr. Boyd had finished speaking, I had this flash. It was like a memory. But, it wasn't a memory of mine. It was like someone else's memory inside of my head."

"Hmmm, that's an interesting way of describing it. What did you see in this flash?"

"It was a man standing at the end of a long counter, like a bar in a restaurant."

"That doesn't seem so unusual. Maybe it was your memory."

"No, I don't think so. The man looked just like the man whose photo was left with me when I was abandoned."

"What was Tom saying when you saw this image flash?"

"He was speculating on what had driven Amburgey to time travel. He said it was the love of a man."

"Is that who you think the man in her photograph is? The man she loved and tried to find?"

"I have no idea. But, Mr. Boyd seems to have actually known

Amburgey somehow, and he thinks she eventually found the man."

"Why does he think that?"

"He thinks I am the proof."

"That's an interesting theory. Do you think he could be your father? Do you have any information on who your father was?"

"No. My birth certificate was issued for a foundling child. It's what is done when a child is found. My birthplace was listed as where I was found and they guessed at how old I was. Neither my mother's nor my father's name were listed on the document. I only know Amburgey's name because of the note that was left with me."

"You must have imagined that the man in your photograph was your father. Maybe that's why you had that memory flash."

"That would seem logical, Marcella. Only that flash was different from a memory. It was different from a dream. It was like I was being shown something. Like there was a purpose in the image."

"Perhaps, you will be shown how to determine what that purpose is. You've obviously been led here for a reason that goes beyond meeting me."

Symphony smiled as Marcella chuckled at her comment. Symphony became lost in her own thoughts while watching her friend gather her belongings in preparation to leave.

"My research has been centered on my mother, since it was her name that I knew. I always thought that if I found her, I would find him. Maybe I should rethink that."

"Since you do not know his name, it would certainly make for a harder quest." Marcella began to walk out of her office and toward the door. Symphony followed. "But, you know, there's usually more than one way to get to a destination. Sometimes, the long way around is worth the trip."

Symphony waved at Marcella. She had a mountain of work to finish before the symposium. Carrying her laptop toward the parking lot in front of the Rock House, her mind kept wandering back to Marcella's final words.

"I wonder if my mother took the long way around to find the man she loved. Maybe that's what I am going to have to do to find them both."

Symphony gave an awkward smile to a gentleman who was walking toward his vehicle a few hundred feet away. She realized that he must have seen her talking to herself. Symphony opened the back door of her Jeep and slipped her laptop bag onto the seat. As she sat down in the driver's seat, she watched the man drive away.

"Grammie Wallace, it's time for another one of those signs. Finding people who know things about Amburgey has not been a problem. It's not gotten me any closer to finding her or my father though. You always told me to have patience. You never told me it would take so much time."

WORDS OF THE GRANNY WITCH

"I've been places no one has the right to be. I've seen things that were not for my eyes. My regrets are as big as the mountains that surround me. Sometimes you go somewhere that you cannot come back from, even when you return. I looked in the eyes of a dead man and saw the life he didn't lead. What happens to your soul when you try to be someone you are not? Does it split or just run in fear and leave you entirely? No one knows who they are supposed to be, if they have never been who they really are.

"I know this child feels like she was robbed of her identity. It may not be something that she consciously thinks about every day. But, it's back there. Back in the darkness of her mind where her secrets hide. It's the thought she never dares to whisper. It's the 'what if' life. It makes her feel guilty to long for something different when what she had was more than plenty. She berates herself for wanting a mother who she does not believe wanted her. The mother tortured herself even when she was sleeping. In her dreams, she watched the child grow and felt guilty for the memory."

Chapter Fourteen

"GOOD EVENING, EVERYONE. THANK YOU for attending our symposium about post-polio syndrome." Allison began speaking from the podium as she smiled at the crowd. To her left was a row of several guests who would, in a few minutes, be included in a panel discussion. "We are pleased to have several distinguished guests who will engage in an informative debate on this important and timely topic."

From her standing position in the back of the room, Symphony had an excellent view of the stage and the audience. She and Marcella were assigned to welcome the guests and monitor the refreshments. After the formal portion of the symposium was over, Symphony would give tours of the permanent portion of the polio exhibit in the Boyd Museum. Almost every seat was occupied, as the audience appeared to be giving Allison their full attention.

"Most of you in our audience this evening are well familiar with Wytheville's tragic, but inspiring, history associated with the polio epidemic of the early 1950s. After the adoption of the polio vaccine in the years soon thereafter, the world breathed a collective sigh of relief. Decades later, however, as those young children who survived the disease approached the midpoint of their lives, symptoms began to resurface that indicated the effects of the disease might have lingered in their systems. Tonight, our panel will discuss this syndrome and how a generation of adults is dealing with a new aspect of survival. We will also hear from recognized experts who will offer some alternative methods of treatment to cope with these sometimes debilitating physical aftereffects."

Symphony took in a deep breath, thinking about the presentation she had prepared that gave an overview of Cybelee's work. It would be the conclusion of Allison's presentation.

"You look quite festive in your outfit." Symphony jumped as Garon came up behind her and whispered over her shoulder. "I know where that outfit came from."

Symphony turned and gave him an inquisitive look. Garon put his finger to his lips in a gesture to indicate quiet before giving her a wink and slipping into an open seat in the audience.

When Nadia returned two days prior, she was thrilled to learn that Symphony was interested in wearing the outfit for the evening. Like Nadia could sense Symphony's thoughts, she briefly turned around from her seat in the middle of the audience and gave Symphony a big smile. While steaming the clothes the previous day, Nadia revealed that the outfit originally belonged to her and that Amburgey loved to wear it whenever there would be school events honoring the 1950s era. Her grandmother did not know the significance of why the outfit was in the suitcase.

The evening flew by and Symphony soon found herself saying goodbye to the last person who had completed the tour. After helping her co-workers clean up, Symphony told Allison that she would lock up at the Rock House.

"I need to pick up a small box that I left in my attic room." Symphony picked up her purse from where she stashed it under Marcella's desk.

"Your necklace fell out." Marcella reached under her desk and picked up the pendant. She looked it over before handing it to Symphony. "I've seen you wearing this often since you have worked here. Did you buy it when you first arrived? It's a BloomSpoons. I wonder if Cybelee noticed that you were wearing one of her creations."

"She did not say anything about it." Symphony took the pendant and put it around her neck. "I took it off earlier because it did not look right with the outfit."

"You looked retro tonight. Several people commented to me that they thought your outfit was a nice touch. Did you tell me you found it in that suitcase of Amburgey's things?"

"Yes. Nadia says that it originally belonged to her."

"Is that a real pocket on the front or a fake one?" Marcella pointed to where the daisy design was on the front.

"I'm not sure. I think it is a fake pocket." Symphony reached up to feel the area. There was a small opening that she had not noticed. "Nadia did most of the steaming." Symphony reached through the small opening and pulled out what she thought was a piece of fabric.

"That looks like money." Marcella pointed as Symphony looked at what she was holding. "Is that a hundred dollar bill?"

"It must have been in this little pocket for a long time."

Symphony shook her head in amazement. It was folded neatly into a small square.

"It looks quite old." Marcella moved closer to Symphony to get a better look. "I'm going to head out as soon as the others leave. You are going to lock up the Rock House, right?"

"Yes. I will. Goodnight, Marcella." As Symphony turned around, she looked closer at the piece of money. The print date on the bill was '1950.' "Considering our program this evening, that just gives me chills."

"What gives you chills?"

For the second time that evening, Symphony almost jumped out of her skin. This time it was Allison who scared her.

"What? I didn't hear you come in."

"I'm sorry. I didn't mean to scare you. I thought you heard me talking to Marcella as she was leaving." Allison moved closer when Symphony started to put the money in her purse. "That looks like a very old piece of money."

"It was printed in 1950." Symphony pulled the bill back out and showed it to Allison. "I found it in the pocket of this outfit."

"That explains what gave you chills. What a coincidence! That bill has seen a lot of years. I bet it is worth more than the face value."

"I wouldn't have any idea about that or how it came to be in the pocket of the outfit."

Symphony watched Allison start to say something, but then stopped herself and shook her head.

"It's getting late. You go lock up the Rock House and get some rest. I am so pleased with how the evening turned out and a lot of that has to do with your hard work, Symphony. You have quickly become quite an asset to our department."

"Thank you, Allison. I am enjoying my work. This symposium research was especially interesting. I only wish that Cybelee would have joined us to talk about her work."

"Cybelee was with us. Her contributions were well represented."

"Yes, I think her information was well received by the group. Many people took some of her literature." Symphony picked up her belongings and followed Allison out the door. "I really wish I could have spent more time with her. She is such an interesting woman."

"I don't think your time with Cybelee is over quite yet." Symphony stood with Allison while the woman locked the door. "You've got to find out the story about the pendant you are wearing."

"How did you know—" Symphony took hold of the necklace.

"You've told me more than you realize. I pay attention." Allison began walking toward her vehicle. "There's time enough to talk about this later. Go home. I'll see you tomorrow."

Symphony made the short walk back to the Rock House. She quickly went upstairs to retrieve what she needed. Walking back down the stairs, she thought about what Allison had said about the pendant. Setting the box at the foot of the staircase, Symphony checked the front door to make sure it was secured. As she did so, the large grandfather clock to the left side of the door chimed, the sudden noise made her jump. It chimed one, two, three. Gripping her chest in shock, Symphony absentmindedly took hold of the pendant and laughed. The clock chimed four, five.

"It's just a clock, Symphony." The sixth slow chime rang out as the handles of the clock slid toward nine. Then, a thought struck her and her eyes grew big. "This clock never chimes. I was told it was broken." The seventh chime rang out. "What in the world is happening?" The eighth chime rang when Symphony's left hand reached for the clock's glass front as her right hand grasped the pendant. A rush of fear shot through her body. The ninth chime rang as a strange feeling engulfed her and she was pulled into a tunnel of light.

WORDS OF THE GRANNY WITCH

"Each tiny piece of the token has a purpose. Each represents something far beyond what the eyes can see. Moss is for the maternal love—the reason behind the journey. It bids the creator with the patience for the passage of time. Purple Statice is for the longing, the missing of the one who was left behind. Queen Anne's Lace shores up the sanctuary of the token—its refuge and security, the drop of blood in the center that unites. Yellow Sweet Clover gives protection while walking between the worlds—time of her own, time of another's. Blue Cornflower breathes power into this life, this journey. Forget Me Not is for remembrance of what shall never be again. Pink Heather gives luck during the long solitude of time. Fern signifies the secret bond that shall be revealed. It gives the confidence to find the answers that fear wants to hide. A few specks of Gold are the magic within, the prize that shall be won. A little Gear to turn the hands of time and connect the wearer with the portal that will lead her to what she must learn. A lock of hair—dark like ebony—signifies the one she searched for and will never again have. And, the Rose, it is the heart of this token—it is the Love that makes it all possible.

"Nobody goes through the tunnel of time and comes out the same. Change takes hold of you and shakes the past out, so that only the truth remains. It's not always welcomed.

"There's a reason why a human rarely sees the future. It's too tempting to try to change it. The same is true of the past. When you have the chance to go back and visit what was before you, your mortal logic says that life would be better if it had gone another way. The truth of the matter is that we all get a certain amount of good and a certain amount of bad—it's our share. If you try to rob your good to fix your bad, you'll end up out of balance and you might just lose the rest of the good.

"The girl who came searching for love, found it. And, as surely as she found one kind, she lost another. She lost the biggest piece of her heart before she even used it."

Chapter Fifteen

S YMPHONY OPENED AND CLOSED HER eyes several times. Taking a deep breath, she tried to shake the feeling that she had been on a long trip. Her body felt like she had travelled on the outside of a vehicle. She felt like the road had ridden her.

"I must have passed out again." Her eyes adjusted and she saw what appeared to be the bright light of sunshine glaring down on her. "If that is sunshine, I wonder how long I was unconscious."

"Just for a few minutes, ma'am."

Symphony jerked around trying to tell where the voice was coming from. Her vision was still blurred and affected by the bright light. The floor underneath her did not feel like the wood of the Rock House foyer. It was cooler and slick like concrete or tile. As her focus became clearer, she made out the outline of a person standing over with a hand extended in her direction.

"Mandy Lee just went to the back of the store to ask the pharmacist for some smelling salts to see if we could bring you around. I wouldn't dare want to take you to the clinic."

The voice was male. There was something familiar about it. Symphony took hold of the strong hand and allowed the person to pull her upright. Once on her feet, the sun's glare was gone from her eyes, but her legs were wobbly. Someone came up behind her with a chair and that same strong hand that had not loosened its grip, eased her down until she was seated. Only then, did the hand release her. Symphony began to take in her surroundings. Nothing looked familiar. She quickly realized that she was no longer in the Rock House.

"How did I get here?"

"Well, darling, the way most people do." Symphony heard a woman's voice a few feet behind her. "You walked right in through that front door. Maybe that's not quite true, is it, Gary?"

"No, Nancy. It was more like she fell through the front door."

Symphony took a deep breath and rubbed her temple. Her gaze followed the sound of the familiar voice to the face it was coming from. A young man came into focus and Symphony let out a gasp.

"Garon, is that you?" Symphony's eyes grew big with amazement. The young man was the spitting image of a young Garon Fitzgerald. It was like looking at a photo out of one of Grammie Wallace's many books about the actor's life.

"Ah, my name is Gary, ma'am. Gary Moore. I sure do like the sound of Garon though. I have a teacher by that name. Maybe I will change my name one day. It sounds more sophisticated than Gary."

"Don't you say such, Gary."

Symphony watched the woman who had been identified as Nancy come around from behind a long counter. Before she could sensor herself, Symphony let out a giggle as she saw the woman's coal black bouffant hairdo and bright red lipstick.

"What's so funny, young lady?" Nancy walked closer to Symphony and looked her up and down. "You've not been drinking, have you? We don't have any of that here at Owens & Owens. This is a family business."

"Oh, I'm sorry. I don't know why I did that. I'm not feeling too good. I must be lost or something." Symphony pinched her lips together and tried to shake off the giggles that were still smoldering inside her. The woman looked like a character out of *I Love Lucy*. She had a feeling that fear would be a more appropriate emotion, but the woman's appearance had struck her funny bone. "Could you tell me where I am?"

"You are in Owens & Owens Drug Store." Gary smiled. "Let's get you something to drink. Would you like a soda?"

"Maybe just a bottle of water."

Symphony began looking around her. Her head was spinning and her mind was racing. She could not imagine how she had gotten from the Rock House to this business that she had never seen before. It was obvious that it was now daytime. Where had she been overnight?

The business had the look and feel of a retro drug store. She remembered being in one in a small town near her college campus. Since she moved to Wytheville, Symphony had been up and down Main Street dozens of times. She did not recall seeing this business. After a few moments, she realized that Gary and Nancy were staring at her. They had puzzled looks on their faces.

"I'm sorry. Did someone say something?"

"What did you ask me for?"

"A bottle of water. It doesn't have to be cold, room temperature is fine."

Symphony watched Gary's head tilt to the side. Despite his handsome looks, the movement reminded her of Tom Hanks' portrayal of Forrest Gump.

"A bottle of water?" Nancy was the one who responded. "Who ever heard of water being in bottles? We get ours out of the tap."

A feeling of confusion followed by fear suddenly overcame Symphony. She looked around the room, eyes darting back and forth, in search for any sign of the twenty-first century. Her gaze finally landed on a calendar on the wall near a cash register. The month was June and the year in big red letters was 1950. Symphony tried to hide her feelings.

"I am just being silly." A nervous laugh escaped as her voice cracked from the strangest feeling inside of her. "May I have a glass of water, please?"

Nancy did not look convinced, but, she walked a few feet away to a small sink at the other end of the counter and filled a glass with water from the tap. Symphony breathed a sigh of relief when her hand found the pendant safely around her neck.

"That's a pretty necklace you have there, young lady."

Nancy commented while placing the glass on a napkin in front of Symphony. Before she could take a drink, the waitress put a paper straw into the water. Symphony did not notice the woman placing ice in her glass, but a couple of cubes were floating around the straw.

"Thank you."

Symphony took a long drink, using the time to look more closely at the woman. Perhaps in her early fifties, the woman was rather tall and slender. Dark circles under her eyes contrasted with the red lip color. Nancy appeared tired, not from a hard day, but from a hard life.

"I don't recall seeing you around before. Are you visiting Wytheville?"

Symphony set down the now half-full glass of water. As she tried to come to grips with her present situation, she was relieved to hear that she was still in her new hometown. She pondered how she should respond to the woman's question. Glancing in his direction, she saw that Gary was listening for her response as well.

"Yes, I've not been in Wytheville very long."

"Visiting family?" Nancy was vigilant in her quest for information.

Symphony's hesitation to reply was rewarded by the sound of a bell ringing as someone entered. All eyes, including hers, shifted in that direction. Symphony did a double take. The young woman looked vaguely familiar.

"How are you this evening?" Nancy gave the visitor a big smile. "I just thought of something." Nancy continued speaking to the woman. "You showed up here the same way this young woman just did. We just found this one about a half hour ago passed out in our doorway. You don't think this is some new symptom of that dreadful polio, do you?"

"Oh, I don't think so."

The woman cautiously looked at her. Symphony felt like she was under a microscope, the woman was looking at her so intently. Dressed in a navy blue A-line skirt and white blouse, the woman's golden brown hair was neatly coiffed in a pageboy style with curls pinned back at her temples. She looked like any number of young women who Symphony had seen depicted in photography from the 1950s.

After a few awkward moments, the woman extended her hand toward Symphony. As she slowly moved to meet the gesture, Symphony allowed her eyes to meet the woman's. A smile crossed the pretty young face.

"My name is Amburgey."

A pain shot through Symphony's brain when the name registered in her consciousness. As the two shook hands, a strange sensation came over Symphony. She could feel the pendant twitch and a surge run through her similar to an electric charge. At the same time, there was a feeling of peace unlike any she had ever known. Symphony fought back the urge to pull Amburgey into an embrace. Staring deeply into her eyes, she sensed that the woman felt something similar. For a split second, she almost thought she saw understanding glimmer in the woman's beautiful green eyes.

It was a surreal feeling to come face-to-face for the first time with the woman who had given birth to you. The woman's eyes narrowed in a stare at Symphony like she was looking deep inside her for more than what was visible on the surface.

The date on the calendar, the look of the environment, the mention of polio, the face of her mother, and now hearing her mother's name confirmed—Symphony could not let her mind ignore these things any longer. She had to face the fact that she quite possibly had travelled in time and had followed her mother to 1950. After another few moments of awkward silence, Symphony could feel Gary and Nancy watching her.

"My name is Symphony."

"What a beautiful name! I don't think I have met someone called such. It's enchanting." Amburgey released her grasp and turned toward Nancy. "I'm sure this young lady does not have polio. She is strong and fit like me. She must be one of the new nurse's aides who have been sent here from Roanoke." Amburgey turned back toward her with what Symphony could only describe as a sly look on her face. "Is that correct?"

"Ah, yes." Symphony's eyes darted to Nancy and Gary to see if they believed the concocted story. "That's right. They sent me from Roanoke. I should have thought to tell you that." Symphony smiled cautiously at Gary.

"Goodness, she must just be tired from the bus ride in this heat. That daytime route stops at every little post office town between Roanoke and here." Nancy's attitude changed like magic. "You must just be exhausted and hungry. Let's get Carter to fix you up a nice plate of food. Are you here for some dinner, too, Amburgey?"

"Sure. That sounds like a great idea." Amburgey led the way to the counter, where she sat down on a stool and motioned for Symphony to sit on the one next to her. When Nancy turned her back to them to head to the kitchen, Amburgey gave Symphony a big smile and a wink.

"Where are you staying?" Nancy was quick on her feet and back with two glasses of lemonade.

"She will stay at the George Wythe Hotel as I do." Amburgey took a long drink from the glass of lemonade that Nancy had put in front of her. Symphony saw the slices of lemon in the bottom of the glass and on the rim. "We have to be as close to the clinic as possible."

"It's a good thing that someone is staying in those rooms." Symphony had not noticed the man at the end of the counter who had just spoken. "I doubt we will be seeing any tourists this summer."

"Well, Lyle, you saw the big billboards that town council had erected on the outskirts of town." Nancy filled up his coffee cup. "It would be worse for those people to come and get sick. Then they would never want to return. At least, our visitors will know that we care about their welfare."

"There are several medical personnel staying at the hotel, off and on."

Amburgey had already finished her glass of lemonade and Nancy was refilling it. It made Symphony thirsty watching her, so she picked up the glass in front of her and took a sip. Her eyes grew big.

"What a face!" Amburgey laughed as she saw Symphony's expression. Nancy and Gary were out of earshot waiting on other customers. Even so, Amburgey still whispered her question. "Don't you like lemonade?"

"I love lemonade. It's one of my favorite drinks. I'm just not used to so much real sugar in it." Symphony watched Amburgey cock her head to one side. Symphony realized that she had let something from her own time slip into the conversation. "My family prefers it on the tart side."

Amburgey nodded her head and started to speak. Gary appeared in front of them and interrupted.

"You know, you two sort of look alike."

Caught off guard by Gary's comment, Symphony knew that her facial expression told more than it should. She took another drink to try to conceal it. She could feel Amburgey's stare. Her heart raced as she allowed her mind to drift away from the conversation around her to the reality of where she was. Everything had happened so quickly, it was now starting to sink in. All those stories about the legend of Amburgey Gibboney were no doubt true. Sitting next to her was living proof; her biological mother had transcended the universe and travelled back in time. Unless this was a total hallucination, Symphony had unintentionally done the very same thing.

A tremor of emotion pulsed through her body while Symphony grasped that the woman she had spent so much time looking for was an elbow nudge away. She was not sure what was stronger inside her—the excitement of finally meeting the woman who had given her life or the utter fear of what she had done to get there.

AMBURGEY STOOD IN the doorway talking to a lady who had walked by as Symphony looked at the small hotel room. By twenty-first century standards, the rooms at the George Wythe Hotel were quite small. About a month earlier, she had taken a tour of the hotel that now occupied the same space—the Bolling Wilson. Her tour had included a description of the remodeling process that had brought the hotel structure back to life. During the tour, she learned that many of the original rooms had a bed and a half bath and were designed for the travelling businessman. Symphony smiled to herself as she thought how different the structure was in her time from what she was seeing now.

These moments of awe and amusement did not last long. Symphony tried to conceal the frightening feeling that was simmering below the surface. Her meager knowledge of fiction stories of time travel told her that revealing you were from another time could be disastrous for ever returning to your own world. It might have been fiction, but she was sure the advice was not false.

"Are you sure it is okay for me to be staying here?"

"You've come here to work at the clinic, haven't you? I mean,

Nancy and Gary said you arrived the same way I did, so that must be what you are here for, right?" Amburgey came into the room and closed the door behind her. "Listen, you seem like a nice girl, not a troublemaker. Maybe you've fallen on hard times and didn't realize you stopped in a town that was in the middle of an epidemic. Maybe you are running from a relationship that turned sour. Or maybe, just maybe, you did get here the same way I did." Amburgey looked Symphony in the eye. "It's doubtful, but not impossible. I'm certainly proof of that."

"How did you get here?" Symphony was amazed that Amburgey was being so open with her. She sat down on the bed and waited for Amburgey's response.

"I went looking for a mysterious person and found a town in the middle of their own mystery instead. I found a place where I could make a difference and it was under my nose the whole time."

Amburgey's words took Symphony by surprise. It had been a frequent imaginary thought of Symphony's to conjure the idea of what a conversation with her mother would be like. Her imagination frequently saw the two of them sitting across from each other over a cup of coffee. Symphony was her current age or thereabout and Amburgey would be twenty plus years older, middle-aged. In her wildest dreams, she never anticipated sitting across from a woman younger than herself.

Symphony had not studied time travel. Up until moving to Wytheville and talking to those who believed it was possible, she never gave the concept much thought short of the occasional fiction novel or movie scenario. Yet, something in her soul told her that what was happening at that very moment probably violated a rule or two, if time travel had such. She was in the company of her mother before the woman became her mother. If it was not just against the laws of time travel; it was against the rules of nature.

"Who were you looking for?" The safest approach seemed to be casual, friendly conversation that might reveal tidbits of what Symphony desired to know.

"The man who loves me most." Amburgey twirled around the room in a schoolgirl fashion. "It's not always who we imagine."

For the first time since she landed in 1950, Symphony allowed her mind to truly travel back to her own time. Her thoughts turned to Jason and how he had so easily entered her life.

"You're thinking about someone right now, aren't you? Is that why you are here? Are you looking for someone who loves you?"

Symphony pondered Amburgey's words and their irony. The woman who stood before her had an entirely different scenario running through her mind. Amburgey did not know that it was the love of a lost mother that Symphony had long been searching.

"What will I be able to do at this clinic you speak of? I don't have any medical training." Symphony knew that the safest route was to make the conversation detour.

"I did not have any training when I arrived. I soon learned that this is an incredible community that is going to great lengths to make something good come from a bad situation. People are scared. There is so little known about how polio is transmitted or why it is the youngest lives that are the most susceptible. You will be trained to help the patients and their families who come into the clinic seeking care. You will help answer questions and offer comfort. History will later say that an epidemic has occurred here. Whatever your reasons were for coming to this town, they will now pale in comparison. You will become part of something bigger."

Symphony sat in silence. She remembered all of the tragic stories she had just studied related to the polio epidemic in Wytheville. It had been a momentous time in the small town. Remembering how the time period now was viewed in retrospect gave her a feeling of calm. There had been tragedy, with an equal or greater triumph in how the community handled and survived such dark days. If she could do something to contribute to that outcome, however small, it might be like Amburgey said, the bigger reason for her being there.

Amburgey had sat down in a chair at a small desk in the corner. She watched the woman take an envelope out of her pocket and stare at the addressed side. After a few moments, Amburgey awoke from her trancelike state and returned it to her pocket, unopened. Without explanation or further comment, Amburgey again made eye contact with her. Symphony saw the conviction in her eyes. Symphony wondered if the strength she felt within at that moment came directly from this woman who braved the boundaries of time. It was proof that nature might, in some circumstances, win out over nurture.

"You don't seem to have any belongings. Did you bring a suitcase?"

The question caught Symphony off guard. Symphony's thoughts went to the small suitcase that contained the outfit she now wore. Was it possible that her mother had meant for her to bring it on this journey? Symphony shook her head.

"Do you have any money? The clinic will pay for your basic expenses, but it will be a while before you will receive your first payment."

Reaching into the little daisy pocket, Symphony felt that small folded bill was still there. She imagined that it too had been left for a specific reason. A script had been written for her to follow.

"Yes, I have some money. I appreciate your concern."

"Let me go over to my room and I will bring you a few clothes to tide you over until you can buy some. Then, I suggest you get some rest. My shift begins at six o'clock tomorrow morning and it will be a long day."

Amburgey left the room for a few moments. It gave Symphony time for quiet reflection. Despite the calmness she felt inside, her hands were trembling. The synapses in her brain were getting a workout with her thoughts jutting in a dozen directions. She wondered if she was missed in her own time or if time stood still during this transition. As was often the case throughout Symphony's young life, her thoughts turned to her Grammie Wallace.

"Grammie, I need your strength and guidance more than ever. I don't know if it is possible, but could you give me a sign of what I am supposed to do?"

A soft knock on the door drew her back to the immediate situation. Amburgey stood with an armful of clothes and held them out to her.

"Thank you. I appreciate your kindness. My predicament probably seems quite foolish to you."

"I've had my share of predicaments. It's funny. I was thinking about what Gary said about us looking alike." Symphony's eyes darted from side to side as she wondered what Amburgey would say next. "I think Gary could sense that we both have an adventurous spirit. Coming to a small town like this during a health scare, it's a characteristic of a modern woman."

"Modern woman?" Symphony wondered how Amburgey would get her way out of that slip up.

"Certainly. I would say that every generation of women has contained a few who thought beyond their perceived station in life. It's no secret that our sisterhood has aspired to overcome obstacles in the way, especially since we got the vote. Who knows what lies ahead in the next century?"

"Yes. Who knows? There might even be a woman president."

"You know that there was sort of a woman president a few decades ago, and she was born in this very town."

Symphony watched a smug look come over Amburgey's face, like the woman knew something no one else did.

"You mean Edith Bolling Wilson."

"Yes. I'm surprised you know that." Amburgey's expression changed to one of surprise.

"You'd be surprised at what I know." Symphony faked a yawn and took the items Amburgey brought her. "This isn't the first time I have been to Wytheville. I appreciate all of your help today."

Amburgey turned and walked over the threshold. The woman's brow was furrowed making Symphony think that she might respond to her last statement, but she did not.

"You get some rest. The front desk will call you at five in the morning. Meet me in the hallway at half past and we will go down the street and grab some breakfast before we head to the clinic."

Symphony nodded as Amburgey started to close the door. Amburgey turned back toward her for a moment.

"Maybe Gary is right." Amburgey chuckled under her breath. "Maybe we were related in another life."

Symphony closed the door. After locking it, she leaned back on the door and let out a big sigh.

"There's no maybe about it. I'm the baby you gave away." Symphony whispered to herself. "It appears that the legend of Amburgey Gibboney is true, and I'm following in your crazy footsteps. Risking my life to learn what you didn't seem to want me to know. I sure do hope this trip in time will reveal some answers to the mysteries of your life." Her voice choked with tears. "And maybe why you decided to abandon your baby girl."

Chapter Sixteen

SYMPHONY AWAKENED IN THE WEE HOURS of the following morning with her first thoughts assuming she had been in a deep dream. It was not the craziness of a dream of her childhood when her biggest fear was forgetting her locker combination. There were no monsters chasing her through the woods or incredible journeys to fantastical lands. This dream had a twinge of reality with a twist that, up until that point, was totally illogical to Symphony. 'Be careful what you wish for'—the old adage prophesied. She had wished a hundred times to meet her mother. Symphony never imagined that she would do so in a time before she was even born.

How could it be possible that she had travelled over sixty years into the past? Travelled to a time that was long before her mother's birth, decades before Symphony's own. Eyes wide open at the edge of dawn; reality quickly consumed her with moments of fear with the realization that she found herself in a nondescript small hotel room in a distant time. She had no idea what she was about to face in the polio stricken town. She had no idea if she would ever be able to return to her own time.

"I wish I had my cell phone." Symphony laughed when she heard the words leave her mouth. "It would probably disintegrate in my hand because it did not exist in this time." The thought pulled a feeling of darkness over her. "How can I survive in a time before I existed? How did Amburgey do so?"

Symphony tried to shake off the feeling as she got out of bed. Grammie Wallace would tell her to make the best of the situation. Thankfully, Amburgey had brought her some clothes and toiletries the night before. After using the toilet and brushing her teeth, she gathered the clothes and quietly opened the door to the hallway. Peeking out, she saw that the darkened hallway was empty and quiet. Amburgey showed her where the shower was located. Symphony slipped into the small room and locked the door behind her.

"This is always where young women die in horror movies." Symphony stood under the showerhead with steaming hot water pouring down on her. With the calming effects of the water, she allowed her mind to assess her situation. In the early morning hours of a summer day in 1950, Symphony was taking a shower in the bathroom of a hotel that still stood a block away from where she worked in her own time of the next century. She wished that she had spent less time questioning the possibility of her birth mother's time travel abilities and more time asking how people thought she did it.

"Travelling to this particular time must have had something to do with the outfit I was wearing at the symposium. Could it be that my mother left me those things so that I would retrace her journey one day?" Symphony shampooed her hair. "The pendant must be the key to making the journey possible. And something to do with that clock in the Rock House foyer. I hope I can find the clock in this time. I have no idea where it originally came from. I wouldn't want to have to ask Amburgey how to get home. If this was her first trip back in time, she might not know herself."

Symphony quickly finished her shower. As she toweled off and dressed, a feeling of calm came over her. Talking a situation out always helped settle her nerves. She opened the bathroom door to find Amburgey waiting outside.

"I've heard of people singing in the shower, but never someone talking in it." The expression on Amburgey's face seemed to be one of annoyance. "You better have left me some hot water."

Amburgey moved past her and slammed the door. Symphony wondered if any other hotel guests on the floor might have just gotten an unplanned wakeup call.

"I guess she's not a morning person. I must have gotten that trait from my father."

A chill passed over Symphony when the words escaped her mouth. She had not allowed herself to speculate too much regarding the identity of the male who had caused her existence. While it seemed like a long shot, the only possibility was that he might be the man in the photograph. Could he have been someone whom Amburgey met in another time? It didn't seem to be a plausible way to procreate. It was more likely her father still resided in the time she left behind.

Symphony tried to shake the idea out of her head. She needed to focus on what was going on in her current present. If she was going to get back to her own time, she needed to pay attention to the signs.

"I need coffee." The door to her room swung open without a knock. Standing in the doorway was Amburgey. The woman was perfectly dressed for the day. But, the look on her face conveyed that she was far from ready for it. "Are you coming with me?"

Without a word, Symphony stood up from her seat on the bed and reached for her purse before remembering that she did not have one. She quickly walked over to the closet and retrieved the hundred-dollar bill that was in the pocket of the outfit she arrived in.

Maybe she was in a shocked stupor from the day before. Or, perhaps, her mind was only allowing her to grasp so much at a time. A feeling of tearful excitement sped through her like an electric current. She took in a deep breath to calm herself before turning around. This was her mother.

"To be such a little thing, you sure do have an appetite."

Amburgey turned toward Symphony and rolled her eyes when the short order cook commented on the second plate of pancakes he had fixed for Amburgey that morning.

"Well, Belcher, I seem to be in a time in my life when I am able to eat all I want without gaining a pound."

Amburgey smiled at the young waitress who poured her third cup of coffee. Symphony wondered if Amburgey's eating without gaining habits really had to do with time travel. It would be a pleasant side effect to what was probably a quite dangerous adventure. She noticed that after her mother had drunk about a cup and a half of coffee, she started acting polite again.

"Is his name really Belcher?" Symphony whispered between

bites of toast. "That seems kind of funny considering what he does."

"You can't make this stuff up. I didn't believe it myself, at first. Then, he showed me his driver's license. Belcher Jones was on it, plain as day. There are a lot of interesting names in this town."

"I guess I shouldn't comment. Symphony isn't exactly Mary or Jane."

"Yeah, what was your mother thinking?" Amburgey laughed. The statement sent a chill down Symphony's spine and caused her heart to race a little. "What am I saying?" Amburgey spoke again, drawing Symphony out of her thoughts. "Mine isn't any better. I will have to talk to old Nadia about it." Amburgey was silent for a moment. "Whenever I get to see her again."

Symphony looked away from Amburgey when she mentioned Nadia. How shocked the woman would be to know that two generations of women after her were together in a time far from the life she currently knew.

"As much as this one eats, you eat that little." Another server stopped on the other side of the counter from where they were sitting to start another pot of coffee. Symphony looked at the small woman who appeared to hop from place to place. She reminded Symphony of a bird, in looks and movement.

"You really need to eat more than that." Amburgey appeared to be waking up and noticing that Symphony only ordered toast. "We will not have time to eat more than a pack of Nabs and a bottle of Coca Cola before the sun sets. You better get some nourishment in you." Symphony started to speak, but Amburgey held up her hand to stop her. "Hey, Belcher. Make my friend here an order of biscuits and gravy, two scrambled eggs, and some bacon. I'll take another order of bacon, too."

"I really don't—"

"You really don't want to pass out later and not be able to help those poor children we are going to be taking care of. Is that what you were going to say?"

Amburgey shot a hard stare in Symphony's direction, giving her a glimpse of what it might have been like to be raised by the woman. An unexpected wave of emotion passed over Symphony causing her to choke back a lump in her throat.

"I'm not much of a breakfast eater." Her voice was barely above a whisper.

"My dear, you are going to have to learn. This experience will be like none other you ever have. You need strength, for your body and your spirit."

"You are definitely right about that." Symphony shook her head and laughed to herself. She could not deny the truth of Amburgey's words. It was already unlike anything she had encountered.

"I put some cheese in your eggs. I thought you might like that." Belcher walked from the kitchen to place the plate in front of her. The man appeared to be in his mid-thirties and he had the nicest smile. It reminded her of someone.

"Jason." Symphony whispered to herself.

"What did you say, ma'am?"

"I love cheese in my eggs. Thank you, sir."

Symphony locked eyes with the man for a moment. He had Jason's eyes, his beautiful violet eyes. It was not just the color, or the man's expression. It was the kindness she saw in them.

"I sure hope you enjoy them." The man appeared shy as he gave Symphony a brief smile before bowing his head and walking away.

The encounter made Symphony wonder if you could possibly

have a connection with someone generations before either of you were born. The thought intrigued her. She quickly shook her head and returned her attention to her breakfast. After watching Belcher resume his cooking in the back, she looked down at the plate. It was a platter of food. It reminded her of breakfast at Grammie's. It was a sign that she should eat. Before she could finish her first bite, an older man sat down on the stool next to Amburgey.

"Good morning, Doctor Moore." Symphony watched as Amburgey glanced at the clock while speaking to the man. "We aren't late for our shift, are we?"

"No, young lady. I'm early. I needed some of Maxine's strong coffee and Belcher's good food before I started another day. I was at the clinic past midnight. A family of four children, all under eight years old, was brought in. I'm quite afraid that their parents waited too long to get them care. I hope we can get them stable enough to be transported to Roanoke."

"Goodness, Doctor. When is this ever going to end?" Maxine poured him a brimming cup of hot coffee and topped off Amburgey's again as she made her way to the other patrons at the counter. "Every week that passes, our town seems more and more like a ghost town. It's a wonder the trains even stop here anymore. Very few get off."

"The conductor didn't want to let me off when I got here last night." Symphony turned to see the man who spoke at the far end of the counter. He appeared to be around forty and his dark hair was slightly balding. "I came from New York City. I followed my girlfriend here. I aim to ask her to marry me." As he turned and met her gaze, he smiled. Symphony was struck by how his whole face lit up like he was laughing inside. His smile reminded her of someone, she could not remember whom. "The man told me I was crazy to get off in Wytheville. I told him that I was crazy if I didn't. My future bride is here."

The man went back to his breakfast. Symphony's thoughts stayed with him for a moment. There was something familiar about his story. Here she was in 1950. She wondered if this man married the woman he had followed to the small town. From his current age, she imagined the man was long passed. Symphony wondered if any of his family remained.

"Maxine, I don't know how to answer your question." The doctor resumed talking after listening to the man's story. "When you've been a doctor as long as I have, you see a lot of bad stuff. I've seen people stricken by influenza, measles, tuberculosis, and a dozen other things that no one ever figured out what they were. Polio has a vengeance to it. Even the ones who survive, I doubt will ever return to normal health. It just attacks the body in a manner that leaves a permanent imprint."

Maxine placed a plate of food in front of Doctor Moore. Symphony watched as the man put salt and pepper on his eggs. Then, he gazed down at them for a few moments before he spoke again. Exhaustion and sadness seemed to have overcome him.

"This disease has hit our town with a powerful force. It's going to get worse before it gets better. I hope we can rise above it." He took another drink of his coffee before he began to eat. "You girls better get on over to the clinic. I'm sure the night staff is beyond exhausted by now. I'll be along directly."

Amburgey took her last drink of coffee and stood up. Symphony finished her glass of orange juice as she saw Amburgey sign their bills and place some money on the counter for a tip.

"I've got yours." Amburgey whispered. "Thanks, Maxine. We'll see you later." Amburgey began to lead the way out the door.

Symphony stopped for a moment behind the man from New York. He turned around on the stool and stood up, wiping his mouth on a napkin before speaking to Symphony.

"May I help you, ma'am?"

"Please forgive me for bothering you while you eat your breakfast. I found your story heartwarming. May I ask your name?"

"Certainly, ma'am. My name is Herb James." He extended his hand to Symphony as he gave her a big smile.

"It's very nice to meet you, Mr. James. I'm new to this town too. My name is Symphony Wallace." Symphony took the man's hand. He had a strong, yet gentle, handshake. "May I ask the name of the woman you have followed here?"

"Her name is Inez Lanter. We met in New York. I must admit that I am quite a few years older than her. I've been a bachelor for forty years. When I met Inez, I knew immediately that she was the one for me. I guess I got too serious too fast. I think I scared her. She left New York and came home. Her family lives here. Her father runs the local lumber mill. I thought that maybe if I followed her and met her family, it might ease her mind some. In my heart, I know she feels the same. I think our age difference scares her a little. That conductor was not about to keep me on that train. I know polio is rampant here. I'm more scared of losing Inez than I am of catching any disease."

As the man's serious look again turned to a smile, it dawned on Symphony why the man's expression looked familiar. She had seen it on another face—a face in her own time. Marcella had a close friend who also worked for the town. While Symphony had only begun to get to know her, the woman had the same smile that made her face light up with a look of laughter. As Symphony was doing her research for the symposium, the woman had stopped by to see Marcella and Allison and related a snippet of her parents' story. Symphony was almost certain that the woman had said her last name had once been James. The woman must certainly be this man's daughter.

"Best wishes to you, sir. I have a feeling that you and Inez will have a wonderful life together. I wish you many years of happiness."

The man smiled once more before Symphony turned to follow Amburgey. She was indeed hopping through time, in more ways than one.

"I can't ever remember a day in my life when I felt my emotions change so often and so rapidly."

Darkness was falling as Symphony and Amburgey sat across from each other in the dining room of the town's Greyhound bus station. One of the doctors had asked them to go meet a ten o'clock bus that was coming in from Roanoke. There were needed medical supplies arriving from the hospital where most of the Wytheville polio patients were being sent for further treatment. Desperate times called for creative measures and using the bus system for a delivery service was ingenious.

"I understand what you are saying." Amburgey responded to Symphony after taking another long sip of coffee. "I don't see how those who work in medicine for a long time do it. It's a rollercoaster of emotion. How can you not feel the sadness of a young mother as she clutches her dying child? How can you avoid being affected by the fear you see in a child's eyes? Or smile as they allow play to take them into a fantasy life that is far more pleasant than their own reality? The emotional toll of this job is far harder than the physical one."

Symphony stared at the woman across from her. Over twenty-four hours had passed since she entered this other time. When she allowed her mind to think about that fact, a sick feeling came over her. It was obvious that her mother had experienced this and survived. Yet, the reality that Amburgey had basically disappeared after her birth was perhaps a sign that life after time travel was not easy, or even possible. Symphony feared that the woman in her presence in the 1950s might no longer exist in her own time. One thing was for certain, if Symphony was going to return to her own time, she needed to learn how to do it, or risk being imprisoned in a time before her existence. She needed to ask questions.

"We really haven't had much time to talk. You hinted last night regarding why you came to Wytheville. I feel like there is a whole lot more to that story though. I love stories."

Symphony watched Amburgey look up from her cup of coffee. A nervous feeling came over Symphony; her mother seemed to be peering into her soul. Amburgey took a deep breath before she began to answer.

"I came here looking for someone." It appeared that the woman was choosing her words carefully. "I thought he was living in this area now. I believe my information was wrong."

"That's a shame. Was this a friend or relative you were looking for?"

"It's complicated. It soon became less important to me as I quickly learned this community was in a crisis and needed help. At my home, I was going to school to work in medicine. I hadn't exactly decided what I wanted to do yet. I just knew that I wanted to help people. As soon as I met the staff at the clinic, I knew that

I needed to stop looking. This was the real reason I was here."

Amburgey's words took Symphony by surprise. From everything she had learned, she knew that her mother had chosen to travel in time. There was no evidence to indicate that Amburgey had stumbled into the experience as Symphony had just done. She assumed that it was to try to find the man in the old photograph. Symphony had planned to try to find her mother in the present. She could not surmise yet why she found herself in another time. Her mother's words told her that there might be another agenda to her personal journey.

"This is a precious moment in time. I can't explain how I know this, I just do." Amburgey covered her cup when the waitress passed by with a steaming pot. "It doesn't seem like it now, but how this little community deals with polio is going to shape its future. Things will get better. They always do. These people need to band together and do what is instinctively part of their nature— they need to take care of each other."

"I've not seen polio in my community." Symphony carefully chose her words. She wondered if, during this time, every community in the country was touched by polio. Her knowledge was limited in that regard. "What I saw today certainly gave me a somber vision of the destructive power of this disease."

"Likewise, I knew little about the disease before I began working at the clinic. Its existence was like a vague mention in a history book to me." Symphony noticed that Amburgey stopped herself when she heard her own words. Symphony made sure that her expression remained neutral. "I think the scariest aspect is that it begins with symptoms that are so common that they are ignored. A mother thinks that her child has a bad cold or the flu as he or she has a sore throat, a fever, a little nausea, or a slight headache. By the time a few days pass and the symptoms continue, the virus has set up residence within the poor child. Sometimes, that is all that occurs and there are no more symptoms, but the virus may still be dormant within the child." Amburgey paused a moment before continuing. "It's not just children either. While their immune systems seem to be the most susceptible to polio, I've seen a couple of adults who have also contracted the disease."

"I suppose there would be the risk that it could cause problems again."

"I believe that those who have been spared the worst parts now may suffer consequences later."

Symphony allowed her mind to wander back to the symposium. The coincidence of her stepping into the time when the foundation for post-polio syndrome began was mindboggling. She could hear Grammie's words in her ears. 'There are no coincidences, my dear. One thing always leads to another.'

"Tell me more about what is happening to these children we are seeing. I want to understand."

"For those whom the virus continues to attack, the symptoms can range in severity from the feeling of pins and needles in the legs to Meningitis to paralysis in the arms, legs, or both. For some, it leads to death because the virus affects the muscles that help a person breathe."

Symphony thought about the iron lung machine that was on display in the polio exhibit at the Boyd Museum. A local man, Lee Hale, who contracted polio in his early thirties, had used the machine on display for over thirty years. At his death in 1976, he held the *Guinness Book of World Records* distinction for living the longest within an iron lung. Her research for the symposium revealed that since Mr. Hale's death, others across the country had gone on to live in iron lungs for fifty and even sixty years. It was beyond her imagination.

"Some of these children will end up in iron lungs, won't they?"

"Yes, I'm sure they will. Children have died and, sadly, more will. This community will help each other out though. The tragedy of this summer will not destroy this town."

"You sound like you are looking into a crystal ball."

Symphony knew it was a statement to make. Yet, she also knew that the sooner she started finding out about how her mother got to 1950 and safely returned, the sooner she could get back to her own century.

"You know, to be a seemingly demure girl, you have a bold side to you." Amburgey's expression was stern for a few moments before a smirk crossed her face. "I like that. Reminds me of myself."

"We are more alike than you know."

Chapter Seventeen

"IT'S MORE ATTRACTIVE WHEN PEOPLE are mingling in the streets."

Symphony turned from gazing out the window to find Gary standing beside her. Despite the fact she had seen him a couple of times since her arrival in 1950, it still made her laugh to see a teenage Garon.

"Wytheville is still a pretty town." Symphony meant her words in both times. "It does look strange to not see a child walking down the sidewalk on such a beautiful summer day."

"It's like we are a ghost town. I've been worried that some of the restaurants and hotels will have to close. All our tourists are staying away. No one can blame them. Wytheville Town Council even put up a billboard on the outskirts of town warning them. I sure hope someone can get this polio stuff under control soon. It's like we are a town without children." Gary paused and shook his head as he looked out the big plate glass window next to the table where Symphony was sitting. "Would you like something else to eat? Geraldine just made a big batch of fresh peach ice cream. It's mighty good."

"That sounds delicious. I would love to have a small bowl. I hope I haven't been sitting here too long."

"Do you see anyone waiting for your seat?"

As Gary walked away to place her order, Symphony looked around. Owens & Owens was part drug store, part restaurant. There were only two tables like the one where she was sitting. The store was fairly busy when she arrived an hour earlier. Several patrons came to have prescriptions filled. The location also seemed to be a gathering place for people to socialize and chat. While eating her lunch, she heard several hushed conversations about whose children were the latest to contract the disease with speculation about how it came to the town in the first place.

"Hope you enjoy it. Geraldine's ice cream is the best." Gary placed the not-so-small bowl in front of Symphony.

"Thank you. Gary, I've heard a couple of people talking about some families leaving town because of polio. Is that true?"

"Yes. I know of several families who have gone to other places nearby like Claytor Lake or who are visiting friends or relatives in other states. Not everyone can afford to do that. But, many who could, left for the summer, hoping for a better situation when it's time for school to start." Gary looked around before sitting down in the chair opposite Symphony. "There have been all sorts of people here from the state health department. No one seems to know why it has spread so quickly here. People from the March of Dimes have come, too. The town council and the board of supervisors don't know what to do. It's an unfixable problem."

"I'm sure it will work out eventually. It can't go on forever."

"I guess not. I just don't know how many people are going to die before it's over. Children aren't the only ones who are susceptible. Don't be surprised if you get a few scared looks once people know that you are working in the clinic. Doc Chitwood has assured us that neither the doctors nor the nurses are carrying any germs out of the clinic. But, if you don't know how it's spreading, how can you say that for sure?"

Listening to Gary's words, the thought passed through Symphony's mind that she was glad she had received the polio vaccine. She could not help but wonder if it would protect her in this time.

"You've been on a long break." Gary stood back up and straightened a nearby shelf.

"Another girl needed to leave to return to her home in North Carolina. Someone in her family passed away suddenly. She is catching the next bus south. I'm going to fill in for part of her shift this evening, so they told me to take a couple of hours off this afternoon. It's no fun sitting in a small hotel room. I walked around town for the first hour or so, but, like you said, there's hardly anyone on the streets."

"I wish you could have seen the town before all this started. It was alive with activity, day and night. People would be lined up all the way down the street to see the latest picture show at the Millwald." Gary looked over his shoulder before he whispered. "That's what I want to do one day. I want to be an actor on the silver screen. Mr. Fitzgerald, my dance teacher, says I have a flair for the movie musical. My feet tell a story. He's been giving me a few acting lessons, too. I know it is a pipe dream. I probably won't ever leave this little town. Still, there's a fire in my gut to spread my wings and try the impossible. I'd like to dance in the movies like Mr. Fred Astaire."

Symphony watched Gary twirl in classic movie musical form. In this young man's face, she saw the great actor he would become— the showman and heartthrob who would captivate her Grammie and a million other women.

"Don't give up on your dreams, Gary. I have a feeling that you can make them come true. Maybe you will have a long and successful career in Hollywood, and then retire back here, back to your hometown."

"It would be nice to think that I could have such a life. I'm not sure that you could get me back to little ole Wytheville if I lived under the lights of Hollywood." Gary looked at his watch. "Gosh, I am about to be late for my class. Mr. Fitzgerald will make me run a couple of miles if I am late."

"Run? In dance class?"

"He says that dancers are athletes and have to be in top shape. I run five miles every morning. I don't want to have to run again this evening."

Gary quickly took off his apron and soda jerk hat and ran behind the counter, almost knocking Geraldine down.

"Where you going to in such a rush, Gary?" The older woman had a deep Southern accent.

"I've got to skedaddle. I'm going to be late." Symphony noticed that Gary's feet barely seemed to be reaching the floor as he ran toward the doorway. "Bye, Miss Symphony. It was sure nice talking with you."

He flashed his Hollywood smile with a wink of his eye, and Symphony felt her heart skip a beat like it did when she was a child watching his movies with her grandmother. There was something about Garon Fitzgerald. Now, she knew that it started with the dreams of a teenage Gary Moore.

No sooner had that thought danced in her mind than Symphony heard the jingle of the bell on the door and saw Amburgey walking toward her table.

"My tired is tired." Amburgey plopped down in the chair opposite Symphony's and caught Geraldine's attention. "Geraldine, I would like a cheeseburger with everything, a large order of French fries, and the largest Dr Pepper you can pour me."

"How did you know that I was in here?" Symphony thought it strange that Amburgey just appeared.

"I was heading in here anyway to get something to eat and Gary about knocked me down on the sidewalk. He said you were sitting at the front table. I assumed you wouldn't mind if I joined you." Amburgey gave her a wide-eyed look that quickly changed to a wink. "Were you expecting someone else?"

"No. Of course, not. I wasn't expecting to see you before I went back to work. Why would you think I was meeting someone?"

"I saw the way that Belcher was looking at you the other morning, and when I was sitting on the hotel porch last night, he came by and started asking me questions about you. I thought maybe he worked up the nerve to ask you out."

"Ridiculous. I came here to—" Symphony suddenly looked down. She had allowed her haste in speaking to back her into a corner.

"You came here to what?" Amburgey's expression was like an animal ready to catch its prey.

"I came here to work, of course. Not to start some romance with a local boy. I have a boyfriend at home, I'll have you know."

"Really? What's his name?"

"Jason."

"Does Jason have a last name?"

"Jason Newberry. Since we are sharing information, how about telling me more about the person you came here to find?" Symphony could not believe that this slipup had opened an opportunity for her to find out more information about Amburgey's intention. "Quid pro quo, my friend."

"It's a long and complicated story."

"I have another half hour or so before I need to be back at the clinic. I might as well keep you company." Symphony gave Amburgey a toothy grin. "Besides, a story isn't really a story unless it is complicated."

Amburgey rolled her eyes and shook her head as Geraldine placed a large glass of soda in front of Amburgey. Her mother took a long drink. She seemed to be studying Symphony.

"What have I got to lose? There's no way you can figure out the biggest complication. Unless you—" Amburgey stopped and narrowed her eyes. "No, it's just not possible. I would be able to tell."

"You are talking in circles." Symphony knew that she needed to play dumb. If Amburgey suspected her mode of transportation to the 1950s, she might clam up or, worse yet, disappear.

"Never mind. I sure hope my food gets here soon. I am starving."

"You are also avoiding my question."

"Okay. You've cornered me. I'm a helpless victim of starvation, so I guess I will talk." Amburgey paused to look around, even though there was no one near them. "I came to Wytheville looking for my father."

"Your father?" Symphony could not conceal the shock in her voice as it went up another octave. She bit her bottom lip thinking about what she had done. She searched her mind for an excuse. She could already see a puzzled look beginning to form on Amburgey's face. "I did not expect you to say that. I thought this might be a complicated love story."

"I love my father and I want to find him." The server returned with Amburgey's plate of food. "I don't believe what I have been told happened to him."

Symphony tried to remember what she knew about Amburgey's father. She remembered that he died when Amburgey was young. Fortunately, the woman across from her was paying more attention to the cheeseburger she was rapidly consuming than the look crossing Symphony's face. She had to choose her words carefully.

"What happened to him? Did he die?"

"Do you think I would be looking for him if he died?" Amburgey's words were muffled by the food she was chewing. Amburgey swallowed and took a drink. "Well, I guess I should rephrase that. I wouldn't be looking for him if I believed that he was dead."

"This is a complicated story. I'm listening."

"I was told that my father died in a plane crash while on a business trip."

"You don't believe that?"

"No. My mother said that the authorities told her that his body was not found."

"Well, I'm sure that is often the case with plane crashes."

"I never saw any news stories about the plane crash. I don't think he was even on a plane."

"Why not?"

"Because he called me and told me that he was taking a trip to the past."

"What?" Symphony's eyes grew big.

"I really have said too much." Amburgey pretended to wipe her mouth.

"You've just gotten started. You can't stop now. I'm a good listener."

"You will think I am crazy if I tell you the real reason I am here."

"You said you were looking for your father."

"Yes, but there is a reason that I am looking in Wytheville at this particular time."

"This particular time? I'm afraid you have lost me."

Amburgey did not respond. Instead she stared straight into Symphony's eyes. There was something about Amburgey's staring that could make a person feel something physical from the encounter. It was like there was something magnetized that came out of her eyes and forced you to keep looking at her. Seconds seemed much longer. It made Symphony wonder if the woman had not only conquered time, but had a way of piercing into another person's consciousness to read his or her very soul.

"You think I'm trying to read your mind, don't you?"

Symphony could not conceal the gasp that escaped from her mouth. She knew it was futile to try and deny it. Amburgey would know the truth.

"Yes. That's exactly what I was thinking."

Amburgey let out a deep sigh and dropped her gaze. Symphony immediately felt different. Like she had been released from someone's grip.

"I read once that your ancestors could read your soul because part of you had once been them. If you pay attention, you can see it happen in families, especially between mothers and children. I think it is one of the senses that we don't know about and haven't evolved into use. I'd love to be able to try it out with an ancestor that was several generations back. Only problem is making the trip to meet them."

Amburgey regained eye contact with Symphony. A sly smile crossed her face. It was a sign—an opening to broach the subject. Symphony must take the bait.

"Time travel. You'd have to take a trip via time travel in order to test that hypothesis."

In an effort to make it seem like a normal conversation subject and hide the fact that her blood pressure was probably rising faster than her mind was racing, Symphony nonchalantly took a bite of the peach ice cream melting in front of her. Conversely, Amburgey almost choked on the bite of cheeseburger she was chewing.

"Are you okay? Have a drink of your soda."

Symphony picked up Amburgey's glass and handed it to her. Her mother's eyes were bulging. It was not clear if she was really choking or just shocked at Symphony's statement.

"What did you say?"

"I thought you were choking, I was just offering—"

"No. Before that." Amburgey stopped coughing. "How did you say I would have to travel?"

"Time travel, of course. It's not exactly a new concept. Albert Einstein was theorizing about it back in the beginning of the twentieth century."

"That's this century."

Symphony tried to conceal the fact she had to stop and ponder what Amburgey said.

"Yes, this century. Einstein first voiced his theories around fifty years ago, I believe."

"You seem to know a lot about the subject." Amburgey's eyes narrowed. No amount of ice cream consumption was going to cool off their piercing stare. "Do you believe it is possible to travel back in time?"

Symphony had a feeling that she had reached a turning point. The way she answered Amburgey's question would seriously affect the rest of her journey. She could keep her mouth shut and see how things played out, or she could knock over the first domino and see if the domino effect would culminate in the results she needed. Symphony was sure it would all come down to trust. She had to trust that the woman sitting across from her set the process in motion by the very fact that she left Symphony the pendant, a ticket for the trip she was on.

"Yes, I do."

"What makes you believe in it? It's not exactly the type of subject that is discussed at most dinner tables." Amburgey put down her food. Her intense look changed to one of wonder. "What do you know that makes you believe time travel is possible?"

"Because my mother was a time traveler." The words were out of Symphony's mouth before she could stop them. She looked around the room. No one was nearby. "I probably should have whispered that comment."

Amburgey's reaction surprised Symphony. Instead of being shocked, Amburgey looked angry.

"You better get back to the clinic."

Symphony looked at the clock behind the counter. She had about fifteen minutes before they were expecting her back.

"I have a few more minutes."

"I think you better get back there now. I'm sure there are things for you to do." Amburgey looked down at her plate and resumed eating.

"Have I said something to offend you?" Symphony took out a few bills and laid them on the table with her meal check. "I'm sorry if I said something wrong."

"No. You didn't say anything wrong. This conversation is just over. I'm ready to relax and finish my meal. You need to get back to work."

"Okay. You enjoy your food." Symphony rose from the table and scooted her chair back into its place. "I guess I will see you tomorrow."

"Yeah. Tomorrow. Hope tonight isn't too busy." Amburgey did not look up when Symphony walked away.

Symphony heard the jingle of the bell on the door as she opened it to leave. A sad and frightening feeling overcame her. She glanced back at the profile of Amburgey. The woman had stopped eating and held her head down. It almost looked like she was crying. Symphony saw Geraldine approach Amburgey, and she quickly looked up at the woman.

"What was I thinking?" Symphony let out a big sigh. She began to walk up the street toward the clinic. "I'm a stranger to her. She's a stranger to me." The sidewalk around her was empty. "All we share is DNA and that hasn't even occurred yet in this time. I wish this was a long dream that I am going to wake up from and be back in the time where I belong."

"Where do you belong, ma'am?"

Symphony stopped in the middle of the sidewalk and looked at a car that was parked on the street. A young boy with a crewcut was leaning against it watching her. There was something familiar about him. Her immediate thought was that she might have seen him at the clinic.

"I'm sorry. Do I know you?"

"Of course you do. Everybody knows me." The boy gave her a big grin. His expression and age reminded her of Opie Taylor. "I'm Tommy."

"Hello, Tommy. You scared me. I didn't think anyone was around."

"You sure were having a serious conversation. Too bad there was no one to have it with you."

Tommy's observation made her smile. He walked with her a few feet before he spoke again.

"Where are you going?"

"I am going to the clinic. I work there."

"That's where the sick kids are. My mother is scared about that. She probably wouldn't want me talking with you." Tommy's eyes were big as he looked at Symphony.

"I know people are afraid. Polio is a serious disease."

"I think it is going to be okay. Someone will figure it out."

Symphony paused to cross the street. She looked down at the child who had spoken so wisely.

"I think you are right, Tommy. I've got to cross the street now and go to work. Thanks for walking with me. I hope I get to see you again."

"Okay. See you later." Tommy began to walk on up the street as Symphony prepared to cross.

"Hey, Tommy. What's your last name?"

"Boyd, ma'am. My name is Thomas J. Boyd."

"I JUST DON'T understand how this happened. Calvin has always been the healthiest of my children."

Symphony could hardly believe that two weeks had passed since she first arrived in the summer of 1950. It amazed her how quickly she became accustomed to the work she was assigned to do at the clinic. She would help gather information from the family of the patient while they waited to be examined by the doctor. It reminded her of recording oral histories. It was an accurate correlation as a pivotal part of Wytheville's history was unfolding before her eyes.

"You said children, Mrs. Williams. How many do you have?"

"Four. Calvin is the next to the youngest. He is seven. I have a son that is twelve, a daughter who is ten. Our youngest is three. I've sent all three of them to stay with my husband's family in Fancy Gap. I hope it was the right thing to do."

"I'm sure it is very hard to make such a decision. Hopefully, they are all well and enjoying themselves and you can focus on Calvin."

"Yes. That's what I thought. I had to try to protect them. I have to save my Calvin." Mrs. Williams brought a handkerchief up to her eyes. She tried to look around Symphony into the examining room. "I would really like to be back there with Calvin. I'm sure he is afraid."

"The doctor and nurses will be very gentle with him, Mrs. Williams. It will be helpful for them to know about all of his symptoms on the days and weeks leading up to you bringing him in today. Let's get all that information down. Then, I'm sure the doctor will want to talk to you. Is your husband with you?"

"No, he is the evening supervisor at the quarry. He started to call off work and come. I stopped him. We don't know what Calvin's treatment will cost. We may need every day of pay and then some."

Symphony watched the mother twirl the same handkerchief around her fingers in worry. Despite her swollen eyes, Symphony could see the bone structure and facial features of a woman whose beauty probably turned many heads. Dark brown hair had a hint of red that would be likened to highlights in Symphony's modern world. What struck Symphony most about Mrs. Williams' appearance was her thinness. The woman did not appear poor or malnourished. It was a thinness that her mother, Mariel—the real nurse, called 'tired thin.' Mrs. Williams worked hard each day, probably expending more energy than she took time to take in.

"Tell me about what Calvin has been like over the last few weeks. When did you first notice something wrong?"

"About two weeks ago, right as school was ending for the year, Calvin started having the symptoms of a cold. I thought it was just from playing in the rain and staying out too late into the evening. That boy loves to get into water. Everywhere except a bathtub."

Mrs. Williams laughed and Symphony caught a glimpse of the younger beauty. Symphony carefully wrote down the key details of what the woman was saying. Down the hall, she heard a child yell in pain from another examining room. It was not Calvin, but the sound of the outcry only deepened the expression of fear on Mrs. Williams' face.

"Go on. What happened next?"

"The cold became worse. He began to run a fever with congestion. Then, he began to complain that his joints were hurting. A few days later, his fever rose even more. That's when I sent the other children away. That was yesterday." Mrs. Williams stopped and looked off into space like she was trying to remember something. "Yes, that was the day that Howard took the kids to his sister's house. Yesterday. After they left, I got Calvin up and walked him around the house a little. He'd been stuck in for about nine days at that point. It was a beautiful sunny day. I thought the air and sunshine might do him some good. Lift his spirits, if nothing else. He seemed so happy, but tired very quickly."

Mrs. Williams stopped talking and looked down at the handkerchief. Symphony followed her gaze. The handkerchief was now torn and one of her fingers was bleeding.

"You're bleeding. Let me get you a bandage."

"No, it's fine. I'm just nervous. Terrified is a better word." Mrs. Williams took a deep breath before she continued. "The kids have a dog. He's a big old Golden Retriever named Copper. He put his paws on Calvin's lap. Calvin let out a horrible scream. Sort of like the one we just heard. Copper immediately jumped down. I had no idea that Calvin was in such pain. I gave him more aspirin and put him to bed. Early this morning, my husband got Calvin up so that I could change his bed. Calvin's legs collapsed under him and he started having trouble breathing. We brought him here immediately." Mrs. Williams' voice cracked. "I hope we aren't too late. Please help my little boy."

Before Symphony could respond, a nurse came out and took Mrs. Williams back to the examination room. Mother and child were taken back into the depths of the clinic and Symphony did not see them again.

"HI, SYMPHONY. HOW are you doing this evening?"

The voice jarred Symphony out of the stupor of her own thoughts. It had been an extra hard day at the clinic as seven children and two adults were admitted to the hospital. With the others already there, the ward was at capacity. She was sure that the children would haunt her dreams for years to come. She longed to have the ability to return to her own time and bring back a stockpile of vaccines. Unfortunately, she doubted that it would help those who were already infected. She was too tired to be surprised by the person standing before her.

"Hello, Belcher. I'm trying to relax a little. It was a hard day at the clinic." Sitting in a rocking chair on the front porch of the hotel, Symphony found solitude in the cool of the evening. "How are you?"

"I just got off work. I had to work a double today because the evening shift cook quit." Belcher let out a big sigh and ran his fingers through his hair. The gesture caused Symphony to think of Jason. She was really beginning to miss him. "I guess I have quite a few long days ahead."

"Sit down and talk to me for a minute."

Symphony knew she did not need to be encouraging any feelings that Belcher might be developing. She did, however, want to get to know him a little better. She had a strong feeling that he had a genetic connection to Jason. She wanted to see what she could find out.

"Maybe, just for a minute. I don't want to bother you."

Sitting down in the rocking chair next to her, Symphony noticed that Belcher looked like he had on clean clothes. Slightly leaning over, she thought she detected the smell of soap and aftershave. His wet hair seemed to confirm her suspicions. After working a double shift, he had showered before he walked up the street. She might have to use that piece of information to her advantage.

"Did you grow up here, Belcher?"

"Yes. I've lived here all my life. My father is from North Carolina. My mother grew up in Bland County. That's just a little north of here, toward West Virginia."

"I'm sorry; I'm not recalling your last name."

"It's Jones." Belcher laughed under his breath. "I guess that is a common name everywhere. My mother was a Newberry, not quite as many of them."

"Newberry. I know a man named Newberry where I am from."

"Oh, yeah. What's his first name?"

"Jason."

"Well, that's a coincidence. My Grandpa is named Jason."

"Small world." Symphony rolled her eyes. She would have to ask about the family tree. "Does your mother have any brothers?"

"Yes. Four. She's the only girl. Poor woman only had boys herself, too."

"What are her brothers' names?" Symphony saw Belcher furrow his brow in confusion. "I like to hear about different names. I'm making a list to name my children one day." She could not believe how lame her answer was.

"That's a good idea. You don't want to wait until the last minute." Belcher gave her a big smile. "Her two older brothers are Lewis and Albert. The younger ones are Johnny and Fred. Uncle Fred works right next door at the Esso station."

Belcher pointed to the gas station that was next door to the hotel. The name 'Esso' reminded her of the uniform shirt that was on display at the museum that was next to the visitor center. Symphony made a mental note of the names. She would have to ask Jason about his family tree when she returned home.

When she returned home—it seemed like such a simple statement. Only a few months into her residence in the town, Wytheville already seemed like home to her. She longed to go back there, only that was the problem, she was already there. Time was not on her side. Symphony looked at Belcher. He was staring at her. She was afraid that if she did not get out of 1950 soon, she might become Jason's mother, or probably his aunt. Neither seemed like a desirable idea to her.

"Belcher, are there any unusual clocks around here? You know, old-looking grandfather clocks?"

For the second time in less than ten minutes, Symphony had seen lines cross Belcher's forehead in confusion. She might not have to worry much longer about his intentions if she scared him away with crazy questions.

"Clocks? Grandfather clocks? There's a really big clock in the courthouse. I think some of the pretty houses on Withers Road have some nice old clocks. I'll have to think about that." Symphony noticed that Belcher was looking at his watch. "It's getting late. I better get on home and get some rest." Belcher smiled and nodded when he rose from his chair and began to walk toward the steps. "Thanks for talking to me. It was really interesting."

"Good night, Belcher."

Symphony watched the man walk briskly down the hotel steps and turn onto the street. Just before he was out of sight, Belcher turned and looked back at her, waving briefly before walking on into the night.

"He has got to be Jason's uncle." Symphony shook her head. "I wonder if he is still living. It would be an awkward thing to meet him in my own time. I might not have to worry about that if I don't find that clock. Where in the world could it be? Surely, it is not in the Rock House."

Not long after arriving in 1950, Symphony walked by the structure. It was still a residence, but she had not been able to determine if someone actually lived in it. Her gut feeling was that the clock was donated to the museum collection. She was not sure though. So deep into that thought, Symphony failed to realize that someone had joined her on the porch. In the darkness, she jumped and let out a soft scream when she turned and saw Amburgey standing a couple of feet away from her.

"What are you doing sitting out here in the dark?" Symphony quickly shook off the feeling of fright and focused on Amburgey. "You look upset."

As Amburgey walked closer and sat down in the chair Belcher had vacated, Symphony saw that Amburgey appeared to be crying.

"Did you find out something about the man you have been looking for?"

Amburgey gave Symphony a long stern look. Symphony searched her mind for what to say to bridge the gap between them—something that might cause Amburgey to start to trust her. The irony of the biological bond they actually shared might kick in if there was something to prompt it.

"We all have our secrets, you know." Symphony spoke hesitantly. "Sometimes we travel a long way to find answers to the deepest questions in our heart. We don't always like the answers."

Symphony knew that the look she saw crossing her mother's face would haunt her for the rest of her life. Whether she ever found Amburgey Gibboney in their own time or not, Symphony had made a connection—their souls met.

"You said that your mother was a time traveler. At the time, I thought you were mocking me. Now, I am beginning to wonder if you were serious." Amburgey reached for her heart. For a split second, the action scared Symphony. "I need to talk to someone about this. I need to talk to someone who I can trust to believe me and keep my secret. My heart says that you are that person. I feel a connection to you that my mind cannot explain."

"We are connected." Three simple words were all that Symphony needed to say. There was magic in the words.

"I don't really belong in this time." Amburgey began her story under a starry night sky. "When I was a little girl, my father would tell me stories about great adventures he had through time. In my youngest years, I thought they were tales from a storybook. Years passed and the stories continued. I began to wonder if there might be some truth in his bedtime stories. He told them with such conviction and detail, and most of them had something to do with this little small town in which we now sit."

Amburgey dropped her gaze from Symphony and looked out into the darkness of the street in front of them. Symphony held her breath, fearing that the woman might stop without telling the rest of the story. She dared not even whisper for fear she would break the spell they were under.

"When I learned to write, I started recording a few of the details in a primitive way with crazy spellings for those grown up words I didn't quite understand yet. It proved to be beneficial later. My father used to travel on business trips. He would be away for weeks at a time. Mother would be cross while he was gone. All would be wonderful again when he breezed through the door carrying packages for 'his girls.' Mother never wanted to hear his stories. It was all I wanted. I prized the stories more than any toy or trinket he brought me. Truthfully, it was the time with him that meant the most."

Amburgey grew silent when a man in a suit and hat got out of a cab in front of the hotel. The cab driver jumped out and retrieved a suitcase from the trunk and followed the man up the steps.

"Good evening, ladies."

The man stopped briefly and tipped his hat. The cabbie looked in their direction but offered no greeting. A few minutes later, the door swung open again and the driver skipped down the steps and was back in his cab in a flash. Amburgey watched him drive away before she resumed speaking.

"He told me that he travelled in time. His stories were from decades before, even hundreds of years. He said that my present time was not his present and that might cause a problem one day. It might separate us. I must be prepared." Amburgey looked back at Symphony. "You are going to break the arm of that chair if you don't loosen your grip. Go ahead and ask whatever question is bulging behind your eyes.

Symphony looked down at her left hand. Even in the darkness, she could see that her knuckles were white from her tight grip. There was a question on her lips.

"Why had he not gone back to his own time and stayed?"

"He met a beauty queen and married her."

Symphony stopped herself from nodding her head. She knew the story of Nadia and her road to Miss America. She almost forgot that Amburgey did not know her connection to the woman.

"A beauty queen?"

"My mother." Amburgey shook her head and laughed. "It

sounds like something out of a movie. Daddy was in the audience of the Miss America pageant. Mother sashayed across the stage and Daddy fell in love. Along came me and the rest is history."

Amburgey grew quiet. Symphony did not interrupt her mother's deep thought until a truck horn broke the silence.

"And then, what happened?"

Symphony heard Amburgey take a deep breath. A sniffle followed. Amburgey leaned up in the chair and rested her elbows on her knees in a classic child position that caused Symphony to wonder if she was travelling on another journey through time in her memory.

"And then, he didn't come home from a trip. Mother said he had died in an accident—a plane crash so bad that no one was recovered. One of Mother's sisters came and Mother took to her bed. She stayed there for several weeks. I went back to school. I wasn't allowed to take to my bed. It's not where I wanted to be anyway. I wanted to go look for Daddy. I knew I could find him."

"Is that what you are doing now? Looking for your father?"

Symphony's question snapped Amburgey out of her trancelike state. Amburgey's head spun around to face Symphony so fast that it reminded Symphony of a horror movie she had once seen. Her wide-eyed expression began to soften when their eyes met.

"Yes. I came to 1950 to look for him. He used to tell me stories about how bad polio was in Wytheville one summer. As I got older, I researched and figured out when it was. He told the stories with such detail, it sounded like a first person account to me. I imagined that he had lived here then."

"That doesn't explain why you were so upset."

"You are relentless, aren't you?" A brief smirk crossed Amburgey's face before she continued. "On the rare times that we haven't been busy at the clinic, I've been trying to go through the records to see if I can find any evidence of my father. I've already tried snooping around and can't seem to find anyone who knew him. Tonight, I found a file with his name in it. The record showed that Tyler Gibboney died of polio. I guess he came back here and died. It's heartbreaking. It only happened two months ago. Right before I arrived."

Tears returned to Amburgey's face. Symphony was at a loss for words. She had accepted the story that Millie had told her about the passing of Nadia's husband. The tragedy of a plane crash somehow seemed easier than the tragedy of dying from polio in another time. Something about it seemed off though. Symphony's gut wanted more information.

"What kind of details did the file have?" Amburgey wiped her eyes while Symphony questioned her. "Did it give any information about his age?"

"I'm sure it probably did." Amburgey furrowed her brow and opened her mouth like she was going to speak. "When I saw the name and the word 'deceased,' I just stopped looking. I was overcome."

"Maybe you should look at the file again. It might have not been him."

"Tyler Gibboney is not exactly a common name."

"True, in most areas. If he had a family connection to here though, it might be more common than you think. Parents sometimes like to name children after other family members."

"Okay. You're right. I hadn't thought of that. I let my emotions get the best of me without having all the data."

Symphony wondered if 'data' as Amburgey was using the word would have been referred to in the same way as now. She thought that computers probably existed in a primitive form in 1950. She doubted that reference to a term associated with them would have been in day-to-day language.

"It's getting late. Maybe we should go upstairs." Symphony rose from her chair and stood next to Amburgey.

"It was hard to see. But, I thought I saw someone sitting with you while I was walking up the street." Amburgey rose and began walking toward the door.

"Belcher stopped by and sat a while."

"Uh huh, Belcher. I told you. He is sweet on you."

Symphony rolled her eyes. There were a few things that Amburgey had down pat for the time period.

"You are probably right. He is a nice man. I didn't come here to find romance though."

They were silent for a few minutes as they walked up the steps to their floor.

"You say you came here to work. Yet, you don't seem to know much about the medical field or even secretarial duties. I've poured my secrets out to you. What is the real reason you are in Wytheville during a polio epidemic? It's not the best time in history to be visiting."

"I came here looking for my mother."

Amburgey tilted her head and narrowed her eyes, deep in thought.

"You said your mother was a time traveler."

"Yes."

Symphony tried to conceal the nervousness that was consuming her entire body. She was treading on dangerous ground.

"Did your mother travel to this time period?"

"Yes."

"How can you be so sure? I thought my father was here, too. Or maybe he was just a child during this time."

"If that is true, then he can't be the 'Tyler Gibboney' who died." Symphony slyly tried to change the subject.

"Why do you say that?"

"Because how could he be your father if he died as a child?"

"Oh, that's an awesome point." Amburgey pulled Symphony into an embrace. "Thank you so much. The first thing I am going to do tomorrow when we get to work is look at that file. I'm buying you breakfast. Meet me downstairs. Maybe we will get Belcher to cook it for you." Amburgey winked and opened the door to her room. "Good night."

"Good night."

Symphony quickly closed the door behind her. Tears were already falling down her cheeks.

"She hugged me. My mother—my first mother hugged me. I've got to find her in our time. She has to still be alive."

Chapter Eighteen

"I OVERSLEPT!" AMBURGEY BURST OUT OF her door and practically knocked Symphony down while she was rushing to put on her shoes and walk.

"So did I!"

They both looked at each other and laughed.

"We stayed up too late talking." Symphony pulled her hair back in a ponytail.

The clack-clack of their heels on the stairs made the kind of sound Symphony had only previously heard in movies.

"I dreamed that I was walking through a clock." Amburgey was almost out the door before she turned back and saw that Symphony had stopped on the bottom stair. "Hey, keep moving. We have got to get to the clinic." Amburgey rushed back and grabbed hold of Symphony's arm.

"What did you say?"

"I said we have to get to work. You must still be asleep." Amburgey turned again and began to walk away. "I don't hear your heels."

"What did you say about your dream?"

"I will be glad to tell you about all my crazy dreams if you will move your feet."

Amburgey was standing inside the doorway holding the tall hotel door open. Symphony relented and walked from the stairs through the foyer to the front door. Amburgey was on her heels, and then running down the steps before Symphony reached them.

"Why are you in such a rush? We still have fifteen minutes before we have to be at the clinic."

"I have one word for you—COFFEE!"

"Oh, silly me. I forgot about the humanizing effect it has on you." Symphony shook her head and hurriedly followed Amburgey down the sidewalk to Owens & Owens. "By all means, let us get you some of the magic elixir. Too bad there's not a Starbu—" Symphony stopped herself before she finished the last syllable. Amburgey stopped walking in front of her and slowly turned around.

"What did you say?"

Symphony's mind raced, searching for some word she could say that would make sense.

"Star what?" Amburgey's eyes were now thin slats piercing a gaze at Symphony that she could almost feel.

"Starbu Coffee. It's a popular brand back home. You've probably never heard of it."

"I think you are making that up." Amburgey turned around and began walking again. "I don't have time to question you further.

This conversation is between me and my first cup." Amburgey pushed opened the front door to Owens & Owens. Amburgey stopped suddenly and Symphony ran into her back. "Don't think this is over though, young lady. We will continue this conversation later. Starbu Coffee. You are lucky we are late and I'm desperate."

Symphony breathed a sigh of relief as Amburgey walked ahead toward the counter, yelling.

"Nancy! I need a large cup of coffee and an even larger one to go. Any doughnuts available? Miss Smarty Pants here probably needs something, too."

Symphony did not feel too smart at that moment. She wondered how she would explain who she was, if Amburgey figured out she was a time traveler. Would her mother's brain explode if it had to process the truth of her identity?

LIKE MANY OTHER aspects of the town that season, Wytheville was unseasonably warm in the summer of 1950. Barely ten o'clock in the morning, Symphony walked down the tall staircase from the upstairs Main Street location of the medical clinic and into what was already a hot day. The air hissed with heat. Her meteorologist father would have called it a 'fry an egg on the sidewalk' day. All Symphony knew was that if people came to the small town to 'summer' because it was cooler, she would hate to have to live through one of the summers where those folks came from.

Despite how long she had spent in this alternate time, Symphony still smiled when she saw the ladies of the town in the 1950s era fashions. As she walked toward the post office to get the clinic's mail, Symphony spied three women chatting on the sidewalk in dresses that harkened of *I Love Lucy*, with polka dots and all. Two of them wore cat eye framed eyeglasses and all were clutching almost identical patent leather purses—one was royal blue, another was white, and the third was a peachy orange color. Symphony was dying to have one of her own, but was not sure if it would survive the trip back to the twenty-first century.

"Miss." One of the women approached her. "You work at the clinic, don't you?"

The heavyset woman looked like she was on a mission. Her expression was not friendly.

"Yes, ma'am. I am a secretary at the clinic."

"I've heard that this polio is being spread in the water and that's why so many of our poor children are getting it. Don't you think you all should be telling people that and getting these sick people away from here. We know that first child who had it was that baseball player's son."

Symphony remembered the story from the exhibit at the Boyd Museum. Johnny Seccafico was the twenty-month-old son of Jim Seccafico, second baseman for the Wytheville Statesmen, a Class D minor league team in the Appalachian baseball league. Little Johnny was the first child diagnosed with polio in Wytheville in the summer of 1950.

"Lord knows this town loves baseball. My husband is at every game. But, if it has brought us such a disease, I don't want it here anymore." There was fear in her eyes.

Symphony was at a loss for words. She sensed that it was less hatred than fear fueling the woman's indignation. It was still a common problem in her time. People developed opinions; often wrong ones, based on hearsay and the fear of what might happen.

"Ma'am, I don't think we know for sure how polio is being

spread or how it spread to Wytheville. The doctors and nurses are trying to do all they can to help the patients and send the sickest ones on to other hospitals for additional treatment. I realize it is a scary time. I think this community can come together and make it better for everyone."

Symphony knew her words were true. Her mind was fresh with the knowledge she had gleaned while researching for the symposium. She knew the stories of the heroic local doctors who would work days straight, tending to not only those stricken with polio, but also their regular patients. Since she had arrived in 1950, she was amazed to meet them face-to-face and watch their dedication first hand. She had read the accounts of the great lengths that the adults went to in order to make a summer when children were kept indoors a fun time for those who were well. The story of a room in a home on Withers Road being filled with sand for children to play in was a legend about the time that was firmly anchored in truth—the truth of kindness.

"GOOD EVENING, SYMPHONY, Amburgey."

Belcher nodded to both of them as he walked across the grass of the hotel in front of the porch where they were sitting. Symphony noticed that tonight he looked like he had just gotten off work. Still wearing a grease-stained shirt and pants, Belcher's shoulders had the stance of tired. The weight of the day's work was on his back.

"Hey, Belcher. I guess you've had a long day, too." Symphony took in a deep breath of still warm summer night air.

"Every day seems long anymore, doesn't it? That new cook we

hired quit already. It seems like there's an anchor around our necks in this town these days, and we can't shake the weight." Hands deep in his pockets, Belcher shifted from one foot to another. "I've heard some of the stories about how long the doctors are working. It's a wonder they aren't sick themselves."

"They've prescribed themselves a strong dose of exhaustion. That's for sure." Amburgey gently rocked back and forth in the rocking chair, which was, for the moment, the only breeze Symphony could feel. "When all of this is over, they will be declared the heroes of this war we are fighting. Them and the valiant soldiers who are transporting these poor souls to the hospitals."

"I've never seen anything like it before. The funeral homes are stepping up and volunteering to use their hearses to transport patients to the hospitals in Roanoke and Richmond. It's like they are on a bus schedule. There's always one coming and going." Symphony shook her head in amazement.

"It's true." Belcher spoke up. "They will even take you down to the hospitals to visit your relatives who are patients. You only need to wait out in front of Leggett's for the next ambulance to leave."

"History will remember this heroic spirit." Symphony could feel Amburgey's eyes on her. "I would think this is the type of situation that's written about in history books."

"I've never heard of anything quite like this happening in Wytheville before." Belcher moved to stand right in front of Symphony. "The reason I stopped by is I was thinking about that question you asked me the other night." Symphony tried to remember what Belcher was referring to. "You know, the question about old clocks. I think the most unusual clock I've seen in Wytheville is right here in this hotel."

"Clocks? Why are you looking for clocks?"

Amburgey's words almost came out as a shout. Symphony
noticed that her loud tone woke up a man who was sitting at the
opposite end of the porch. The man grumbled before standing up
and walking toward the front door to go inside.

"I like clocks." Symphony did not make eye contact with
Amburgey, even though the woman was boring holes in the side
of Symphony's head with her intense stare.

"You like clocks?"

"There's no crime in liking clocks, Amburgey." Belcher came
to Symphony's defense. "I remembered that there's an unusual
grandfather clock in the back of the first floor of the hotel. It's in
a sitting room. I forget what they call the room, but some of the
businessmen who stay here sometimes sit back there to drink and
smoke cigars. I imagined that you probably had not been in that
part of the hotel, Symphony, so you wouldn't have had a chance
to see it."

"Thank you, Belcher. I appreciate you telling me about it. I will
have to take a look."

"Why don't we just go and take a look right now?" Amburgey
stood up. "I think it might prove to be quite revealing."

Symphony finally met Amburgey's gaze when she stood up
next to her. For a split second, it seemed like Symphony could hear
Amburgey's thoughts. Her eyes seemed to dance with questions—
deep complicated questions.

"I don't know why you two are getting so excited about a clock.
It's pretty and all, but it's just wood and gears and such." In her
peripheral vision, Symphony could see Belcher shaking his head
and starting to walk away. "I'm going to head home now. I hope
you like the clock, Symphony."

Breaking her eye contact with Amburgey, Symphony walked

to the edge of the porch. Belcher's long stride had almost reached the sidewalk.

"Thank you, Belcher. I appreciate you stopping by to tell me about the clock." He turned back and gave her a slight smile. There was something about the expression on his face that reminded her of Jason. It tugged at her heart. "I hope to see you again soon." She realized that he might take the comment as a sign of interest. Yet, her heart needed to say those words to Jason across the expanse of time. Maybe his heart would hear her.

"You're going to tell me why you are so interested in old clocks." Symphony felt Amburgey's hand encircle the top of her arm as she pulled her toward the front doorway. "I think you have a secret, and it's time for you to tell it."

Being pulled made Symphony quicken her steps when they entered the lobby of the hotel. The jerky movement caused her steps to create a clattering sound across the tiled floor. The sound drew the attention of a man standing at the front desk. His appearance caught Symphony's eye. Even in the humid weather, the man was dressed in a dark suit and hat. Still being dragged by Amburgey, Symphony watched the man turn and glance in their direction. He turned back to the desk clerk. As if by reflex, the man's gaze returned and focused on Amburgey. A wide-eyed expression of recognition passed over his face. Glancing at Amburgey, Symphony saw that she did not appear to see him. Just before Amburgey pulled her through another doorway, Symphony glanced back at the man. He was still staring at Amburgey, like she was the only person in the room.

"This must be the room Belcher was talking about."

Symphony turned around and found herself in front of two heavy wooden doors. There was a small eye-level window in each one. Amburgey was peering through one of the windows.

"It must be a slow night. I don't see anyone in there." Amburgey waved her hand in front of the door. "Open sesame." Pulling the handle toward her, the large door opened. "That must have been the magic word."

Symphony remained silent watching Amburgey walk ahead of her into the dark room. It reminded her of a cigar bar that was near the campus of the college where she received her undergraduate degree. Lots of wooden furniture and dark leather adorned the décor. Remembering the design of the clock that was her time travel portal, she could see why it might be in the room. She had barely moved across the threshold until Amburgey's voice jarred her from her thoughts.

"Finally! I've been looking for this everywhere."

Symphony held her breath. As much as she was hoping to find the clock so that it could possibly take her back to her time, she was hesitant to view it with Amburgey in the room. From the comment that her mother had uttered, it must have been her portal, too. Symphony knew that neither she nor Amburgey awoke near it after their journeys, and she wondered why they had not. Another mystery to a mysterious journey.

"I'm really tired, Amburgey. I think I'm going to go to bed." Symphony took a few quiet steps. Now, she quickly tried to back up to the doorway.

"Stop! Don't you dare try to sneak away. You've got a secret. I think it's the same as mine. Come in here."

Symphony wondered if there was some genetic link that could make a child listen to a parent even if that parent had not been in the child's life. Symphony felt a pull of obedience take over. Her mind was screaming to run. Her feet had other ideas and proceeded to take her right into the back section of the room where Amburgey's voice was coming from.

As soon as Symphony turned the corner, the clock was in full view. It looked just the same as it did in the front foyer of the Rock House. The sight of the clock calmed Symphony's core. The look on her mother's face stirred a fear unlike any she had ever felt. She knew nothing of the laws of time travel, if such existed. But, the laws of nature screamed in her ear. Both she and her mother were in the wrong time. Worse still, at that moment, they were there together. That time portal had brought them there separately. Symphony could not imagine where it would take them together if they got too close.

The stream of thought made Symphony instinctively reach for the pendant. As soon as she felt it in her grasp, she knew it was a mistake—a mistake that her mother saw.

"I've caught a glimpse of that pendant before. You don't wear it outside of your clothing. Yet, you reach for it like a security blanket." Amburgey moved toward Symphony. "Let me see it."

"It's just an old necklace." Symphony moved away from Amburgey, backing into a chair and almost falling.

"If it isn't anything special, you shouldn't mind showing it to me." Amburgey continued toward her. She was backing Symphony toward the direction near the clock. It was exactly where Symphony did not want to go. "It looks quite unusual to me. There seems to be flowers in it and specks of gold."

"Belcher is right. This is an unusual clock. It looks like there are flowers worked into the design of the face."

Symphony succeeded in getting Amburgey to glance momentarily at the clock. It did not give Symphony the time she needed to move further away.

"Flowers. Yes, blooms, they could be called. Quite a coincidence that the clock and your pendant both have such. You seem to have a lot in common with this little town for someone who claims to have never been here before."

"I never said that."

"Aha! You have been here. Was it in your time or someone else's?"

Symphony's heart rate accelerated. She was running out of space and distractions.

"I wonder how long this clock was in this hotel. Maybe it came here from a country far away."

Amburgey moved closer. Her stance was like an animal readying to pounce.

"Where did you get that pendant?" Amburgey locked eyes with Symphony.

"I wonder how old the clock is." Symphony broke the gaze and turned her attention to the clock inches away. She was afraid to touch it. Yet, she wondered what might happen if she did.

"I want to know who gave you that pendant."

Symphony was still avoiding eye contact when she felt Amburgey lunge toward her and grab the pendant. Her grasp was so forceful and sudden that it caused Symphony to lose her balance and begin to fall toward the clock. Her reflexes kicked in causing her to reach for the clock to break her fall. As she did, Symphony turned back toward Amburgey and a tingling feeling came over her.

"Who gave it to you?" Amburgey was almost screaming at her.

"You gave it to me."

Their eyes locked. For a split second, everything stopped. Visions passed before Symphony's eyes. Snippets of her own life.

Snippets of the lives of others. Just enough to stir her thought process. Not enough to give her any idea what she was viewing. She caught her breath and blinked. Suddenly, Symphony felt like she was in a wind tunnel. A silvery wind was encircling her. Everything was moving. Looking down from Amburgey's shocked expression, Symphony saw that her mother was still clutching the pendant. Everything seemed to slow down. Symphony looked back up and locked eyes again with Amburgey. The woman's mouth was open like she was in the middle of a sentence. Before either of them could say anything, the sound of the wind increased to a deafening level. Glimmering silver dust swirled around them and, in a split second, everything went black.

Chapter Nineteen

A T FIRST THE VOICES WERE WHISPERS, then they grew in amplitude. Symphony could not make out what anyone was saying, but the voices sounded familiar to her. She tried to open her eyes. They felt like they were glued shut. It was an effort to open them. She had to consciously think about it.

"It looks like she is trying to open her eyes." The woman's voice was soft and comforting. It hinted of nervousness and fear. "My darling girl, please open your eyes."

"This is a sign, Symphony." That was the voice of Grammie Wallace. It was coming from inside her head. "Open your eyes and see it."

Symphony's eyes flew open. Hovering over her was the face of a woman. She blinked her eyes and saw a young face. The same woman who had been with her a few minutes earlier. As her eyes began to focus, the face changed. An older woman was smiling down at her. It was Nadia. The woman Symphony recently learned was her grandmother.

"Oh, Allison, she's waking up." Nadia looked off to the side before returning her gaze to meet Symphony's. "My darling Symphony, you gave us quite a scare."

"I am so relieved." Allison came into her view. "The rescue squad is on the way."

Hearing Allison's last statement caused a reflex action in Symphony. She began to sit up.

"I think you should continue lying down until the ambulance gets here. If you fell, you might have broken something."

Symphony's eyes darted back and forth taking in her peripheral view. Her mind tried to catch up with the situation. She was on the floor of the foyer of the Rock House. Inches away, from her head, was the clock. The realization made her suddenly sit up and scoot away from it toward the staircase.

"What's wrong, Symphony?" Allison squatted down next to her. The woman picked up a washcloth that had been on Symphony's forehead. "What happened to you?"

Symphony looked deep into Allison's eyes. The woman furrowed her brow and her expression changed to concern and fear. Symphony could not come up with the words to answer Allison's question.

"You've been somewhere, haven't you?" Allison's voice was barely above a whisper as she reached out and clasped Symphony's hand.

"You've taken a trip like your mother." Symphony had not seen Nadia leave the room until she reappeared behind Allison. "Did you find Amburgey?"

Symphony still could not manage the strength to form the words. She slowly shook her head affirmatively.

"Did you find him, too?"

Allison stood up and gave Nadia a questioning look.

"Surely, Allison, your research about Amburgey led you to the conclusion that she was not the only time traveler in the family."

"What? Are you a time traveler, too?"

"Of course not. It doesn't run on my side of the family." Nadia handed Symphony a bottle of water. "Amburgey's trips away were in search of her father—Tyler Gibboney, my first husband."

"I've never heard that before from any of those who have researched Amburgey. That's not come up at all."

"Well, no one ever asked me." Nadia walked around Symphony and sat down behind her on the stairs. "I guess everyone assumed that I would not believe such an outlandish story associated with my missing daughter. They had no idea of how mixed up with time travel my life was before she was even born."

"So, ALLISON FOUND you lying on the floor in the foyer of the Rock House?"

Symphony had slept in the following morning, before returning to work in the early afternoon. Allison wanted her to take the whole day off. Once Symphony awakened from a deep sleep, she had an anxiousness inside her that could only be tempered by keeping busy.

"Yes, Marcella, it appears that I decided to take a nap after the symposium last night."

The words 'symposium' and 'last night' made a fuzzy feeling

return to her brain. It was much longer than a few hours. A few decades was more like it.

"That's a pretty smart answer coming from someone who caused her supervisor to be awakened in the middle of the night."

"I know. I know. I'm just mortified. Do you think she will fire me?"

"Fire you? No. Hire you a bodyguard? Possibly. Drew told us that last night wasn't the first time you had collapsed in that foyer."

"Drew promised he wouldn't tell."

"Give the kid a break. He kept your secret for several months."

"I'm not a fan of secret keeping." Symphony lunged toward Marcella's desk as Allison came up behind her. "I'm sorry. I didn't mean to scare you."

"I guess I am a little jumpy." Symphony took a deep breath to try and calm her racing nerves. "I'm still a little tired."

"I would guess so. You made a long trip." Allison ended her statement with a slight laugh.

"Trip? Where did you go?" Marcella looked from Allison to Symphony. "Did I miss something?"

"Oops. I guess I said too much." Allison gave Symphony a wide-eyed look and shrugged her shoulders.

"It's okay, Allison. I would have told Marcella eventually."

"Is something wrong? I thought you were okay. Allison said that you weren't taken to the hospital."

Symphony watched a look of concern cross her friend's face.

"I am fine, Marcella. No worries. The thing is that I did take a little trip last night. It seems that I have inherited a tendency toward a special type of travel."

"Like Amburgey did?"

"Yes."

"No wonder you look like you have jet lag." Marcella chuckled. "I'm sorry, I couldn't resist. I am very relieved. You worried me for a moment."

"It's a good thing that she wasn't really injured with that fall." Allison shook her head. "I can't imagine how I would have filled out the workers compensation paperwork for human resources regarding injuries sustained travelling to 1950."

"1950!" Marcella's voice raised an octave. Symphony could almost see the wheels turning in the woman's head. "You really didn't have to get into your research that deeply. The symposium is over. I've got to hear this story."

"I've got to get to a meeting downtown." Allison put on a lightweight jacket and picked up a large notebook. "You fill Marcella in on what you told me last night. We can talk later." Allison started to walk away before stopping and turning back to face Symphony. "I feel sort of responsible for you making that journey. If I hadn't assigned you to learn about the summer of polio, you might not have been put into the position for this to happen."

"Don't worry about that for a minute, Allison. It appears that Amburgey put this scenario in the works long ago. It may have even started before I was born. I think if it hadn't been this research, it would have been something else. The good thing is that I had some background into the time period and more of an understanding about what I was seeing happen around me."

"It's so amazing." Allison seemed lost in thought. "To be able to travel to another time, it's like something out of a movie. I never dreamed I could ever believe it was possible. Even with all we knew about Amburgey, there was a part of me that continued to discount the possibility. I guess I saw too much science fiction to believe that hidden within it there could be any truth."

As Symphony watched Allison leave, Marcella sat down at her desk.

"You sit down." Marcella pointed to a chair. She retrieved a small lunch cooler from under her desk. "You are going to tell me about this unbelievable experience of yours while I eat my lunch. I love dinner and a show."

A half hour later, Marcella's lunch was gone and her mouth hung open with a shocked expression.

"I did not know it was possible to render you speechless, Marcella." A little nervous laughter escaped Symphony.

"So, you went back in time and found your mother who was also travelling back in time." Marcella tilted her head as her expression of shock turned to one of confusion. "This sounds like a dream you have after a night of too much alcohol."

"I suppose that is a good comparison. I must admit I do have a hungover type feeling." Marcella continued to stare at her. "Yes, I seem to have met Amburgey Gibboney in 1950. I guess the legend is true." Another nervous laugh escaped. "I don't even know what to think about the experience. I know it sounds like a crazy dream. But, I swear it wasn't. It was as real as you and I sitting here now. My mind cannot grasp how I got there. But, I've seen Wytheville during that dreadful summer of polio, and it was everything that history has painted it to be. All the good and all the bad rolled into one hot and scary summer."

"As interested as I am in what was happening in Wytheville, I really want to know what you thought of Amburgey."

"I liked her. She was smart and funny. She had quite a sassy personality. I was a stranger to her and she took care of me." Symphony let out a long sigh and turned her gaze to look out the window. "Now that I think about it, it was like she instinctively knew I was connected to her. We bonded instantly."

"Did you tell her that you were her daughter?"

"No. I don't know if there are laws pertaining to time travel. If there are though, I'm sure we were breaking some just being there together. I tried to not tell her too much about me. But, as I told you, the end of my journey was quite eventful. I did not tell her who I was. I did tell her that she was the one who gave me this pendant."

Symphony took hold of the pendant and pulled it up to look at it. She had worn the necklace, off and on, for most of her teens and early twenties, spending plenty of time staring at its unusual design. As she looked at it now, something seemed different to her. Her memory could not pinpoint what changed. Perhaps, it was her mind playing tricks. She felt the same type of electric prickly feeling that came over her right before the time travel journey. She released the pendant and looked back at Marcella.

"You've remembered something, haven't you? You've been staring at the pendant for several minutes. You looked lost."

"Time seems to have the ability to slip away from me these days. I don't know how to describe the feeling that comes over me. It's as if I am here and in another place simultaneously. I fear that there may be side effects. It certainly must be an affront to nature to mess with the rules of time."

"Sometimes great things occur when people break the rules. I daresay it's when some of the biggest discoveries our world has seen were made." Marcella reached over and took hold of Symphony's pendant. "It's a beautiful piece of art. The person who created it must have a little magic in her soul."

"If this really is a BloomSpoons pendant, as everyone seems to think, I wonder if Cybelee would remember making it." Symphony got up and moved toward the doorway. I'm sure that she and her staff have made thousands of pieces of jewelry since, but I would imagine that this had to be one of the early versions. Maybe it was a custom piece."

"Since you know her now, perhaps, she might be willing to see you again and take a look at it. I've got to warn you though. Even a custom piece might be a fuzzy memory to her."

"You're probably right. Even if Cybelee remembers Amburgey, it's doubtful that she would have any information concerning her current whereabouts. There's nothing I learned in 1950 that will get me any closer to finding her in this time." Symphony picked up her belongings. "I'm heading to the Rock House. Now that the symposium is over, I have a ton of information that I am behind on in the logging of the archives."

"You seem so nonchalant about it all. Last night you spent several weeks in another time and now you are worried about catching up with your work. If it was me, I think I would be hiding in my bed today with the covers over my head."

"After such a surreal experience, I think I want to get firmly planted back into the here and now as soon as possible. I will immerse myself into work. Allison might not like me taking 'trips' while working."

"You should be glad she didn't have to fill out any paperwork on your 'accident.'" Marcella gestured with quotation marks in the air. "She's not a fan of paperwork when it makes sense. Including time travel in the description would put her over the edge."

Symphony laughed and headed out of the building. As she walked around the building to the sidewalk, she glanced at Withers Park. For a moment her mind jetted back to her time travel experience. The Wytheville Statesmen called Withers Park home in 1950. While the polio outbreak had shut the team down soon after she arrived, one night after work Symphony had stood on the very same grassy bank and saw the end of a game. She could still hear the crack of the bat and the roar of a small crowd.

"It's going to be great to have baseball played here again."

Symphony jumped. She quickly turned and saw an older gentleman. There was something familiar about him.

"I'm sorry. What are you speaking of?"

"The vintage team that will begin playing soon. They've been practicing all spring. Don't you work for the Museums? Allison Emerson started the organization of the team."

"Oh, yes. I remember someone telling me about that. I guess it's been a long time since baseball was played here."

"Several decades, at least. I grew up in the 1950s, but moved away in the 1960s. I sure do have some fond memories of watching games on this field when I was a kid. You make sure you come out to a game. The sound of a bat hitting a ball in this park is a special thing."

"I will certainly do that, sir." Symphony held out her hand. "I'm Symphony Wallace."

"Calvin Williams." The man gave her hand a firm shake. "Time to get to my walk."

Before Symphony could reply, the man turned and began making his way down the bank toward the walking track. She noticed that he had a pronounced limp to his stride.

"Calvin Williams. That name sounds familiar." Symphony turned to head toward the sidewalk and a thought hit her. "Oh my goodness. Could it possibly be?" Symphony smiled. "I guess Mrs. Williams did save her Calvin and maybe, just maybe, I helped."

"I FEEL LIKE YOU are avoiding me."

The following morning was Saturday. After Symphony rose from a night of deep sleep, she found Nadia sitting on her front porch with a large mug of coffee and a carafe beside her.

"I would be a liar if I told you that you were wrong." Nadia looked up when Symphony sat down in a nearby chair. "Over the last twenty plus years, my mind had put time travel away in a firmly taped up box in the corner of my brain. I have thought about Tyler and Amburgey every single day since they left me. There's no forgetting them. But, I had managed to selectively remember what took them from me. I suppose I have given off such an anti-time travel vibe that's probably the reason that people rarely remember that Amburgey was my daughter."

"Was?"

"Is. Was. What does it matter? When someone leaves your life by choice, maybe they cancel out their right to it. I can't imagine that you, of all people, wouldn't partially agree with that."

"I spent a lot of time with her. I spent weeks with the woman who gave birth to me, long before she even knew that I was a possibility."

Psycho got up from where he was sitting next to Nadia and sat down next to Symphony.

"He likes you better than me now. I guess it is because he was Amburgey's dog first."

"What? How is that possible? That would make him—"

"At least twenty five years old. Yep. That would be correct. Psycho came back with Amburgey from the last trip she took before you were born. I guess the laws of time are kind to dogs or maybe his system just doesn't know how old he is."

Nadia rose from her chair and picked up the carafe. She filled up Symphony's mug as she began to walk back inside.

"I have to go town for a meeting. Jason called about an hour ago. I told him you were sleeping. He asked for you to call him after lunch. He's working this morning. He would like to have dinner with you tonight."

"Okay." Symphony took a deep breath. Because of his work schedule, they had only managed to exchange text messages since her return. "He doesn't know anything about my trip."

"Are you going to tell him?"

"I don't see how I can avoid it. I think I met one of his relatives in 1950." Nadia backed up and gave Symphony a wide-eyed look. "Actually, I probably could have stayed in 1950 and married one of his uncles if I had wanted."

"That's an interesting idea." Nadia shook her head and laughed. "Perhaps Jason is genetically predetermined to be attracted to you."

"It all makes my head hurt. I don't see why my mother wanted to travel more than once."

"A mystery in one's life can be a powerful thing. Looking back on it now, I don't think Amburgey ever intended to stay back in time. I know that Tyler did not. He wanted to be here with his daughter and me. I think time reached out and pulled them both back. I blame him for my daughter's disappearance. She wanted to find her father, just as surely as you wanted to find her."

———⊰✤⊱———

DARKNESS HAD BEGUN to fall when Symphony finished her story. She had asked Jason if they could pick up some food and sit in one of the town's parks to eat their dinner. He listened patiently and ate while she poured out her heart with the tears and laughter that so needed to escape her soul.

"So my Uncle Belcher hit on you?" A smirk crossed Jason's face. "I guess I'm going to have to keep an eye on you two at the next family gathering."

"I've just told you that I travelled over six decades in reverse during an epidemic and stayed for several weeks and that's what you are concerned about?"

"In my defense, you obviously returned safe and sound, and you look fabulous. My uncle has been married three times and is currently single. You must be the one who got away. Yes, I'm concerned. He's charming and good looking, like me."

Jason winked at Symphony. She had put her guard up with Belcher, but his nephew was right. Even the young shy man had the magnetism that drew her to Jason.

"I don't think I should meet him. Belcher knew my real name and I would look the same to him. It might make him have a stroke or something. At the very least, he will think your girlfriend is an alien."

"My girlfriend?" Jason raised his eyebrows and smiled.

"Well, you know, older people automatically think that single people are in a relationship."

"Stop trying to back pedal. I like the sound of girlfriend. Besides, you have to continue dating me now; I know that you're an alien. Obviously, the men in my family find that attractive."

"You must be crazy. I seem to come from a long line of time

travelers. I'm amazed that I didn't accidentally travel as a child. It's appears that I had my passport all the time." Symphony held up her pendant. "There's something magical about this thing, especially when you get it near a clock."

"I've been thinking about that since you mentioned it earlier. You seem to think that your mother used that clock as a time portal, too, right?"

"Yes, I'm fairly certain that she did. I think she actually travelled back when I did, to whatever time she had come from."

"But, she didn't have this pendant."

"What?"

"Amburgey didn't use your pendant as her token."

"You are not just good-looking. I don't have any idea what she used. I wonder if it could be something that she left here with Nadia. I wonder if that could help me find her. If it would lead me to her."

"In a past time or the present?"

"Either."

"Well, I understand that you may be genetically predisposed to that sort of thing, but I would rather you stayed here in the present."

"Jason, I was speculating. I don't have any intention of taking any trips outside of my, hmm, time zone." Symphony laughed at her comment. Jason was not laughing. "Seriously, I never intended to go to 1950."

"That's my point. It wasn't your intent. It's scary to think that it could happen again, and you might get stuck somewhere. It would appear that this Tyler Gibboney person got stuck."

"We don't really know that. It was a theory of Amburgey's."

"A theory that Nadia seems to have confirmed." Jason stood

up and followed Symphony to where she was now pacing. "I'm not trying to interfere in your quest to find your mother. I know that is important and I want you to find her. In the here and now, so that you can have an ongoing relationship with her without jeopardizing your future." Jason pulled Symphony into an embrace. "I would hate the thought of you becoming my aunt."

"I get it. I don't have any desire to take another one of those trips. As interesting as it was, I had a sick feeling in my stomach the whole time that I was going to be stuck there." Symphony gave Jason a quick kiss. "Don't worry, I wouldn't have married Belcher."

"How do you know that?"

"Because I had already decided that if I still was stuck in that time by the mid-fifties, I was going to head to Memphis."

"How come?"

"To discover Elvis. And, then, well, he would have been so grateful."

"Elvis and Symphony doesn't quite have the same ring as Elvis and Priscilla did."

"Oh, but it would have."

"So, you would have moved to Memphis. You could have met him in many different locations."

On Monday morning, Symphony found Garon on the porch of the Rock House waiting for her to come to work. A brief preliminary chat about her weekend led her to tell Garon about her alternate plans if she had been stuck in the 1950s.

"Memphis is Elvis' home. Home is where the heart is."

"You sound like a song."

"See. I have songs in my heart. He would have loved that about me."

"Elvis was quite the southern gentleman."

"I've heard that."

"I knew him."

"Really? Well, Grammie Wallace would have been impressed with that as well."

"We would cross paths quite often on studio lots in the 60s. I was very busy then. It was really the shining decade of my films. Elvis had impeccable manners. I mean I grew up in the South and I learned it as well. You just don't shake the whole gentile manner. Elvis' manners were as much a part of him as his sex appeal. It would actually get on many of the younger actresses nerves to be called 'ma'am' by him. He couldn't help it, bless his heart."

"Now who sounds southern?" Already in the Rock House, Symphony almost ran up the steps to get away from the clock in the foyer. "Are you going to help me search for information for the next temporary exhibit or are you here to work on the jewelry archives?"

"I came to hear a complete account of your trip to days gone by, especially all of the portions that star me." Garon flashed his Hollywood smile as he turned to inspect his reflection in the large mirror that permanently hung in the upstairs storage room. "You know that Allison had this mirror placed here just for me."

"I know that Allison would love to put it on display somewhere downstairs, but cannot seem to figure out a way to get it out of here without breaking it."

"Yes, the mirror is landlocked. That makes it mine."

"Quite frankly, I would have more quickly imagined this impressive mirror to be a time travel portal than that clock downstairs."

"My dear, anything can be a time portal. I read this lovely book series last summer that was based on one of the mansions in the eastern end of the county. It was a time travel mystery and a closet, of all things, was the portal. I took a tour of the mansion after I finished the series. I walked into that same closet, nothing happened."

"I bet you didn't have a token. That's the key to making it work."

"So, I've heard. Okay, let's get to that story."

"I think you mean, let me help with your research, Symphony, and you can tell me snippets on our breaks."

"Okay, if you insist. But start with the parts about me."

Garon spent the whole day with Symphony. True to his word, he helped research the topic for the fall temporary exhibit for the Boyd Museum—the 1924 Wytheville fire.

"This clock." Garon opened up the glass door and peered inside at the pendulum. "This clock is a time travel portal. I remember this old thing when it used to sit in the bar at the George Wythe Hotel. I never imagined that it had any function other than time keeping. Makes you wonder what other inanimate objects might be capable."

"I don't know about other objects, but this is the way I went to 1950 and back. And, it really makes me uncomfortable to be near it now."

Symphony inched down the stairs and stayed as far away from the clock as she could. Once a safe distance away, she took a deep breath and raised her head, sniffing at the air.

"I wonder where it will take you next." Garon closed the glass door and turned the key in the lock. "Maybe I should say *when* it would take you." Garon chuckled and looked around at Symphony.

"I have no intention of it taking me anywhere ever again. I think I will stay in my own time. I appreciate you helping me with the research today. It gives me a great head start on the information for the exhibit panels. Next, I will need to comb the photography archives for some photos from 1924."

"I don't imagine that will be too hard to find. There should be some newspaper accounts of the incident. It was a large fire for a small town. I was amazed as I read about it today. I had forgotten how devastating it was for the community." Garon watched Symphony sniffing around the foyer. "What are you doing? You look like a bloodhound."

"I guess I have delved too deep into the research about the fire today." Symphony sniffed the air again. "I keep smelling smoke. Do you smell it?"

WORDS OF THE GRANNY WITCH

"Be careful what you wish for. It's closer than you think. Be careful what you avoid. It will find you. Time knows the secrets of your heart. You can try to avoid them, but they will follow you just the same. Call it destiny. Call it fate. You cannot change time. It will change you."

Acknowledgements

As a fiction author of several books, I'm often asked where I get my inspiration for stories. There is probably as many different answers to that question as there are ideas. For me, a story spark often comes from deep within dreams, through chance encounters with strangers, or a tidbit of a news item that crosses my path. For this particular story that you have just read, a sizable portion of the inspiration came from the creative fingertips of my dear friend, Amanda Slaughter—the owner, designer, and creator of BloomSpoons jewelry. Her beautiful pieces of handmade jewelry have the unique combination of nature, nurture, and magic needed for a token to transport you to another time. Her creative soul and reverence for nature is the epitome of the characteristics personified by the original Granny Witches—the true Queens of Appalachia. The pendant that enabled Symphony to travel through time was created by Amanda and adorns the cover of this book.

While she does not create herbal remedies, at this time, BloomSpoons is a very real company and you can have your own special one-of-a-kind piece of jewelry by visiting Amanda's website at www.BloomSpoons.com. You never know, it just might send you on your own journey through time.

Wytheville, Virginia is a real place. As the story tells you, there is only one community with such a name in the whole world. Most of the businesses mentioned in this book are real. The community did experience a tragic incidence of the polio epidemic during the summer of 1950, gaining the small town much media attention for the unusually high number of cases of the disease and the way the community came together to help each other. While this is a work of fiction, much of the historical information contained within is factual. To learn more about this wonderful community, look it up on the World Wide Web at www.VisitWytheville.com.

For the most part, writing is a solitary task. There comes a time though after long hours of creation that you must allow others to join you on your journey and help you fine tune your work. I am blessed to have four strong and talented women who are the first ones to read my words and offer their thoughts on how I can improve my story. These four talented and caring women are: Carole Bybee, Pam Newberry, Marcella Taylor, and Donna Stroupe. Each of them possesses a different level of editorial prowess. This book would not exist without them. I am grateful for their critical eyes and loving suggestions.

They say you can't judge a book by its cover. Unless you have a cover designed by Cassy Roop of Pink Ink Designs (www. pinkindesigns.com). Despite the fact that Cassy and I have never met face-to-face, she has some magical insight into how I imagine the covers of my stories and beautifully brings them to life. Her talented fingers are also behind the formatting of the pages within.

Many thanks to every person who takes the time and spends the money to read one of my stories. Without you, these voices would stay in my head. I am grateful for the opportunity to share them with you.

About the Author

Rosa Lee Jude began creating her own imaginary worlds at an early age. While her career path has included stints in journalism, marketing, hospitality & tourism and local government, she is most at home at a keyboard spinning yarns of fiction and creative non-fiction. She lives in the beautiful mountains of Southwest Virginia with her patient husband and very spoiled rescue dog. Learn more about her other books and writing journey at RosaLeeJude.com.

Want more? Sign Up for Rosa Lee Jude's mailing list. It's for new releases and fun giveaways only, no spam. https://www.rosaleejude.com/newsletter-sign-up

Other books by Rosa Lee Jude can be found on her Amazon Author Page (https://www.amazon.com/Rosa-Lee-Jude/e/ B00E6TYRGE)

Please consider following her to keep up-to-date on new releases.

Or connect with her on her Facebook page Rosa Lee Jude, Author (https://www.facebook.com/rosaleejudeauthor/)

Did you enjoy this book? You can make a big difference by leaving a short review. Honest reviews help convince prospective readers to take a chance on an author they do not know. I personally read each review and appreciate the time that the reader has taken to tell me why he or she enjoyed it. Thank you.

Made in the USA
Lexington, KY
03 May 2018